not go

"EVOCATIVE
Publishe

"A woman's trek back to origins, hers and western culture's, in an attempt to make them jibe with the images she dreamed as a girl . . . Karen Lawrence maps out the way with humor, intelligence, wit and tenderness."

San Diego Tribune

"The book includes some stirring passages about the death of loved ones—especially parents—and about how those deaths liberate and abandon us to our own lives."

Detroit News and Free Press

"Attempting to deal with a strained relationship with her sister, and trying to understand the troubling love she feels for her father, Min creates scenes that are like glittering gems. There is much that is tender, the emotions are never strained; they, like everything in this compelling story, are born from an honest passion."

Richmond Times-Dispatch

"This candid lyrical novel will touch sophisticated readers with its truth about the mysteries of intimacy."

Booklist

Karen Lawrence won the prestigious
W.H. Smith Award for Best Canadian
First Novel for *The Life of Helen Alone*

Also by Karen Lawrence
Published by Ballantine Books:

THE LIFE OF HELEN ALONE

SPRINGS
OF
LIVING
WATER

Karen Lawrence

BALLANTINE BOOKS • NEW YORK

Library of Congress Catalog Card Number: 89-40198

ISBN 0-345-34827-3

This edition published by arrangement with Villard Books, a
division of Random House, Inc.

Manufactured in the United States of America

First Ballantine Books Edition: March 1991

Cover photo © 1990 by James Robinson

For my grandmother,
Minnie Davis Lawrence
1893–1956
not unremembered

and our Great Uncle Alf
always at the top of his form
an inspiration to us all

Above all, he thought of his childhood, and the more calmly he recalled it, the more unfinished it seemed; all its memories had the vagueness of premonitions, and the fact that they were past made them almost arise as future. To take all this past upon himself once more, and this time really, was the reason why, from the midst of his estrangement, he returned home. We don't know whether he stayed there; we only know that he came back.

—Rainer Maria Rilke,
[The Prodigal Son], from
The Notebooks of Malte Laurids Brigge
translated by Stephen Mitchell

many thanks
to Christa Van Daele
spiritual midwife to this book

and Peter Gethers
éditeur extraordinaire

The Garden

It occurred to Min that thinking about your family is like gardening. The mood hits you, the sun is beaming down, the smell of wet black earth coming in strong through an open window, and you say to yourself, Why not? I've got a few minutes. So you go out that door. Maybe the timing is bad, maybe you aren't dressed for it, but the air is so sweet and full of life—and you then look around, and suddenly realize that things have changed since the last time you were here. *How did this happen so quickly?* The plants look weedy, overgrown, confused, as though they, too, have been caught unawares by time running on, have grown and spread wildly in their sleep, their visible parts, the leaves and branches, racing to keep up with the eager reaching roots and rhizomes down below, that were planted here so long ago. Like your memories, they feed on almost nothing—underground streams, air, an occasional generous burst of light. A letter can send you off rooting around for days. Desire. Guilt. Anticipation. *Loss.* You stand there staring, stopped in your tracks like a space traveler just arrived from your home planet, your own present, freshly landed in the middle of something you thought was finished, complete, a deserted world. *This shouldn't be here.* There should be a small square of pavement, a single evergreen tree, a neat path leading to the present and, off distantly, to the future. Pruned, orderly, taken care of: a low-maintenance area of your life. Not this accelerating accretion of textures and colors, these

1

woody stems and sinuous vines, these *life forms*, swelling and nodding and blistering in the heat.

For there is heat here, the billowing heat of vegetative growth and crawling things, the high humid steam of a private jungle—Amazonian, shocking, close. Stems, spikes, pistils, pedicels, inflorescences—so many parts, so many old faces, crowding around you, making your skin itch, your sinuses swell. This is anthesis: the fullness of existence. Down, down, down, the single-minded roots keep driving. However are you to make sense of this, to see your life as separate from the others? To sort out this rangy plant from its neighbors, from its own dying superseded leaves, its suckers and runners and seedpods? Certainly you had not planned on this. You were looking for a brief diversion, a little exercise, a stroll down Memory Lane, the sun warm on your back, dirt lining the tiny cracks in the skin of your hands. But there is so much to be done here that you fall to your knees, rooting furiously, driven by something far deeper than pride in appearances. What about those dreams you have now, of dark tunnels, clogged drains, of voices calling from the long ago, echoing like your best friend's from the other end of a pipe in a ditch? If this can happen to your past, what could become of the present? How self-forgetful might you become, what losses must you forestall, right here and now, before it is too late?

Rina's letter set Min off like this, nudged her back into memory, where she was brought up sharply by the unexpected, the wholly forgotten, a chiding chorus whispering of her unfaithfulness and neglect. What am I supposed to make of *this*, she thought—surprised, and not a little dismayed by a sense of doom settling about her shoulders like a well-worn sweater.

You should know that among other things, Dads' not his self. He drops things, he forgets. I say he should *not* be driving because he still won't wear those glasses he got, they pinch his nose he says. Jerry Lefave (remember the Lefaves on Birchwood, one of them use to think you were cute—Maybe not) says the shingels are shot, which I don't know a thing about. Its' so hot here without no air cond. I think you should come home for a visit.

Not that I want to interfere with your *lifestyle* or anything.

As usual, she tried to overlook Rina's spelling and concentrate on the message embedded in her words. *I don't really like you but I need your help.* Was that it? Her little sister. Min remembered the long period—or it had seemed long, maybe it was only a matter of a few months—when Rina had needed her help to pee. After sitting on the toilet for two, three, five minutes sometimes, with nothing coming out in spite of tickling her sacrum with two fingers and running the tap, she would call Min to the bathroom door.

"Say wee-wee."

"Drop dead, Rina."

"Come on, say it."

"No way. What for?"

"Just say it. Please? It helps me go."

"You're sick."

"Please?"

"Wee-wee, wee-wee, wee-wee. All right?"

A trickling sound from behind the closed door.

"Yeah. Thanks a lot."

Her family. Home. Doom. Min understood doom. She had been acquainted with it from an early age. Of course she tried to live as though it didn't exist, as though on her own she could effectively mold her life into a shape that pleased her. "Creating your own reality," they called this in California. Here they believed that everyone possessed this lordly, ingenious power. You just had to snap out of that other way of thinking and it would come naturally, like buoyancy in salt water.

But fate was much more rigorous and inescapable back in Wyandotte, where she was from. There, you found out early that certain things had been decided long before you were born, set in motion automatically. You operated from that knowledge; it was as common and enveloping as the sheets on your bed, or snow in winter. A simple Fact of Existence.

She did her best to explain this to Peter.

"Hey. You don't have to go, you know, if you don't want to," he said. Earnest, caring. Oblivious. A born Californian.

"It isn't a question of have to, Peter. It's my family."

" 'Shoulds' usually come from a person's family."

He must say that a million times a day, she thought. Peter was a counselor. That was one of their problems, in Min's opinion. She hadn't grown up around words like *options*, *growth*, *personal space*. *Should* had a much more familiar ring to it. She really wasn't crazy about having her feelings examined, either, her comments footnoted, her motives remarked upon. Her friend Katherine told her Peter was just trying to be supportive, to demonstrate that he cared. Min actually believed that could be true. It was just hard to get him to understand certain things. He had no context for them. No context at all.

"We're not talking about the same kind of family, Peter. At *all*. I've tried to tell you that. Your family talks. They *understand* things. Mine doesn't. They wouldn't understand it at all if I said no. Dad would be hurt and Rina'd be pissed off and then I'd feel bad and it wouldn't be worth it. What I'd have to go through to say no. So I'm just going. I can fit it into this trip. And it's been years. It's time I went back there anyway. I guess."

When she went down to the basement to sort and pack her camping equipment, she came across her old purple box. It was round, covered in some kind of faded but elegant patterned silken fabric (moiré? taffeta?) and lined with pale yellow satin. She had found it years ago in an antique shop near Orillia, when she first started buying things of her own, things she thought distinctive. *My silks and fine array.* It had moved with her many times in her travels, safekeeping her few treasures: her mother's engagement and wedding ring set, a pouch of foreign coins, her university diploma, her baby bracelet—tiny pink and white beads strung together like baby teeth spelling out the letters of her name, some photographs, two small gilt-edged volumes of Shakespeare's sonnets an old boyfriend had given her, several full sketchbooks and journals. Her portable property. From the small stack of photographs she drew out one in a brown cardboard cover. A beautiful, sad-faced young woman stared back at her. She had masses of fine pale baby hair gathered at the back of her neck, a delicate mouth, a broad intelligent brow. Her eyes shone dark, clear and keen. They looked as if they had seen sorrow, and were perhaps trying to look past it, toward something hopeful, or at least new.

Min's parents had taken her and Rina as children to visit their grandfather every month or so, after Sunday School. He lived in a small town about two hours from Wyandotte, past green rolling acres of corn and tomatoes, just this side of the marshy edge of the lake. It seemed no one ever really wanted to make that trip: her parents silent in the front seat, Rose tap-tapping her cigarette against the clasp of her purse, Rina squirming and threatening tears or throwing up, Min herself counting out the coins in her clear plastic change purse, or the number of blue cars passing them on the highway. But she loved the movement, the asphalt unrolling behind them like a black velvet carpet, the idea of really *going* somewhere, alongside all the other people in their cars on the highway.

Grandfather McCune's rambling wooden house smelled of dry rot, and was deeply, permanently shaded by a stand of gigantic black spruce that nearly hid the house from view. There was no lawn or garden of any kind, only these great spreading trees. Min would sing and dance under them in the summer, confidently unseen, on a secluded, fragrant stage of crunchy dead needles.

And why didn't anyone want to go there? Was it some loony fear of being sealed away forever in those gloomy deserted rooms, surrounded by lumpy furniture and odd knick-nacks: heavy brass bells, slavering porcelain boxers, pressed tin coasters, handleless mustache cups? Was it that there was really nothing to do, after you said Yes, please, to a beverage in a sweating red aluminum tumbler, no interesting books or toys, the three murmuring adults sitting stiffly in front of the console television, staring for an hour every visit at the same program, which showed men shooting into herds of wild animals—deer, Sumatran tigers, impala, bison? Was it the sound of that shooting? Of the animals thudding so heavily to their knees, over and over again? Perhaps it was her grandfather himself, roused from his torpid private world, his baggy pants smelling faintly of urine, his crooked outstretched hand squeezing yours too hard, clapping a secret quarter into your palm until it hurt, until you were sure you could feel the outline of the queen's head there. Or having to climb eighteen broad creaking stairs to reach the bathroom—which was nothing like their own: vast and echoey, the footed tub and toilet, and the sink you could barely reach, all white, and cold, and reproachfully clean.

After she peed, Min would tiptoe across the hall runner to her grandfather's dim, musty bedroom. This picture was in there, shining palely against the mahogany dresser, the only feminine thing in the hushed male atmosphere of those mysteriously darkened upstairs rooms. Every time they visited she said she had to go to the bathroom, so she could go up and stare at the picture. At times it seemed to move, to grow larger and hover above the wooden surface, vibrating ever so slightly in the sultry changeless air. Sometimes she thought she heard a faint voice in the room, beckoning her from up near the ceiling. *Come here, child. Come over here to me.* Once Min and her mother climbed the stairs to the bathroom together, and Min asked her who the woman in the picture was.

"Your grandmother."

"Daddy's mother?" Her tall, solitary grandfather, paired with such a delicate wife? Crushing her with his big heavy body, those clamping hands? Never.

"Daddy's mother, yes. She died having your father. And don't ever mention a word about it. It would upset him."

Upset *who*?

But Rose didn't explain. A stiffness came over her when she spoke of her husband's family; she looked off to one side, at something invisible on the nearest wall.

At that time Min had only the most rudimentary information about the sexual act, babies, childbirth. "He sticks his cock up your ass, dummy," Rosalie Simon had told her one day at recess. Rosalie couldn't believe Min didn't already know about this. Cock and ass were Sunday School words to Min: *The cock crowed thrice. The ass bowed down.* But she knew that wasn't what Rosalie meant. Someone else said to look up "concourse" in the dictionary. "1. An assemblage; a throng: *a mighty concourse of people.* 2. A railroad station." More puzzling. The copy of *The Canadian Mother and Child* hidden in the hall closet strongly suggested that a woman selected her infant out of rows of them, lying in little boxes in the hospital, swaddled like papooses. Min had no idea that having one was something that could kill you. She had tried to grasp the idea of her father being a baby, that woman's baby. *Of him killing her.*

The picture of that woman became something tragic, private, irresistible to her. Something inexplicable had happened in her family, something which suggested, however darkly, that she herself might someday walk a path that led someplace other than to the IGA at the corner. Beauty, childbirth, death even, seemed desirable, shone with that same luster that fell over the streets at night, after she had to be in bed by nine and could only gaze through the venetian blinds at all that mystery, all that glory, lying out there shimmering, just beyond her reach.

She had no idea what the woman's name was, nor much hope of ever being told. Annie Laurie, she called her, the name of a tune in *The High Road of Song* book they used in choir. *Her brow is like the snowdrift, Her throat is like the swan, Her face it is the fairest That e'er the sun shone on. That e'er the sun shone on, And dark blue is her e'e, And for bonnie Annie Laurie, I'd lay me doon and dee.* Her grandmother was nothing like the short plump women with gold teeth and big cracked leather purses, who came to visit their daughters' suburban households on Sunday afternoons, who didn't speak English and pinched their grandchildren's cheeks and needed help getting out of the car. *Grandmother* contained grandness, was something shimmering, exotic, majestically sad, much larger and finer than a mere mother.

When her grandfather died, they stopped driving out to the big shady house. All those knicknacks were stored away in boxes in the McCunes' basement. One night when her parents were both gone from the house, Min took a flashlight down there, and searched through a box at a time until she found the picture. She hid it away between UVW and XYZ in the *Britannica* set. It wasn't stealing, she reasoned. You couldn't steal from your own family.

She would take the picture out from time to time and study

it, looking for a message in her grandmother's features that would account for her father's black silences, the hush over her grandfather's house, his clutching crooked hands, the way they had sat there silently every visit and watched those animals being killed. And beyond that, some explanation of this dark, doubleheaded secret of a woman's body, the mysterious way in which she could contain her own death in the shape of a child, and be cracked open like a nut, her life spilled out irretrievably. *The Canadian Mother and Child* said nothing about this. The pictures of bootees and bedjackets and bottle sterilizers hinted at benign processes, of no more consequence to the young beautiful mothers in those pages than putting on a fresh coat of lipstick, or getting a perm.

Min invented a life for Annie Laurie, which paralleled the one she herself lived inside, that had nothing to do with her house on Huron Street, or its inhabitants. It took place in the same land where Heidi, Anne of Green Gables, the March girls and Tess lived, where a girl's life was shaped by trouble, poverty, happenstance, grace. And sometimes, magic.

Annie Laurie slept in the loft. Every night of her life she passed up through that narrow little hole, that dark opening which was her passageway to the other world, the planet of herself. The room, once she had ascended into it, seemed to drop up somehow, to leave the rest of the house and become part of the night. It reeked of mouse droppings and old hay and pungent timbers half rotted with damp. Her bed was cosied off in one corner, the covers tumbled, surrounded by a jumble of her private things: leaves and dead insects she had found and brought in from the fields to study, clothes that no longer fit, books she had received from the rector at church or the lady her aunt worked for, a few precious pencils, a hairnet dangling from the corner of the mirror like a broken spiderweb. Mostly the corner was filled, crowded to the rafters with her dreams, whose webby presence brushed against her face as soon as her head came up through the hole. Don't think we haven't noticed you were gone. *She was comfortable with them, sank back into them as you would into a soft mound of furze. They multiplied up here like pieces of her mother's knitting, elongating and filling themselves out into garments she slipped into. Wearing her dreams she was not aware of the damp, of the wood heaving and sighing in its half-vegetable state, of hunger or the ever-present shame of her growing body. She was other-than-that, wrapped in the lovely warm miracle that waited here for her.*

No need to take the purple box this time. She had to pack carefully, for the long months she would be on the road: traveling halfway around the world—Central America, Canada, Europe—working on a set of photographs for a book she had planned, making notes, now taking this additional trip to see her family. And thinking. For when she had outlined her journey to Peter he acted hurt, raised objections, told her he was tired of her indecision, there was too much uncertainty in being with her, he needed a shape, a definition of what the two of them were.

"This has been going down for over a year now—we come together, move apart, back closer together. And now you're leaving for God knows how long. You have to decide, Min. Are we a real couple, or not? If we are, then I want to know where we're going here. I know where *I* want to go. I want to live with you, to get married. You obviously know that. I've said it a hundred times, haven't I? I keep saying the same thing."

"So a real couple lives together, or is married."

"Well, yeah. After a certain amount of time—yeah. That gets to be the only thing that makes sense."

"So what if we're not one?" she asked, not daring to look at him.

"If we're not—if we're not, then I can't do this anymore. It's too confusing. Too painful. I need to move on. I want you, but not like this. I don't want to date you anymore. So you decide. Yeah, I'll wait for you while you're on this trip. I don't think it's such a hot idea, frankly. I'm not happy about it, it's not going to be easy for me—but I will, all right? But that's it. Then you have to tell me for sure. You have to decide."

As she listened to him, all the joy and lightness and open space she usually felt when they were together suddenly seemed to fade, like a backdrop at the end of an act, before the stage went dark. She felt heavy in her chair, diminished, as if there were no air to breathe and she had been walled into a small, dim closet. Six months of planning had gone into this trip; she wanted to do it very badly, thought of it as one of the most important things she had ever attempted. Now he had cast a long shadow across it: she might have to pay a high price for leaving. She had not been prepared for this, for hearing that kind of finality in his voice. *Decide*. She had no idea if she could do what he was asking. He was talking about family, having a home. *Doom*.

There was something about the absolute *literalness* of living with someone—what she thought of as a downward spiral into dailiness, crumbs on the counter, a ring in the bathtub, juiceless lovemaking—that frightened her, felt like a kind of death. Her parents had had that kind of existence, seemed to know—or want—no other. Their domesticity was organic and unreserved. They needed one another so peculiarly, out of such opposite natures, it was as if they had been joined together in order to make a single complete, decently functioning unit. A set of hot and cold taps. Rose hollered, Alex caviled, Min and Rina scurried to keep out of the churning vortex at the center of their home. There was never enough room to get away from the others in her family. They were stranded together on a raft of misery. The recollection of all that pointless turbulence lived at her core and still did its work, chewing at her steadily. Her images of family were of being cornered, hounded, deeply unhappy. From time to time, when she thought about all of it, about Rose especially, she would say to herself, I could be like that, and she could feel shards of her mother sticking up from the deepest loam of her self, like pieces of an old, broken pot. She would have to dig into that to say yes to Peter—and who knew what was down there, what might be uncovered?

She put the purple box back up on its shelf, then pulled it down again, and drew out the picture of her grandmother that had been a silent, steady companion through some of her worst years. She slipped it in with her other gear. She would take it back home with her. Maybe after all these years, she should return it to her father. Or at least show him that she had saved it: a piece of his life too, after all. She sensed him waiting, sitting in his old chair in that cold, drafty house, waiting for her, for all of them, his girls—Rina, Min, their mother—to come back to him.

Hot Springs

Her van had been climbing through massive clutches of greyish rock for most of the day, so that when she crested a hill and finally saw the valley spread out before her like a small green world all its own, Min let out a gasp and murmured to herself, Incredible. Will you look at that. Just incredible. Wasn't she always looking for exactly this kind of place, a pocket of beauty her eyes could move into gradually, with the kind of slow, drinking reverence she felt when she walked into a church in a foreign country, that quiet expectancy of a small miracle or revelation of grace, which might change her suddenly, perhaps forever? She counted on change happening like that: unexpectedly, a broad arm circling, enfolding, gathering force from hidden corners. As much as you could count on the unexpected.

Above the valley like this, looking down from the side of a rounded green mountain, she took her time, slowed the van, let herself sink into the scene bit by bit. Gently weathered farmhouses flecking the hillsides. A faded cluster of taller, red-roofed buildings, which must be the town. A silvery slip of a river parting two dark masses of trees, then winding off to the east past her line of seeing. And all of this basking in the light of late afternoon, her favorite hour: a thick vegetative haze brightened by the moisture collecting in the air above the trees, the kind of light that endowed every rock and leaf and dully gleaming bit of railroad track with a seeming inner perfection: luminous, complete.

She let the van roll to a stop in a gravelly turnoff where she could get out to stretch her limbs and have a look at the map. Was that the town she was looking for, down there? She paid scant attention to maps when she traveled; she liked to establish a destination in the morning, then take whatever side roads suggested something out of the ordinary—something that perhaps couldn't be shown on a map—and were headed in the right general direction. The right direction during most of this trip had been north, then had veered toward the east a couple of weeks ago. She was shooting rolls of photographs for the book she had been thinking about for so long, a book on hot springs. After months of poring over guidebooks and geological surveys, digging up old maps and references, she decided to track down the major springs she hadn't yet visited in North and Central America, then as many as she could in Europe. She had first driven south, into Guatemala, then wound her way up back up through Mexico and California, tracing the great vertebrae of the continent on into the coastal range of western Canada and toward the Rockies, seeking along those undulant spines the hidden openings from which hot water seeped, gushing or drying up at the earth's whim. *Ojos*, some people called hot springs. Watching, recording, reflecting eyes.

She had been drawn to springs since she first stepped down into a steaming pool at Banff, years ago, on a family trip through the mountains. She stayed in the water for hours that day, completely at home, and did not want to come out when her parents called, ready to leave. It was the rare enchantment of a pool scooped out of the side of a mountain, of other people's faces disappearing in the steam, of the way her body felt, puckered and slithery with minerals, that bewitched her. Ever since, she has looked out for springs on her travels. They have become another kind of aperture for her, another lens, geological events that open onto a particular diorama of human history, first sought out by native peoples, then by the infirm, the crackpots, the hopeful, the aged whom no other source could warm. People need such places, she has come to believe, where there is some promise, however evanescent, of transformation. Around many of them sprang up entire towns, development schemes, cults; masses of tourists poured in, who sometimes disappeared as quickly as they had come, owing to a fire, a landslide, bankruptcy, rumors of an Indian curse.

Rich, her editor at the publishing house that had brought out her last volume of photographs, had been highly skeptical of this project, and paid her advance with considerable reluctance.

"There's absolutely no readership for a thing like this, Min, nobody out there. Zero. *Nada*. I might as well flush this right down the toilet," he had said, waving the check in her face. "Why such a completely obscure topic? What's wrong with buildings, all of a sudden? You do great buildings. People *buy* buildings."

"I'm tired of buildings. I know this seems off the wall, but it—there's something there, something I want to do. I'm not really sure why."

"So what are you going to call it? *Cracks in the Planet? Soaking Your Cares Away? How Hot Is Hot?*"

"I'm still shooting film, how do I know what I'm going to call it?" she replied, hoarse from arguing for her project. "Just trust me, Rich. Something's there. Trust me on this, all right?"

So there she was, after six weeks on the road, somewhere in the interior of British Columbia. There was a spring at the bottom of this mountain, hidden in all that alluvial lushness spread out before her. A civilized, orderly spring, no doubt, nothing like some she had seen, just this side of volcanic in their maddened, explosive heat. A woman she had met at Radium Hot Springs last week told her she'd find this spring a few miles past the center of town, on a side road winding off to the left. The place was rundown, unpopular. It was no longer on any maps.

The ripe, fertile light of late summer, golden shading to ocher, stretched endlessly toward a lingering twilight. Hauling out her bag, she changed lenses, set up her tripod, and shot two rolls of film quickly, deftly, as the light shifted, dissolved, and re-formed over the valley. She was not a sparing, two-shots-a-day photographer. She had all the restless appetite of someone still learning the reach of her craft. In a place like this she felt like a cow standing in a pasture, up to her knees in the middle of all the food she could eat. I could have been fiddling around with that frigging tape deck and completely missed this, she thought, measuring her luck. Alert, antenna-like, her eyes and fingers sensed, recorded, reached, gave her the place for a few moments, an hour, etching its shapes onto some back part of her brain where they would live in storage, where she could feed off them later, when there would be time to choose, savor, digest.

The first time she'd ever seen mountains Min had been ten, slouched down in the back seat of the salmon-colored Mercury trying to ignore her sister. Her mother had been prodding her for the last two thousand miles to get her nose out of that book and look at some of the scenery it was costing her father an arm and a leg to drive them by on this vacation. Her mother was always trying to get Min to look at what *she* was looking at, to see it the way she did, agree that it was cute, or funny, or magnificent, whatever.

The back window of the car was tinted a tropical turquoise, and moved up and down at the touch of a button next to her father's left arm. Min was certain this distinctive modern feature was the sole reason he had bought the car.

"Put it down, Dad."

"No, it's too windy, put it up."

"Halfways then. Big baby."

The rear window was the only one she cared to look out of, half-twisted around on the seat and gazing backward, as if where they had come from was the only landscape that could possibly be worth looking at.

"Have you ever seen anything so magnificent in your *life*?" Rose McCune crowed, craning her neck all the way out of her window and turning her head skyward. Surely if her father's hands suddenly tugged the wheel an inch or two sideways, her mother's head would be knocked right off by the greasy-looking black rocks rising wall-like on both sides of the car. It could happen; everyone knew her father wasn't a very good driver. Her mother was taking a big risk, watching the scenery instead of her father's driving. Her mother always used words like *magnificent*, *spectacular*, *majestic* when they were on vacation, words she never used at home. She had a special little traveling atomizer of Tigress that made her smell different, too. A vacation made her feel like a new woman, she said. All the

Rockies meant to Min on that trip was a sudden shadow on the pages of *Swamp Angel*, a darkness that loomed up beside her in the car. Chilly earth-tainted air, which smelled as though they were driving through an underground tunnel, an ancient deep-freeze. She already knew how to block out her family, the way the mountains blocked the sun. She concentrated all her attention on what was closest at hand: the minute, the barely visible. Pages of fine print, the gradations of color and texture in the brown mole on her left arm, the tiny tracks of dirt that were already established in the pores of the new salmon vinyl upholstery. She was growing nearsighted. The larger world meant nothing. It was merely something you had to act like you cared about in order to please your parents. Mountains. Fresh air. Wildlife. *Sensational.*

By the time she packed her equipment into the van and finally descended into the valley, the deep bluish shadows of the mountains were moving with her, gradually staining the landscape a darker, saddened hue. Here were the farmhouses, the weedy yards and overgrown gardens, at close range. Everything looked to be of an older, poorer time—the forties, perhaps, her parents' time—the valley a likely victim of the agricultural slowdown that had spread blight-wise across the rural areas of the country since the seventies began. It was picturesque, until you remembered that people still had to live here, put food on the table, buy tires for the truck, new jeans for the kids to start school in.

In the gardens she could see the old-fashioned plants of her childhood, strong-smelling varieties that liked to sprawl out of control: hollyhocks and snowball bushes, spirea, rose of Sharon, buddleia. Plants nobody grew anymore. Her mother had grown them. She taught Min all their names, rolling them off her tongue like they were a pack of crazy relatives. Speedwell, heliotrope, mignonette. *Rose of Sharon.* One of those had grown next to their front porch: deep pink, nearly hat-sized blooms with scarlet throats and long, furry yellow tongues. Min had loved its exuberant tropical flash, its abundance. She claimed it as her own special plant, giving it drinks from the hose every night in summer, yelling *Look out!* at the other kids when they jumped off the porch. She had thought that would be a lovely name for a daughter: Rose of Sharon.

At the edges of the fields huddled clusters of rusty machinery, discarded tires, sagging clotheslines, broken plastic buckets and toys, tractors waiting to be put to use—not modern tractors, but those of childhood storybooks, the red ones with scooping metal seats, huge corrugated tires, exhaust pipes that tooted out musical puffs of smoke behind Farmer Brown. On the outskirts of the town, wooden signs were posted beside driveways. FERT. EGGS 4 SALE, CANNING TOMATOES, FILL DIRT WANTED CHEAP. Two ratty-haired children were hauling something out of a drainage ditch with a rope, the only people Min saw until she neared a gas station on the main street.

She decided to pull into the station. It was old, the pavement blackened with oil, with four of those human-looking rounded pumps, and a large stucco canopy suspended over the service area.

"What exactly do you mean, hot springs?" asked the hoarse teenaged attendant through her window, as though she must be speaking of some specialty auto part. Jeez, maybe I'm not in the right town after all, she thought. The place was starting to feel more and more like a movie set than anywhere real. The kid was wearing suspenders. There was a beat-up looking pop machine that showed bottles, not cans, lying on their sides in the little compartments. She went inside to talk to an old man she saw leaning against a fly-specked wall-sized map of the area, which filled half the front window.

"Oh, you must be thinking of Tinsley's, young lady," the man said, rubbing his stubbled cheeks. "Used to be a popular place, years ago. Never went there myself. Nobody goes there anymore, not with Radium aways up the road."

"I've just come from Radium," Min explained. "Now I want to visit this Tinsley's."

He looked at her as if she'd just left heaven, and was asking him how to get to hell. He gave her directions doubtfully, reluctantly, shaking his grizzled head. Clearly she wouldn't be going there if she had any idea what it was like, if she was in her right mind.

"There's the Sleep Inn on the way out of town, you know," he shouted after her as she went out to pay for her gas. "They remodeled it in '83. It's a lot more up to date."

His directions proved confusing. Maybe he'd made them deliberately so. Some people just didn't want you to get where you were going if they didn't think you should be going there.

After several wrong turns she figured out where to cross the railroad tracks to get to the turnoff, and three blocks later saw the faded red letters spelling out TINSLEY'S RESORT. The sign stood beside a large, crumbling three-story wooden house, quasi-Victorian, done in irrevocably weathered, peeling shades of blue, the upstairs balcony and downstairs porch both sagging dangerously in the middle. Damn! she thought, feeling a surge of disappointment. What a hole. I wanted something nice tonight. Comfortable. Clean. Surroundings mattered less when you were traveling with someone else. You could always joke about the appalling carpeting, the funky bathing-cap smell in the bathroom, the bugs lined up on their backs along the windowsills. When you traveled alone, as she usually did, a dreary room often turned hostile: the peeling veneer on the pullman grabbed at your underpants, the dust and mildew came to roost on your chest as soon as you lay down, you moaned and ran great distances in your sleep. You learned to reason with yourself, devise rituals for your own comfort, remind yourself again why you had come, why you kept doing this. You promised yourself a bottle of wine with dinner, a special breakfast tomorrow morning. She'd been camping out of the van for a week now. Luxurious would have been unrealistic in this part of the country; she knew that. But this place hardly looked open.

It seemed remarkable, then, that the large pool near the back of the property should be filled with steaming, strong-smelling water. She parked in a scruffy-looking area dotted with anthills and bits of trash—likely the parking lot in better days—and wandered over to investigate the bathing facilities. There was a ramshackle changing house next to a small pool, which must have been built for children to wade in. Chrome railings, which looked recently installed. A red wooden box displaying a faded life preserver behind glass, like a saint's collar. The big pool was lined with chipped yellow ceramic tiles, bordered around the top by a band of dark blue. Though its surface looked a little green and scummy, the water tested hot. A good sign.

She had traveled long hours to any number of springs, only to find cold water—sometimes no water. Finding springs was often a matter of deciphering hints, allusions, directions, prodding at vague memories, contending with dead ends, wrong turns, mistaken guesses. Her first summer in Greece, she and her traveling companion—a man whose eyes and hands still flashed vividly in her memory, a Spaniard who possessed a spellbinding potency of expression in his own tongue—had spent two nerve-shattering days climbing over rocky, parched hillsides on an ancient Vespa, searching out a place marked LOUTRON ELENIS on her map. When they finally arrived with a bone-dry gas tank at what should have been the right spot, they found two buildings that could have been stores and six or seven white houses, all tightly shuttered against searing noon heat and dust, and nearby a long low building that looked like a storage shed or small animal pen. The Spaniard sank down into the dust, clutching handfuls of it up in the air and uttering some harsh-sounding phrases—one was *"Traigame tierra,"* which meant, approximately, "Bring me dirt (to eat)," and betokened an utter loss of hope, an exaggerated shame and reviling of oneself. "Loutron Elenis? *Nero*—hot?" Min asked an old man who finally peeped around the corner of a building. She pointed at the map and made washing, dousing motions. Her question was heard by invisible ears pressed to the shutters and doors, for several old people—everyone in the town appeared decrepit, and was wearing the inevitable black—came out to shake their heads and wag their fingers at her. The first man pulled at her arm and led her over to the shed building. (The Spaniard was still kneeling in the dirt.) Inside were small, square cement enclosures, built around some rough metal troughs. Then she saw the pipes that emptied into them—these were the hot baths, then! Or what had been. The man pulled a rubber stopper out of one of the pipes, and a gush of brackish water ran cold over her outstretched hand. Several old people who had crowded into the low doorway after Min were clucking their tongues in their toothless heads, gesturing up at the blue patches of sky showing through the window openings as if to tell her that the Olympians had one afternoon cast their disfavor upon Agua Thermi, and the water had been running cold ever since. They acted pleased when she pulled out her camera and began taking photographs, as if she had been specially sent to record their story, as if there was a possibility that justice might finally be coming, that heat once again would find its way up to all their aching bones from the middle of the earth. Min spent two days there, sleeping above the town's taverna/general store in a bare white room with a rusty cot on one side. The room had a tiny balcony that looked out over the sea, and, inexplicably, a large octopus flung over the railing. The Spaniard disappeared on the Vespa. She taught the owner's daughter, who could count but not converse in English, to play cribbage. When the octopus began to really smell, she hitched a ride out of town with a group on an English tour bus, a nice air-conditioned Mercedes.

She climbed the creaking steps of Tinsley's Resort and rapped loudly on the bleached-out front door. After several knocks, it opened. She was appraised wordlessly by a stooped, sad-looking woman in a flowered housedress and a raveling blue cardigan.

"Mrs. Tinsley?" Min enquired politely.

"No, no," the woman said softly, shaking her head and nervously tucking a few strands into the heavy white coil of hair at her neck. "She's passed on nearly fifteen years back—the mister too. We'd be the only ones here."

"Well—no matter. I'm not actually looking for the Tinsleys. I'd like to find out about the springs, if I can, perhaps take a few pictures. And I'm looking for a room for the night. If you still have rooms available."

The woman smiled.

"This place has twelve rooms, and they're all available except for our two, and there's a couple staying up on the second floor. They're all clean. You can pick any one you like upstairs. Downstairs is family. Are you alone then?"

"Yes, I am."

"Well. We charge twenty-five dollars a night, including your breakfast if you don't need eggs."

She ducked back into the hallway and took a card from a low table. Handing it to Min, she murmured, "I'm Maida Jones, like it says there."

The paper was fuzzy and well-fingered—was it her only card?—and it read:

TINSLEY'S HOT SPRINGS RESORT

Hot Sulphur Therapy Pools
Showers
Crippled Facilities
TV In Every Room
All Ameneties

Bill & Maida Jones, Props.

I wonder what other amenities are being suggested, Min thought. Mrs. Jones stood there twisting the top button of her sweater—left/right, left/right. She had a slight, lilting accent that Min couldn't quite place—it wasn't exactly Scottish, or English either. The way she stood—stooped forward, sheltering herself—made her appear timid, overworked, as though she had lived in cramped, closed-up rooms all her life, and would no sooner dive into that pool outside than take off all her clothes in a roomful of strangers. But Min thought she saw a flicker of something else in her face: a hopeful girlishness, the expression of someone with a life yet unlived waiting before her.

A feeble noise came from the hall behind her, the sound of a whimpering dog or cat, perhaps. Mrs. Jones turned toward it, buttoning up the top buttons of her sweater, pulling it down at the hem.

"I have to tell you we don't have the TVs anymore, the way the card says," she said, turning back toward Min for a moment. "That makes all the difference to some. There's just the one set now in the parlor. You're welcome to look at it if you want. Go up and take a look around, if you're not sure."

The last streaks of long summer twilight were fading from an indigo sky. From where Min sat in the pool, the mountains loomed dark and silent at her back. The moon, not yet visible above the peaks, sent ahead a silvery glow. A portion of the valley lay in front of her like a dimly lit corridor, a few boulders and shrubs and a once-painted bench nearby shining softly, as if from daylight stored within. After the sun set behind the mountains the air had cooled instantly; steam now rose thickly from the water's surface, coiling up toward the first faint stars, forming tiny beads on each of the hairs on her arms when she let them float out of the water. Stillness. *Now fades the glimmering landscape on the sight, And all the air a solemn stillness holds.* This valley is old, old, old, she thought. It has aged, faded, been forgotten by everyone. The peace is comforting. I could live in a place like this, just for the sheer abandoned beauty of it.

But that wasn't true at all. Who was she trying to kid? She could no more live here than on the moon. She'd be bored out of her mind; beauty wouldn't be enough. It never was, even though sometimes she thought it ought to be. Hadn't Proust lived on it for years, like a communion wafer, an energy-charged molecule? No; that was the *memory* of beauty: something quite different. Beauty itself could wear on you, do in your adrenals like sugar. After a while you just couldn't look at it anymore. You had to go away and look at something else for a while, or you wouldn't even see it, because you were bored, your eyes had nothing to strive for. There was that kind of beauty where she lived now, in California. You had to really watch out for it.

When you came right down to it, that was one of the reasons she'd left this country, more than ten years ago. Boredom. That waiting for something to happen and the near-certainty that it wouldn't, because it was happening to somebody else, someplace far away, and would never happen here. Or if it did, it would be too late for it to make any difference. To her. Oh, the countryside was beautiful, in its scruffy, haphazard sort of way; she had grown up near broad open fields strewn with waist-high Queen Anne's lace, milkweed, and red willow, where you could take your lunch and walk for miles and not see anyone—not be afraid of anything bad happening, either. But you could spend only so much time walking through fields.

She used to feel permanently, closely surrounded by what she now thought of as a special Canadian variety of blankness, a lot of empty space. *In this vast land of ours*, began all those National Film Board documentaries they had to watch at school.

Millions of square miles of uninhabited land. Slabs of endless tundra, prairie, polar ice cap, squeezing you slowly from all sides. In the middle of all this lay the familiar wasteland of her own neighborhood, in which she imagined herself to be like one of the dots on a connect-the-dots page in her coloring book. There was her house, then a big bare place until you got to the Silvers' house, then another space before the corner house. Those vacant gaps had been cleared for building, but were as yet unused scrubby patches of ground, baking in the bright sunlight or blanketed by snow, awaiting their inhabitants. Then came a treed, overgrown place called The Bush. Across the street from The Bush was The Ditch. Before the roads were paved you wandered pathlessly across these blank places; you did not make a straight line to connect house: house: corner house: Bush: Ditch. When you played at The Ditch, your house was someplace far away, completely out of your seeing. It might as well not even have existed. If your mother called you, you couldn't hear her. You only went home when you got hungry, or stung or bitten by something, or if you saw your father's car go by and realized it was already dinnertime and you were probably in trouble.

Usually it was your mother you were in trouble with; she was the fixed point in the broad spaces of your life, a goalpost, a flashing red light. Your father—a much vaguer entity, hard to locate—was saved for special occasions. Min had experienced her mother as a push from behind, something sharp between the shoulder blades—a stick, the bony end of a finger, a jutting edge. She had not been put on this earth to be amused, sheltering, indulgent. Rose saw a mother's duty as keeping things moving; she did her utmost to steer Min the way you steer a car on an icy road, prod along a balking pony. *Toe the mark* was a favored expression of Rose's. *You'd better learn to toe the mark, Miss.*

The mark, of course, had been invisible to Min; she could neither perceive nor understand it. She imagined it as a faint wavering line, a dark speck hovering above her in space, antimatter, the stuff that ran up and down on the television screen before the stations came on. Like Rose herself, it was erratic, heavy, outside reason, infinite. It stretched, indelibly, to the farthest reaches of space, beyond the edge of the sky you could see at the lake. Aglow in the dark, its gleaming silver-black edge used to cut through her dreams like a knife through water, through air. Standing on the other side of it, the wrong side—as she often did—Min was given to understand that she was adrift in a vast ocean of sin and recklessness, deep into the stuff that could break a mother's heart. She was not walking the paths of righteousness. She was sinking into the opposite of goodness, of everything they told you about at church, of Gloryland, of love. Sinking away from the sun, and into deep, cold shade.

Why was she there? Why had she been told for so many years that she'd better shape up, sit up, smarten up, listen up, or else? Or else *what*? In her heart she had not been a bad child, bent on fouling the nest through malice, deceit, thoughtlessness. Like every child, she wanted the love, the approval, the pats and nods. But she didn't want to be drowned by them, or suffocated or choked, either. Rose's love was enveloping, fierce, eruptive; when it came out it surged over everyone in a hot lava flow. Min felt it right from the first, pumping into her straight from Rose's breast, from a strong underground stream in her mother. No one could say a word or lift a finger against Rose McCune's children, save for Rose herself. Me and Mine, she called them. *Nobody's gonna do that to Me and Mine.* The day Min came home for lunch sobbing over being smacked on the leg and sent to the corner, her mother yanked on a sweater and marched all the way back to the school with her, to tell Miss Murdoch—startled in the act of raising a fried baloney sandwich to her skinny mean lips—exactly what was what. That never happened again.

Rose herself, of course, had been about as far from toeing any mark as you could get. But something about her own half-squelched, that's-all-behind-me-now willfulness must have scorched her somehow, left her afraid, for she fought against it the way you fight a brushfire—beating it back in sudden fits and surges—especially against any signs of it flickering to life in her daughters. It left her standing foursquare against certain kinds of people and certain kinds of behavior that could have been found threaded snugly through her own past, had anyone cared to look there. It had moved her to marry a quiet, reasonable man who stood utterly remote from the Mediterranean glitter and tempest of her own family, the Minellis, who imported her from a brawling slum into the ordered neutrality of the suburbs, the blandness of Protestantism.

Those neighborhoods were filled with women like Rose, a scant generation removed from their own parents' miseries, which they visited faithfully on weekends, bearing tokens of their New Lives: cakes made up from mixes, frizzy permanents, bottle-fed babies. After these visits they came back home to their gravel driveways and lawn chairs shaking their heads, damp with tears and smelling of cooked cabbage, shaken and proud, even more determined that their children would not grow up the way they had. Certain things were to be avoided at all costs: dirt, illness, smart-aleck kids, shabby clothing, ethnic foods, sleeping more than two to a bed. Filled with the resolve of pioneers, they grew shrewd with money, fierce in love. They had plans, a map of the future. They knew perfectly well it was all up to them. There would be no back talk.

To their children they were steadfast sources of heat and light, the blazing molten centers of the inexplicable solar systems all children revolved in. To a certain extent they could be hung onto, leaned against, counted on: but they must be obeyed. Not to agree with them was a deliberate invitation to catastrophe, a wild spinning out of orbit, a deadly choice of wrong over right, danger over safety, the rotten over the pure. There was an ideal family somewhere—with certain furniture and appliances, the kids' hair water-combed and parted, a particular pattern of linoleum gracing the kitchen floor, an overall, meat-and-potatoes *correctness* to the thing—which their mothers had never exactly seen, but carried a vision of, knew they must strive to emulate and uphold.

Min could not see how she fit into any of this. She could hardly wait to get away, certain that she was living in an unswept corner of the civilized world, a grubby, linty little pocket that had simply failed—for some sad, awful, unjust reason—to evolve. In her teens, when life was exploding everywhere else, when people her age were running away from home and flocking to love-ins and be-ins and taking acid like vitamins, she was still stuck in Wyandotte, where you couldn't even order a beer until you were twenty-one. She was able to work herself up into a state of inspired, watery melancholy over this: listening to the requiems of Verdi and Mozart, Strauss's last songs, Gregorian chants (all borrowed from the library and played at night by candlelight on the record player in the basement), consuming large amounts of muddy, tremor-inducing coffee, making Beardsleyesque drawings or writing grotesque lyrics in her sketchbook. Of course she was an artist. She knew she belonged somewhere else. Sometimes she stayed up all night, so she could walk around the next day feeling lightheaded, nauseated, seeing everything in a tight halo of throbbing light.

What sustained her through those years was imagining a life for herself in a place where things really happened: in New York, say, or Paris. San Francisco, London, Florence—she constructed a wild, satisfying existence in each of them during the long Saturday afternoons she spent at the public library downtown, drawing, dozing, looking at pictures, watching dust motes move in the light beams that gleamed across the wooden tables. She would be a visionary painter in New York, hurling ideas at canvas into the small hours every morning, her hair dotted with paint, her kohl-rimmed eyes burning as she hallucinated from the fumes. Or she would study voice in Boston, training herself for the gilded halls of Europe, where audiences would cheer and sob openly as she dragged them with her through the poisonings, reunions, betrayals and suicides of the great operas. No, she was too tall for opera. Well then, perhaps the quieter, more scholarly life of an art historian in Paris. Her stockings would be textured, her dark unruly hair would magically have straightened out and hang to her shoulders, perfectly cut, she would wander the avenues in the brisk evening air, sip absinthe while she made notes on bar napkins, attend a salon on Sunday afternoons—no, no, she would *hold* a salon on Sunday afternoons. In her apartment. The one carefully decorated with rich fabrics, tribal art, mysterious heavy objects in glass, stone, metal. Where she would cook delicious, beautiful-looking meals for her lovers—themselves as passionate as she, people of learning, underground habits, and artistic flair, of both sexes, many races, who loved her deeply, if for the moment, and would never forget the time they had spent with her for as long as they lived—to eat with their fingers.

No, leaving the country had not been difficult. It never occurred to her that another city in Canada might have been any different from her own. All she could visualize were more neighborhoods like hers: then prairie, tundra, ice cap. Rose's family—including her mother and all six of Min's cousins—had moved to the States, and their Christmas cards bespoke wonders: cheap cars, drive-in restaurants, no-iron Crimplene dresses. Sunday shopping! Beer in grocery stores! When she finally made it as far as Malibu, which seemed Wyandotte's opposite in every way, she felt it was so much more a move *toward* something—a vision, a future as richly textured as the wallcoverings in her imaginary apartment—than away from anything. She could discern no important way in which the landscape of those original, vacant suburbs figured in her imagination, nor the seasons there, except as conditions to be suffered through: too hot in summer, too cold in winter, the modulations of the neighborhood everlastingly tiresome. What did it mean, after all, to have a home? To say, I am from X. During that first year she used to interrogate herself, trying to discover whether some necessary part of her had been forsaken, had left a great hole gaping somewhere in her psyche. But she could never feel anything like that. What was left back there, anyhow? Only her family, a few friends, a teacher she still wrote to. And she could always visit, or her father and Rina could come to see her anytime, anyplace she chose to live.

Of course, they hadn't. They felt betrayed, abandoned, left alone with each other in that house on Huron Street like two orphans on a raft. Their suffering, accusing voices on the phone those first few months had driven her nearly wild. Rina had sobbed and pleaded, hiccuping across the miles that she was lonely, she didn't know where anything was, she didn't know what to make for dinner, Dad just sat there night after night not saying anything it was driving her crazy—and then her father would take the receiver, and say in a distant, leaden voice that he and Rina hoped that *she* was doing fine.

Rina had always been fretful, needy, unsure of herself, desperate to be liked and included. After their mother died, she fastened onto her sister like a mouth on a nipple, greedy for reassurance, sustenance, continuity. She ran to keep up when Min walked to school with her friends, hung around the fringes of Min's class at recess, leaped to her feet with a trembling lip whenever her sister made a move to leave the house.

"Please let me come. *Promise* I won't say a single thing. I won't say one solitary word, I won't even look at you."

"Come on, Rin, don't be a pill. Why don't you go over and call on Denise or somebody?"

"Denise is at her grandmother's for the weekend and Joanne can't come out, she hit her brother too hard."

"What about Debby then?"

"Debby has to help her mother clean house on account of company."

"Jeez Rina, it's not my problem, you know? Get your own friends. We don't always want some little kid tagging along. We can't *do* anything."

Then Rina would look frantic and start scratching away at the scabby red patch on the inside of her elbow.

"You can have all my allowance. Please? I'll make the bed every day this week. Let me come, okay?"

Feeling hopeless, Min usually relented, because the times she hadn't she imagined Rina sitting alone in the living room all day, kicking at the couch, scratching her arm and crying. Rina's devotion irritated her; it was like being followed around by some scruffy little dog she didn't want. With Rina around she could never forget about *home*, pretend she was really somebody else. It was always Rina's dream that when they grew up Min would really like her, want to be with her all the time, let her wear her clothes, take her on trips. When Min finally left, Rina could not believe she had been left behind.

But what else could Min have done? She had acted to save herself, finally, from the loneliness of waiting, of longing for a real life to happen to her. By the time she was twenty she had known that it would not happen in Wyandotte, not in that house with the three of them watching one another the way they did. Living there had become unbearable; though at first the guilt and uncertainty, the sudden cold shivers of turning her back on all of it, seemed hardly better. *I can't give them their lives*, she told herself over and over, trying to convince herself it was true. After some years Rina had finally left, gotten a job and her own apartment. Several years went by when she would not talk to Min, or write back to her. In her occasional letters now she sounded cheerful, impetuous, if not exactly confident. Oddly, their father sounded much better after Rina moved out. Calmer. More like his old self. Or what she thought she remembered his old self as being like.

No sign of the couple who were supposed to be staying on the second floor. Maybe they didn't like bathing in the darkness, the secretive deceitful steam. Perhaps they were one of those couples she'd seen who created encapsulated worlds of familiarity for themselves when they traveled, making it almost unnecessary for them to relate to strangers, new surroundings, unexpected weather. They came to places like this so they could tell themselves and their friends at home they'd been somewhere; perhaps they'd go for a swim, or a walk, or look at a mountain, always pointing out to each other what to notice, secure in the knowledge that there was something to see if they wanted to go out later, but quite content to stay put, eat dinner, watch TV in their rooms, arrange their clothing in strange drawers. The same kind of predictability that used to make her mother call out excitedly, "Oh look, girls, there's a Howard Johnson's!" that put the four of them on orange plastic banquettes, staring at the same menus they'd seen a thousand miles ago.

She relaxed onto her back, drifting, rippling, moving randomly, the warm water lifting her, holding her up. Idly she wondered if her grandmother had ever visited a hot spring. From her research she knew that they existed in Ireland—or had, at one time. "Hydropathic establishments will cure patients suffering from chronic gastric or hepatic derangement, or some of the protean forms of cutaneous, strumous, or gouty and rheumatic affections and of certain complaints peculiar to women."

Her Aunt Binnie, who before this afternoon she had not even known existed, had come for her in a black carriage, in which they made their way, squeaking and thumping over the rutted roads and bridges, to Dublin itself, and beyond, further than Annie Laurie had ever traveled in her life. Her aunt had a large square face like a man's, enormous rough hands, a dark path of hair wandering across her top lip. After a thorough questioning of her niece regarding her education, her brothers and sisters and the business of the farm, she spoke little, only now and again to revile the turn the weather had taken.

At last they drew up in front of a long white-pillared building, separated from the river by a promenade along which strolled a great many finely dressed people, half hidden under swaying, glistening black umbrellas. Her aunt grasped her firmly by the arm and led her past a luxuriant terrace of flowers to a tall iron fence. The bars of the fence streamed with droplets of moisture. Looking down through them, Annie Laurie saw great draughts of steam rising up from the ground and dissolving into the grey mist above. She realized the figures moving in the steam were the heads and shoulders of men and women, gliding above the surface of an enormous pool. An awful smell, as of animal parts rotting in a bog, came to her nostrils. Why would anyone bother to bathe so near to such a smell as that?

"Come now, child," her aunt ordered, nudging her toward the gate. "We've come to take the waters, not to stand gawping. This is certain to cure you of your nerves."

Min automatically began rubbing her fingertips with her thumbs, in an effort to remove some of the permanent yellow stain the photographic chemicals left on them. Her hands always looked rough and discolored—working hands, their veins already knobby and dark, the way her mother's had been. The slithery layer of minerals bathing her skin felt like silk, or feathers. She could almost feel what it would be like to have another kind of body completely: a fish body, a bird body. Something other than heavy bones, flesh, hair; a body that moved effortlessly in other elements. She was aware of this sense of difference each time she removed her clothing and yielded herself to a pool of water like this, let herself be made invisible by the mist.

Not that she had anything wrong with her, anything that needed making over. But she changed, subtly, will-lessly, the longer she floated, and soaked, and let her mind drift the way her body did. She didn't have to think anymore, she could become a more primitive creature, moving from instinct, memory, pleasure. With her ears underwater she could hear bubbling, gurgling sounds, her heart pumping, the coursing of her own invisible fluids through her trunk and limbs, the far-off swishing of her paddling hands. Floating this way, that way. Tonight it seemed that as she floated her body was swelling in the water, her cells soaking it in, she was getting larger, filling the pool, even as she felt herself becoming younger and younger inside: drifting back, into a timeless, weightless place, floating murmuring endless space. Cradled, rocking, dreaming, bathed in warmth. Her younger self a companion creature in the water, fluttering and rolling and moving inside her.

Something floating to the surface: a watery image of a foot. A white foot on a rock.

Then her chest felt as if it was dissolving. Sudden warm tears swam under her eyelids. There was no contraction, no spasm, no wrenching sob. The tears simply washed out of her body as if the water in the pool was washing into her and out of her again, of its own will. And two words bobbed on the surface of her mind as she bobbed, suspended in the water, two separate realities that came together to form a thought.

I   want
I want   I want   I want

Mrs. Jones was standing in the doorway when Min came in from the pool with dripping hair, wrapped in her robe.

"Goodness you're tall. I mean I hope you don't mind my saying so. But you look even taller now that you're wet."

Min smiled at her.

"Five eleven. When I'm wet."

"Oh my, that's tall for a girl. Anyway. I wanted to tell you I've made ourselves a light supper and thought you might want a bite—there's no place open in the town on a Wednesday night. Those other people had to drive clear on over to Elk Lake. I thought . . . I didn't think you'd want to be out on the road alone at night like this."

"I hope you haven't gone to too much trouble—"

"Nothing special. Come down to the parlor after you get out of your wet things."

Min came back downstairs to a gateleg table set with a well-mended white cloth and the kind of yellowed crockery that has a dainty flowered border and a surface of tiny cracks, like old dry skin. Mrs. Jones brought in a big brown pot of tea, bread and butter, sliced tomatoes that looked fresh from her garden, or somebody's, and two boiled eggs. She served Min shyly and awkwardly; she could have been bringing private items out of her closet, one at a time. The whites of the eggs were still clear and runny, barely cooked.

"You have some remarkable things here," Min said, looking around the parlor while she ate. The room had an air of abandoned improvisation, a forgotten, elegiac look that shuttled her eye back and forth between the turn of the century and the present. Rubber-banded piles of plastic bread wrappers spilled from a low table whose legs were made from the curving, silver-tipped horns of some animal. Pictures were stacked three deep on the mantel, a crowd of silent observers. The lampshades wore cracked, yellowing plastic covers, and there was a corrugated plastic mat over the carpet in front of the doorway. The whole space was dominated by an enormous sagging red-velvet couch nearly buried under an assortment of embroidered pillows, pillows depicting Princess Elizabeth's coronation, a person going over Niagara Falls in a barrel, the Seattle Space Needle, pillows from Sault Ste. Marie and Daytona Beach and Gatlinburg. From the corners of the room emanated various old house/old person smells—mothballs, dry rot, unwashed sweaters, mouse droppings, horsehair. Min had to make an effort to keep chewing and swallowing her food.

"Just what I've lived with all my life," Mrs. Jones sighed, wiping her hands on her apron. "Doesn't seem remarkable to me. A lot of dusting and looking after, things nobody else cares about. Did you ever see one of these?"

She handed Min a heavy frame, with a sort of wreath under the glass, and LAVINIA PHELPS R.I.P. 1856–1927 cross-stitched on a black velvet background.

"Made that from my mother-in-law's hair after she passed on. The undertaker cut it off for me. Off the back part. You couldn't tell it was gone by the way she was resting when they laid her out. She'd been growing that braid her whole life. People used to do things like that when someone died. Death meant something in those days. And collecting tears at the funeral—I'll bet you never heard of that, did you?"

An old person's favorite question.

"Now my mother," she continued, not waiting for an answer, "she used to have the most beautiful gold and onyx tear bottle. Up on her dresser. I don't know whatever happened to that bottle, I haven't seen it for ages. . . . People make tapes of funerals now. My sister sent me a tape of her husband's last March. Terrible organist. She had him play 'My Way' at the service. Can you imagine? On one of those cheap little keyboard things. Right there in the chapel. Just as well I couldn't go."

That curious whimpering noise again, from down the hall.

"Did you just hear something?" Min asked.

"No, no, let me do this, it's what I'm here for," Mrs. Jones said, intercepting Min to pick up the dishes. "Don't like eggs, eh? Yes, that's Mother. She usually wants me for something around about now."

"She lives here with you?"

"Mmmm. Going on ninety-two, poor soul. Bedridden. Not much anyone can do for her anymore. Myself, I told Bill to get out the shotgun if I ever get like that."

She cleared her throat, and Min expected she would now mention the extra charge for the meal. She didn't mind, even considering those eggs; it had saved her dressing and going out somewhere, losing the mood of the place. Maybe she would photograph Mrs. Jones here in the parlor tomorrow morning. No. Definitely too Diane Arbus-y. Maybe standing out by the pool. Next to the life preserver.

"I was wondering," Mrs. Jones said. "Now you're certainly not obliged in any way, shape or form. But I was wondering if you would mind very much stopping a moment to say hello to her. It's just that she used to love to meet the guests; when she was well, she'd always be right out there on the porch chatting with everyone and toweling off the children and now, you know, she only sees myself and my husband. And she knows we have guests this evening. She heard the others go out, and I—"

"Sure, Mrs. Jones, I'd be happy to say hello to her."

The mother's room was at the end of the hall. In it stood a bed, a table with a lamp on it, a rocking chair. A tall dresser, filmy white curtains at the single window. At first, in the dim light, Min couldn't see anyone in the bed. There was a strong smell of camphor, fainter ones of urine, and chocolate, from an open box by the bed.

"Mother. I've brought someone to see you. Min—you don't mind if I call you that, do you?—this is my mother. Elizabeth is her name. Isn't it, Mother? Your name is Elizabeth. Lift your hand up now, so we can see where you are, there's a love."

Min laughed as Mrs. Jones said this, for the tiny figure had indeed disappeared into the soft feather pillows and comforter. When a face emerged, Min could not say whether she was looking at a man or a woman. The person in the bed appeared sexless and ageless—old, but of indeterminate oldness—a dry, wrinkled armful of humanity. Min's voice must have registered, for the old woman's eyes opened slowly and very wide, the way a turtle's would. She turned her head—and Min had an image of an egg on the end of a stick, so smooth and white and fragile it looked atop her bony neck—and said wonderingly, "The lady laughed."

A crack widened in the lower half of her face—it was a smile—and she said again, "The lady laughed at me."

Mrs. Jones squeezed Min's hand beside the bed.

"She loves to hear someone laugh. Don't you, dear? I get altogether too serious, always worrying if she's eaten—she hardly eats a bite anymore—or slept, or had her pill. I'm a bore, aren't I, Mother?"

"Hello there, hello Elizabeth," Min said, bending close to the woman's ear, taking the cold, nearly transparent hand that was wavering up from under the covers like a feeler. "I've just been for a lovely swim, and your daughter made me a nice supper." Welsh, she thought, finally placing the older woman's singular accent. She felt awkward, much too large for the room. She was trying not to shout; she had no idea what you say to someone this old, what she might care about. The grip of the woman's thin hand was powerful.

"Been swimming, have ye? Well you watch out, there's deep water around this place. Deep water."

The old woman's eyebrows lifted and her jaw worked up and down, as if she had just found something in her mouth to chew on.

"So. Did you bring me anything then?" she asked Min.

"Oh, Mother—" Mrs. Jones said in a sinking voice.

Feeling around in her pockets, Min pulled out a small flacon of cologne she used when traveling. She pressed this into Elizabeth's papery hand.

"Some scent. I brought you some scent."

The old lady considered this.

"Put some on me then, so I can smell it."

Min dabbed a little on the inside of Elizabeth's wrist, into the webby hollows of her throat.

"Mother—" Mrs. Jones was fussing at the ammonia-smelling sheets, clearly embarrassed by the turn things had taken. "Have you had your pill yet, then?"

"Eh?"

"Your pill. Did you take your pill?"

"What pill?" Elizabeth drew back and looked sharply sideways, as if she'd been cornered in bed by a lunatic.

"I've never taken a pill in my life," she declared. Squeezing Min's hand, she whispered, "You tell her that. You—what's your name?"

"Min."

A kind of fierceness rippled over the old lady's face, animating it.

"I know a lot about you," she said.

Min's own hand suddenly felt icy.

"Yes I do. I've seen your name in a great book."

"Now Mother, let's not, you're getting silly again—"

"Min. Yes. You've come looking for something, I know. But you're looking in the wrong place."

Boy, you can say *that* again, Min thought. Now she didn't know whether to laugh or run out of the room. She was starting to feel giddy, with the old woman's foolish, old-country conjurations, her grip on her hand, the lack of air in the smelly, overheated room—she wanted to get out of there.

Elizabeth gave her bony shoulders a little shake, then fixed her eyes on a spot on the ceiling. In a quavery, distant soprano, she began to sing.

> *There is Someone waiting for me*
> *In an old shanty down by the sea*
> *There is Someone waiting for me*

Mrs. Jones touched Min on the shoulder. "Do let's leave her," she whispered. "She'll be singing that for hours."

With some effort Min released her hand from the old woman's, almost roughly, in a mild panic now to get away. What on earth am I doing here? she wondered. Suffocating in some weird old house, making small talk with two crazy women. She and Mrs. Jones tiptoed out of the room; the tiny singing woman didn't seem to notice.

As they walked back down the hall, Mrs. Jones was twisting the buttons on her sweater again.

"I'm sorry. I shouldn't have taken you in. I hope she didn't upset you."

"No, no. Of course not."

"I'll get that perfume back for you first thing in the morning."

"It's all right. Good night, Mrs. Jones."

"Good night."

Min paused at the front door before going upstairs. She had the kind of disoriented, off-balance feeling she had once after walking through a funhouse, when she tried to stand up straight on the uneven plank floors, saw herself fat, skinny, and squashed in the wavy mirrors, heard unreal laughter coming out of the walls. What was the old woman talking about? There was no reason to pay any attention. But it was unnerving all the same. Nonsense. Old people got to be like children, didn't they?, making up silly stories, talking nonsense to amuse themselves. Crazy as loons. She stroked the skin on her arms, tried to imagine being so old, imprisoned in a leaking, helpless body, lying in bed all day, waiting for nothing, singing at the ceiling.

She could hear Mrs. Jones murmuring in low tones with a man: the invisible Mr. Jones. A loud thud, something heavy—a book, or maybe one of his workboots—dropping to the wooden floor. Then a cough, bedsprings creaking directly over her head. The invisible couple. Going to bed. Pairs of people, couples, talking, undressing, rolling over, performing nightly rituals with one another. She thought of Peter back in Malibu, dwelt longingly for a moment on his features, on silky sand-colored hair, the stiff ruff of his mustache where it hid the curve of his lip, the sea-blue eyes that went light or dark with the shifting of his internal weather. Eyes that didn't look away, that held your gaze as steadily as gravity keeps planets to their orbits. What is he doing? Is he in bed, is he thinking of me? She wanted to talk to him, to take her usual measure of comfort from his kind, steady voice. He had always had a knack of knowing precisely how she felt, of meeting her there somehow. From that very first morning, when they'd both been waiting for a table at Rama Lama's, it was as if he'd always known her, had just been waiting for this opportunity to speak up.

"Might as well sit together," he'd said with a pleased sunshiny grin, touching her arm as naturally as if it were his own. I wouldn't say that in a million years, she had thought. I've been coming here for breakfast every Saturday for six months and I've never talked to anyone but the waitress. Peter had a breezy, boyish confidence about him. *So American*, she had thought at first, unsure whether she liked him or not. It was clear from the way he barely looked at the menu before ordering, steered his way through their conversation easily, humorously, with scarcely a pause, that he knew instinctively what he liked, or didn't like, and hardly gave it a thought. He didn't agonize over things the way she did. For some reason, he had simply decided he liked her. And in spite of her cautious, evaluating nature she found herself liking him too, unaccountably giving in to the situation and discovering it to be pleasurable, easy, absorbing. And—oddly—touching. As they talked she thought how she had suddenly found a friend, feeling so warmed by Peter's interest and understanding, so *seen* by him, so undone, she'd nearly burst into tears. He took it all in stride, squeezed her hand, and finished her toast and fruit salad for her. Somehow they ended up walking the beach, watching sea lions sunbathing on a flat black rock, driving up the coast, eating another meal together, seeing a movie.

"I never do this, you know," she said at one point during that afternoon, sounding prim even to herself.

"Do what?" he asked.

"Just go off like this, with someone I've just met, someone I don't even know."

He flashed her a smile, the ocean glittering and calm behind him.

"Oh, that's okay," he said. "Neither do I." Peter made going with the flow seem like a most reasonable proposition. She was the one who later started to worry that it was all going too fast, maybe they were becoming too attached. How did you gauge those things? Hadn't matters proceeded at a steadier, more conservative pace with other men? She was sure they had. There had been more of a sense of order, a well-modulated sequence of acquaintance, social interaction, mutual evaluation, deepening of intimacy—or not, depending on how the evaluation went—and then the predictable erosion of interest, increasing discomfort, and eventual termination of the attachment. Or sometimes, less predictably, one of them would become far more attached than the other, and a decision would have to be made, the whole thing nipped in the bud before it became too messy and unmanageable. With Peter, however, she had seen none of those familiar markers along the way.

"You just tell me, if it stops being good," he would say, whenever she raised her doubts to him.

But it hadn't: a fact that continued to bewilder her. It was inconsistent with all her experience that their connection should go on being so good, so easy. Yet given such evidence—their continuing happiness—what was she afraid of? Why couldn't she simply say yes, and yield to a life together with him? Tonight, she wondered if it was simply this: that she *was* happy with him, very happy, and couldn't think how to expand her image of herself to accommodate such a spacious, radiant feeling. Instead, she went back and forth, back and forth, thinking of every bad thing that could possibly happen. Or losing herself in that dark well that opened up when she thought of family. Her family. She had tried to explain to him how she felt about them; they weren't alcoholics or child molesters or vicious, soulless people, they were just, they were just—and then she would spread her hands helplessly in front of her, and say, "I don't know. I just don't know." *Irrational*, a voice inside would say. *You're being irrational.*

Peter. No way to call him, tonight. She shivered, and her breath caught in her throat, in a little quiver of a sob, the kind that can ripple over a child even an hour after she's done crying. Standing there in the hallway, looking out, she felt sad, suddenly. Alone. In front of her, on the other side of the glass door, everything was drenched in full silver moonlight, nearly as bright as day. The pool lay silent, and still, a steaming mystery at the foot of the mountains.

Lumps

All the staff at the Ananda Healing Institute had red hearts embroidered on their white jackets. Not valentine hearts—anatomically correct hearts, which looked like boxing gloves with tubes sprouting out of them. Min was attracted to the concept, only she thought they could have gone a lot farther with it—pink nipples, quarter-moon shadows to suggest breasts, bright scarlet penises on the front of the men's pants, curly dark pubic hair done in a fancy chain stitch. Surely their hearts couldn't be that much more important than the rest of them? The motto at the Institute was HANDS THAT HEAL, HEARTS THAT CARE.

It was the summer she turned eleven. Her sexuality was in full, mad blossom. The world was saturated with genital suggestions, rich triggering smells, snatches of music that left her feeling swollen and itchy. It was depressingly apparent that she had been brought to the worst place on earth for developing her sexual powers, which was her goal for that summer. Everybody at Ananda seemed to be doing just the opposite: denying and punishing their bodies, shuffling around in shapeless gowns, displaying their sores and malfunctioning parts with incomprehensible pride, filling the dining hall with talk about their bowel habits, their kidney stones (the size of walnuts, tennis balls, GRAPEFRUIT!), their Higher Selves. *Really.* She had never seen so many weird people in one place at one time. It was like *The House of Frankenstein.* Even the staff had these kind of staring, buggy eyes; they looked at you as if they were trying to see *your* anatomical heart right through your skin. Their skins were Martian shades of green, or orange, like peoples' skin on one of those cheap color TVs.

Only one other person there was even close to her own age, a blond fourteen-year-old boy who was supposed to have leukemia. From what she'd seen of him so far, he looked pretty hopeless. He wore pajamas most of the time and sat in a wheelchair with a vacant smile on his face, his mother hovering over him like a big fluttery moth. The mother wheeled him up to them the first day, introducing themselves as "Mrs. Winger, and my only son, John"—like she was God, or Mary, wheeling around her pale, sickly Jesus. Min thought of leukemia with a D after it, for Death. Every time she heard about an ailment here she tried to evaluate how serious it was, whether or not to give it the D.

"What a place!" her mother had exclaimed, when they finally arrived after almost a week of driving. "Sensational! Smell that? Eucalyptus trees! Mother of God, I feel a hundred percent better already, I swear it. And a big nice pool for you—two of them, will you look at that. Now how could anybody stay sick in a place like this, I ask you?"

"How could you get better is more like it," Min grumbled. "Everybody's so *creepy*."

She walked over to examine the swimming pools, and wrinkled her nose in disgust.

"The water stinks."

"Miranda, you give me a real pain in the neck."

"*Mother*. Don't *call* me that. It does. Smell it. I can't help it. It smells like rotten eggs."

"A Royal Canadian pain."

Rose walked over to the pool slowly, as if her feet hurt, and leaned her nose over the edge, sniffing critically.

"Miss Picky. A little *tiny* smell of sulphur. But that's the *therapy*. That's what it's supposed to smell like if it's going to cure you."

"Yeah, right. And if you're not sick already it makes you sick. No way am I going in that stinky stuff."

For most of the trip across Canada and down into the States, they had nattered at each other like this. Rose had brought Min here—kidnapped her, was how Min thought of it—to keep her company while she underwent the Ananda Cleansing and Rejuvenation Program, which was supposed to cure her cancer. In Min's opinion she had been taken hostage from the family because Rose wanted a witness to something that her husband would not share—would not even hear of—and that Rina was still too young to really comprehend. So she was chosen. She was still angry about this: doubly angry, because her summer was being completely ruined, and because she couldn't even really be angry with her mother for ruining it. How could you be angry at someone who had cancer, who could get so sick they might die on you any minute? One anger was sitting atop the other inside her, like a poisoned sauce bubbling away in the double boiler on the stove.

"No way am I going to be cut," Rose had said emphatically to the doctor on the telephone. "I'm going to a san." "The san" was what she called this place, this cluster of aging stucco buildings set against masses of trees with hanging, peeling bark, with outdoor therapy pools, a huge organic garden, and wooden "contemplation benches" scattered strategically around the grounds. The staff was trained in water therapy, body massage and colonic therapy, and something called "Radiant Light Therapy." There was a certified raw foods specialist, a nutritional counselor, a life skills coordinator. For eight weeks Rose would be undergoing juice fasts, high colonic coffee enemas, olive oil and lemon juice liver flushes, rejuvenant diet therapy.

"Learn how to stop violating the Laws of Nature and Health, and how to live in perfect harmony with Universal Principles," Min read aloud from the brochure on the nightstand in her room. "Purify the Blood, flush out the Liver, rid the Colon of years of putrefying waste material." Makes you sound like a toilet, she thought. A great big toilet. A septic tank. Ma's spending a fortune to have enemas and eat grass. Meanwhile I'm going to *die* spending the whole summer in this creepy place. Nothing to do. Weirdos everywhere. Health food. Thank God I have my own room.

While they were traveling and stopping overnight at motor inns, Min had to share a room with her mother, although she insisted that, when it was possible, Rose get them twin beds, at least. Upon their arrival, the admitting doctor had said, "We welcome your daughter to Ananda, Mrs. McCune. However, we feel it best that family members be housed separately, especially while the patient is undergoing a healing crisis." Now, she had no idea what a healing crisis might be. The two words meant different things, didn't they? For both of their sakes she hoped it would be mostly healing and not too much crisis. And no D after it.

Lying back on her cot, she stared at the huge map of the large intestine that covered the hospital-green wall at her feet. Actually, it was a map of *two* large intestines: a healthy one, in pink, and a sagging version in dark grey, shadowing the original and labeled IMPACTED. The healthy intestine looked gigantic, with symmetrical little bulges along its length, like a python that had swallowed a beaded necklace. Red arrows targeted the flexures: potential trouble spots in the intestinal world. A small diagram in the top corner of the chart showed a person sliced in half, with his digestive system detailed in multiple colors, like a complicated pinball machine. The empty hairless head was turned sideways; you could see that the entire digestive apparatus was really a long winding tube, open at the mouth and rectum. How revolting. Min could not believe such a bulgy thing wormed its way through her own slim body. She remembered an article she saw once in one of the *Reader's Digest*s her father kept down beside the toilet—"I Am Joe's Prostate." I Am Min's Colon. Gross.

Here she was in California, where some of the cutest boys in the world were supposed to be living, looking at a colon. Probably not a beach within a hundred miles. How was she ever going to improve her personality? At home she had been working on her laugh and her mouth, both of which, according to her best friend, Kathy Greene, lacked S.A.—sex appeal.

"The trick is," Kathy had said to her seriously as they stood in front of the mirror in Kathy's bedroom, where they went to practice these things after school, "the trick is when you laugh, not to make any noise. Like this." She expertly crinkled her lips and eyes in a sudden, radiant smile, and rhythmically puffed air out of her nose, shaking her shoulders prettily. "Boys don't like it when you snort and stuff." Kathy was the second most popular girl in their class; Min practised the noiseless laugh devotedly.

Fortunately, besides the colon chart there was a full-length mirror in her room—probably for checking how deformed you were, where your colon was ready to bulge right out of your skin—and standing in front of it now she slowly outlined her lips with the tip of her tongue. I am *not* going to let this whole summer go to waste, she told herself in the mirror. I'm still flat-chested; I can't afford to. A lot of other girls already have way more to work with than I do. That was how Kathy described lips and breasts and eyebrows: *What you have to work with.*

Min decided to concentrate on just her tongue for the first week, on using it the way she had seen older girls and women do: subtly caressing your lips, letting its glistening point linger just behind your top teeth while you pretended to think about something serious, your mouth open exactly the right amount, the wet pink mystery within merely hinted at while the position was held a second too long. Miss Waters, the seventh-grade teacher whose first name was Elizabeth and who looked exactly like Liz Taylor when she married Nicky Hilton, did this with her tongue while she waited for the line to straighten up before she let her class into the building every morning. The elegance of the gesture was completely wasted on the grade seven boys— who were more interested in hammering each other in line— but it was not wasted on Min. Miss Waters was petite, raven-haired, voluptuous; she wore tight, two-piece suits in colors like hot pink and lime green, and high, high heels. Min could have watched Miss Waters and her tongue all day.

While she stood in front of the mirror, she took inventory. She usually did this three or four times a day. Forehead: average. Eyebrows: too straight, growing together in the middle. Should be plucked, Kathy said, but she had tried it and it hurt too much. Eyelashes: long, dark, curving. Eyes: best feature. Deeply set, indigo blue, clear. Unfortunately hidden behind ugly glasses. Nose: ski nose. Freckled. Impossible. Mouth: more problems. As nondescript as the eyebrows, a pale nothing. Thinnish lips, which she continually tried to bite and lick into some sort of fullness. Overall face: small and plain. Body: much too tall, thin, flat as a board. A pencil with clothes on. Arms and legs: hairy. Kathy called her Spider. Spider McCune. She'd tried peroxide on the hair on her forearms, but it still

looked like she had hairy arms, just blondish hairy ones instead
of dark. Maybe she should shave them.

Rose now allowed her to shave her legs, after months of
pleading, because of what happened on the way out here. Min
had finally just gone ahead and done it, one night while her
mother was out picking up some Chinese food for them to eat
in their motel room. When she returned Min was white-faced
and at the point of fainting, stanching blood from a deep four-
inch gash on her shin where her mother's razor had slipped
sideways in too much lather. All that blood made a swift
impression on Rose, made her alert as a nurse. She became
that self whenever anything bad happened, the one who sat on
the edge of the tub and cradled Min's forehead in her cool hand
while she threw up all night from eating sour cherries, or who,
the time Rina was snatched into the lake by a sneaker wave,
ran in fully clothed, the spatula she'd been flipping their ham-
burgers with still held aloft in one hand, dragged Rina back
onto the sand, and pumped gushes of greenish water out of her
until Rina started to cough, and then sat up, crying. She didn't
scold Min. She bandaged the cut expertly, and cleaned up the
mess in the bathroom without saying a word. She seemed to
have recognized something in her daughter, and treated her
with a quieter, more detached respect from that night on. Min
had deliberately crossed one of her mother's lines, and hurt
herself doing so. Rose acknowledged that purpose, female to
female, and stepped back. She even let Min order a cup of
coffee for breakfast in the restaurant the next morning. Min
had come to look forward to beginning the day with a black,
furry, bitter taste in her mouth, like an adult.

Of course they didn't give you any coffee for breakfast at
the Ananda Healing Institute. They saved it for the enemas.
This morning there had been jugs of murky tea brewed from
some kind of brown roots, and the little paper cups of wheatgrass juice, which smelled exactly like when she and Mac did
the lawn. How could a human being *drink* it? Bowls of soaked
grains, a tangled jungle of sprouts, some dark slimy things
made out of seaweed, nuts with the shells still on. The only
thing Min could eat were the apple slices. She ate all the apple
slices for their whole table. Rose didn't say anything to her
about it, either. Min was always hungry, moaning that there

was nothing to eat here but *plants*.

"I'm just so glad to see a young person here," the woman sitting next to her this morning had said. Min despised being a Young Person. The woman was gigantic, draped in a white cotton muumuu that suggested her body had been put into storage, like an old couch. She had little gold thongs tied onto her puffy bluish feet.

"Are you doing a healing, honey?" she had asked. "Well, never mind, you'll learn a lot about healthful living anyway. I wish I'da done something like this when I was your age, I can tell you. If I'da only known how I was perverting the food I cooked—like all those delicious pink fantail shrimp I used to deep fry, with that creamy horseradish sauce on the side—you know, literally *robbing* everything I ate of its life-giving properties, why I'm sure I never woulda ended up here, the way I am. Look at those legs. Look at them. And they're not a quarter the size they were when I came. Phlebitis," she said confidentially. No D. "Oh honey, you've never seen anything like it. They were swelled up like an elephant's, all black and blue."

Of course Min had never seen anything like her legs, which were so distorted and discolored they did not resemble legs in any way, except that the woman stood up on them when she was finished eating. Another woman, sitting across the table, was pretty normal-looking, only her lips and the ends of her fingers were quite grey. She nodded eagerly at the muumuu woman.

"Isn't it a miracle?" she said in a breathy voice. "My word, when the poison started coming out of me it was black as the hole in your eye. And foul! I never ate a bite of anything for three weeks—*three whole weeks*—and it still kept coming. You'd never believe a human body could be filled with so much garbage. Just *filled*. When my husband came to visit on Fridays I'd tell him it was still coming and he'd stand next to the bed shaking his head; he couldn't believe it either, the poor man. The doctor said I got here just in time. Barely in the nick of time."

The first woman leaned her bulk onto the table, nearly crushing Min's arm.

"Death starts in the colon," she said darkly.

You heard that a lot. It was just about the most popular

saying there was around here. Most people's talk measured sickness, sizes of tumors, amounts of waste products, the extent and severity of invisible, internal damage. Even her mother had started to sound this way, as if her cancer was a specific, delimited thing, a small creature that had lodged itself inside her, fastened onto her breast with its claws, that must be flushed out, exorcised, driven off before any further damage could be done. Sort of a little monster. Collectively, the patients here were battling a host of mutant, greedy, rampaging entities, like the scientists in the Japanese science fiction movies Min watched on Friday nights while she babysat. Except that from the way some of these people looked, the creatures were winning.

Every afternoon she floated in the thermal pool, her one refuge from the strange people and doings at Ananda. Since she was five—when they spent a week at a cottage by the lake and her father taught her to swim—the water had been hers, the bodiless freedom of floating still bound to those first stirrings of pride and power as she kicked steadily toward Mac's open arms.

She was by the wall at the far end, where the hottest water came seeping through the rock. Her hands floating down from the surface passed many gradations of temperature, layers of heat and coolness, stirring up the smells of dissolved minerals, the superheated sulphur-and-iron breath of the earth's depths. She was doing the Dead Man's Float. Pretending to be an amoeba. To do this, you needed to concentrate—hard—on not feeling your body or hearing your thudding heart. Then there was the added effort of not having a mind, of not thinking, especially of not thinking that you were not thinking. Sometimes, when she came back after losing herself in this way, she wondered, Is that what it will be like when I die?

> *I have no mind, no shape, no voice.*
> *I have no mouth, no feelings, no family.*
> *I have no past, no heart, no thoughts—*

Movement. A foot. A white foot moving like a bass on a rock, barely an arm's length in front of her. Min spluttered into the air. John, the leukemia boy, was sitting on a rock ledge, up to his chest in the water—*her* water—his slender white arms floating aimlessly at his sides.

"I thought you might have passed out or something, you were just lying there for so long," he said, the barest outline of concern etching his features. The water in her eyes made her see almost as well as she did with her glasses on. The lines of his face were delicate and clear in the steam, as if drawn with a finely pointed pencil, and his skin pale white, translucent. His skin reminded her of skimmed milk, the way it is bluish where it meets the glass.

"No. Oh no," she replied, rolling and bobbing away from him with the assumed indifference of a leaf, a stick of wood. "That's just something I do sometimes. Nothing to get excited about." She didn't say how he had startled her with his foot like that. She didn't say anything about amoebas. It wasn't the kind of thing she thought you were supposed to say to a boy.

He smiled then, a lopsided half smile, which looked as if maybe he was afraid to let go with a full one. His face was hopeful on the smiling side, sad on the other. Min had noticed lately that a lot of people looked different on the two sides of their faces. Could leukemia be something you got just on one side, maybe? Then he was looking straight into her eyes, in a way that the boys at school never did. His gaze was frank, curious, persistent; it suggested that he already knew certain things about her and was merely waiting for some act of confirmation of her part. That look made her feel naked. My cheeks must be totally red, she thought, panicky, and quickly sank herself up to the chin.

"I've watched you in the cool pool before. You're pretty good," he offered.

"Can you swim?" Oh God what a mean question, I could die. It just popped out before I had time to realize it would sound like that.

"Oh yeah. Well, not so much any more. I used to a lot, before. Our swim team was in the state finals."

"I start swim next year. Everybody says swim wrecks your hair but I could give a care, mine's a wreck already."

"You have nice hair," he said softly. "I like your hair."

Instantly she wanted to deny that she had nice hair. That she had any hair at all. She was quite unprepared for him to *like* anything about her. Let alone say so. But that was how he talked to her. He seemed exceptionally gentle and kind. Min had not heard any boys talk this way before.

"Where are you from?" she asked, a little wildly. *Change the subject.*

"San Francisco. Where are you?"

"Wyandotte. Ontario. I know, I know, you've never heard of it, no American has. It's near Buffalo and Detroit and Cleveland, all those places."

"Oh. I've never heard of it."

"Yeah, I know. So how long ago did you guys get here?"

"Mmmm, guess it's been about three months now. I missed spring term. My mom's—well, you've probably seen how she is. She kind of worries about me a lot."

"I kind of noticed. Doesn't it drive you—you know, having her around all the time like that? I mean, *God.*"

John shrugged.

"She doesn't know any other way to act, I guess. The only kid she ever had is me. My dad never lived with us, so she sort of made me her specialty." He shrugged lopsidedly, as if there was a hand on his shoulder.

"Mine drives me. Sometimes I honestly think she's crazy."

"All mothers are crazy," he said reasonably. "They care too much about you and it makes them that way. You know, you're a little baby and they have to look after you all the time and everything. It's sort of like they never grow out of it. They don't know any better."

Min sniffed loudly.

"What are you, some kind of psychiatrist or something?"

He laughed, with his whole face this time.

"It's just, I've seen a lot of mothers with their kids in the hospital and stuff and they're all the same. They're like mine is, like yours. You know, can't leave you alone for two seconds."

Hearing John say "hospital" reminded her that there was something wrong with him, something serious. With a D after it. To look at him in the water, you might not guess it. He was very white, there were deep smudgy shadows under his eyes, but you could think he stayed indoors a lot, maybe reading too much. Blond hair, greenish-brown eyes—you could definitely say he was cute. Kathy Greene would give him big marks for those eyes, actually. Min was already working up what she would tell Kathy about this guy she met in California. Bedroom eyes, she'd call them.

"Does it hurt a lot, what you have?"

"Not really. Except for all the needles they poke you with at the hospital. That was a total drag. That's one of the reasons she brought me here. The staff doesn't do much of that. She doesn't believe in drugs or transfusions."

Min didn't know anything about drugs or transfusions, but she didn't ask. After that first day, they didn't talk about Ananda, or what was wrong with him, what kind of treatments he was getting. She thought they talked about funny things—insects, the books they'd read, what it was like when they were little, dreams.

"I had a dream about you last night," she offered shyly one afternoon when they met in the pool. "I dreamed you were riding by on a horse, a big black horse. You weren't sitting on a saddle or anything, just a red blanket, and you were galloping really fast. I tried calling and waving at you but even though you weren't very far away, it was like you couldn't hear me. You just kept riding, straight up into this mountain. I watched until I couldn't see you anymore. I couldn't understand why you didn't hear me or see me."

And then, she couldn't believe it, but they talked about her dream. As if it really happened.

"Do you believe in dreams?" John asked her solemnly.

"I don't know. I guess so. What do you mean, do I believe in them?"

"Do you believe they come true?"

"I don't—I'm not sure about *that*."

"I do. I believe they all come true, sooner or later. Not exactly the way you might think. But sooner or later. Some of mine already have."

She didn't ask him about that, either. She didn't want to know, in case he was talking about bad ones. A person could only think about so many bad things at one time. And she didn't necessarily want to think of bad things in relation to John. She liked him. The way she could talk to him about whatever came into her mind—about anything, like you talk to yourself. She had even talked to him about Rose's cancer, which she had not done with anybody except Rina, who at six was really too little to count. And though she was totally humiliated when tears began rolling down her cheeks—she couldn't seem to stop crying once she had started, and was grateful that at least they were in the pool, where all the snot and stuff could float away—John hadn't acted in the least embarrassed. He just kept nodding quietly while she blabbered on and on, about how she didn't know what to tell Rina, or her friends at school, how she was terrified that Rose would have to go into the hospital and stay there, and what would happen to them all then? She didn't know one single person her age without a mother. Life without Rose in it was unimaginable: the house without her smell, the sound of her voice, her crashing around in the kitchen every night. Of course Rose drove her nuts—everybody's mother did, didn't they?—but she was still her *mother*. Everyone had a mother.

John was nothing like any boy she had ever met at home. Between the boys and girls at school there was always some kind of war going on, as if they were creatures from Mars and Venus, say, who didn't understand one another, who couldn't decide if they liked or hated one another. There were rules and factions and score sheets. But with John she felt none of that strangeness, that pushing and pulling. There was a calmness in him, a warm sense of suspension, as if he was floating a little outside of everything, just far enough so that nothing bothered him.

Maybe some of it was the pool. Without agreeing to it, that was the only place they met. At mealtimes they smiled uneasily at each other in the dining hall, but sat on opposite sides of the room. She thought he might be embarrassed now for her to see him in the wheelchair, with his mother pushing him around. In the afternoons she tried to arrive at the pool a few minutes after she thought he would, so he could get himself out of the chair and into the water with whatever awkwardness might be necessary, without her eyes on him. It must have felt like undressing in front of somebody. And then that other part of him—the sick part of him, as she thought of it—was underwater, out of their sight. She wondered if he thought of it that way too, of showing her his best parts and hiding the rest. His upper half seemed well enough. His face looked fine. Really. It looked just fine.

For once, Rose seemed not to care what Min was doing with herself; she was too occupied with all her treatments. Much of the time she looked as if she were concentrating, trying to pick up a message on a station she couldn't quite tune in, or that was broadcasting in a foreign language. Freedom from her attention confused Min, left her pushing against nothing, against air, the way everybody in the neighborhood did when the automatic doors were installed at the IGA, one person after another hurled forward into the shopping carts by that unexpected release. She felt she had been given a dangerous gift: one she had longed for, true, but now felt ashamed to accept, because of the cost to its giver. She went to Rose's room every day after breakfast, dreading yet at the same time almost hoping that Rose would be back to her familiar, ranting self: cursing a burst and clearly defective zipper, a daughter who gave her lip, a meal that wouldn't keep a hamster alive. But day after day she dismissed Min with an absent wave of her hand, a blank look that seemed to say, *Why are you here? Do I know you?* That look shook Min to her core. She didn't know how to look back, to make it disappear from Rose's face. She would stand there, touching her own face, as if she could no longer know who she really was, because her own mother was looking at her in that distant, uncomprehending way. Then leave, because she couldn't think of a thing to say.

One afternoon, another afternoon, and the next—time drifted past Min and John as they floated in the pool world together. Min had been in different worlds before, but never with another person, the way she was with him. The water, their bare limbs, and not wearing her glasses made everything intimate and unreal. The world outside the pool was a fuzzy blur, a mass of green. They sat, they paddled, they gazed at each other's features through the meandering steam.

"Let's see your hands," she said to him.

He was submerged to just beneath his eyes. Slowly he raised his hands, the fingertips curved toward her like claws.

"Aaauuughhhhh! The Mummy! The Creature From the Black Lagoon! The Thing That Wouldn't Die!!!" she screamed, mocking horror at his flesh, puckered and bleached from hours of soaking.

"You are now in my power," he croaked, slowly bobbing up and down. "You have only a few moments. Do as I say, or face the terrible consequences. The AWFUL consequences!"

"Anything! I'll do anything you say!"

"Good. Very good. First. You must put your hands behind your back."

"Okay."

"Next. Next you must back up against the rocks behind you, then DO NOT MOVE."

"Okay, I'm backed up, okay."

"Now you must close your eyes."

"Closed." The tingle of fear, the shiver along the spine, even if it was pretend, even if nothing—

His lips on hers. Wet, and soft—incredibly soft. Briefly she panicked, thinking I don't know what to *do*, I need to practice on my arm first. But there she was, doing it, and it was sweet, and wet, and ever so softly *interior*. His lips imprinted themselves on hers like a duplicate pair, perfectly matched, perfectly timed, their lips came together in a long endless wave of movement. Then he rained hundreds of tiny soft kisses all over her mouth, delicate as petals, and she felt—grateful. She felt grateful that this was happening to her, that someone was kissing her like this, that it was John, because she hadn't known what it would be like, she was actually afraid of it, and now there was this warm shower of little kisses and it was nothing like what she imagined it might be—some sort of collision, a clashing of teeth and skin—this was wonderful, it was perfect, it was *good*. It feels so good, he feels so good. This is it, then, this is why they all practise smiling and running their tongues over their lips, for this. His lips were parting, his warm sweet breath was breathing on her, she inhaled his essence. And then his mouth was there, his mouth and tongue. He was entering a dark moist cave in the back of her somewhere, that she had not known existed before this, a pleasure cave of soft nudgings and ticklings and stirrings. His tongue was silken, pliant, it was a sea creature seeking her, teasing her, calling to her own tongue to come out, to play.

And when her tongue enlivened in her mouth it swam into his, she went swimming into his mouth, her whole body alive in her there, rolling, floating, diving, surfacing, the way she did at the lake that summer, stroking and fluttering toward a man. She had entered his cave now, and he was opening to her, to the fish in her, the sweet mermaid. He was her baby, her father, her fish lover, they were feeding one another their juices, giving one another their softest parts.

Amoebas.

Min had never done anything so exciting in her life.

When it stopped, she couldn't wait to do it again.

"Ma, what's wrong?"

Min had come to Rose's room to get her for dinner. Rose looked really awful, really *sick*, today: the dark circles under her eyes, the greenish discoloration of her gums and lips from the wheatgrass—"my cocktail," she called it—had combined to give her tired face a ghoulish appearance. There *is* something inside her, Min decided. Something is eating my mother from the inside out.

"I feel like absolute hell, that's what's wrong. These treatments might be knocking the poison out, but they're knocking the life out of me too. Look at me. I've got no strength, my legs feel like a ton of bricks—I used to be full of piss and vinegar and now I don't even know which end is up. The doctor says—oh jeepers. What the hell difference does it make what the doctor says? Just look at me. I'm not getting any better, am I? I look worse every day. Don't I?"

What could she say? What her mother was saying was true. Most alarming was the way Rose's shape had changed in the weeks they'd been there. She had always carried extra weight, but in Min's memory her mother's poundage had a springy firmness to it, a jounce; it was packed onto her frame in such a way that she had simply grown larger and more solid over the years, was never flabby or squishy anywhere. But now extra flesh hung from her bones dispiritedly, as if it could not be bothered keeping to a woman's shape anymore. Her belly had somehow become unanchored; the way she was slumped on the edge of the bed this afternoon it flowed into her lap, onto her thighs. Ironically, her breasts still stood out from her wasting core, two solid round harbingers of illness. Some cancers never become visible or palpable; they lurk under the skin, inside the skeleton, doing their work in secret. But Rose had the other kind, the kind that was assertive, that hurt when it was touched, that showed. She felt her daughter's eyes on her breasts.

"Can you believe it? The rest of me's deflating by the minute, while they keep getting bigger and bigger. Can you explain that? Nobody here seems to be able to explain it to me. 'We're not really sure, Mrs. McCune.' 'I'm sorry, Mrs. McCune, but we just don't have any data on that.' "

"Well, at least you've lost some weight," Min ventured helpfully, trying to inject something positive into Rose's dark mood.

"Oh, there's no doubt about that, is there?" Rose laughed bitterly, shaking her head. "I've finally lost that ten pounds, and then some. That ten pounds I always thought was going to change my life, make a new woman out of me, give me what I've always wanted and never had. Oh yes. I've lost some weight, all right. But *look* at me, will you? *Look at me!*"

She stood up, holding her arms away from her sides, eyes blazing red with rage.

"I've lost most of what I was. Can't you see that? I'm losing my goddamn *self*. What am I now but this cancer? That's it. Nobody talks to me like a person anymore, let alone a woman. I've turned into a disease. I'm cancer. A big ugly lump of cancer. It's practically all that's left of me. My arms are even shriveling up. Look here—I used to have the smoothest whitest arms, just like my mother's. Your father loved my arms, you know, he loved to just lie there and run his fingertips up and down on my arms—"

Rose stopped abruptly, cutting off the memory. Then she started pacing the small room, back and forth in front of Min, who was still standing in the doorway, not sure whether to come in or stay out.

"I've gone through every one of these rotten treatments and the thing's still there. 'Let's give you another physical,' they say. 'We think the mass may be receding.' Like it's a glacier or something. Brother. These people don't have a blessed clue what they're doing, believe you me. *I* know it's not receding. I can't even sleep on my stomach anymore; it's the same as when I was pregnant, with two big boulders out in front. Ha! Pregnant. What a joke. Pregnant with cáncer. And how did I get it? Nobody can tell me that, can they? The doctor said it could have been in there for years, growing away, and I never even knew it, never felt a thing. How can you have something like that growing in you and not even know it? I've never been sick a day in my life except when I had you kids."

"I know, Ma, I know. Look, you're getting so—maybe it's not good for you to get so depressed about it," Min suggested. Her mother's talk was making her feel queasy, as if they two were alone on a dangerously rocking boat out in the ocean, and had lost sight of land.

"Depressed? Who's depressed? I'm madder than hell. We drive clear across the country for this magic cure and I end up looking like some green-lipped zombie. I feel worse than ever. The damn thing's getting bigger. Nobody knows what to do. My counselor this afternoon tells me I have to use my *imagination* more, I have to think of surrounding the thing with Radiant Light. *Radiant Light!* Will you get a load of that? What does she think, I'm Tinkerbell or something? I could have imagined her a fat lip right then and there. Jeepers. Why don't they say it's hopeless? Why don't they just up and tell me that and get it over with? There's no point in hanging around here, I can tell you. These people are idiots. Eating grass. I should have had my head examined, that's what I should have done. We might as well turn around and go home and let old Dr. Mason cut the whole thing off."

Cut *what* whole thing off? What about John, what about the pool? What about *me*?

"That's what we're gonna have to do. What the hell else can I do? It doesn't look like there's going to be any other way to get rid of this damned thing. Oh damn," Rose cried, collapsing onto her cot. "Damn, damn, damn. What am I going to do without my breast, Min? I'll be mutilated. I'll be a freak.

Your father will never look at me again. He'll never want to touch me again.''

Min sat on the edge of the cot and awkwardly put her cold trembling hand on her mother's heaving back. Rose had stopped talking; the room was filled now with her sobbing, her heavy sorrow, that had a brownish, singed, hopeless smell to it. Min had never actually seen her mother cry before. She knew about her Moments because Rose would mention them now and again. *Oh I've had my Moments, don't kid yourself*, she would say, dragging deeply on her cigarette, then blowing two long streamers of smoke out of her nostrils and looking at you like you didn't have a clue about anything. What should she do now? She patted Rose's back rhythmically, carefully, the way her mother did when you threw up, or woke from a bad dream. Min's throat was dry, her head ached, she was confused. She'd always been convinced that Rose had absolute power, could control anything. But here she lay, helpless and fearful as a child living a nightmare, beyond comforting. Min longed to be at home—or just about anywhere else. Back in the pool with John, the way they were that afternoon, the sun sparking off his golden hair, their mouths open, active, seeking. She tried to take herself there, to make the walls fade away, to feel light and floating. But Rose's heavy body kept getting in the way. Min couldn't seem to take her hand from it, even though her palm had gotten warm and was starting to itch. She was stuck in the small green room with her mother, stranded on a rock, an island of pain far away from the rest of the world. She, and her mother. And no help in sight.

"Is there any cure?'' she had asked him that afternoon, out of the blue. She had lately become obsessed by the idea of him dying, something they never talked about, by the idea of kissing and tasting the mouth of someone who was actually going to die. Didn't he shake his head too easily, didn't the word *No* fly from his lips without any consideration of what he was saying, what he was *telling* her?

"They say I'll get worse before I get better.''

"But what does that *feel* like?'' She was at a complete loss. "Aren't you *depressed*? I mean, God. To know you will never drive a car. Or graduate. Or get married. I would be so depressed if I knew that. And you just say, It's going to be over, it's going to end. Like it's the World Series or something. Aren't you afraid it's going to hurt?''

"Well, let's see." John considered her questions thoughtfully, unselfconsciously. Honestly, she could have been asking him about someone else.

"I'm not afraid it will hurt, no. I think I've already felt the worst I could feel.''

Min flinched. I will never ever be this brave, she thought. Never. I couldn't even stand getting my polio booster.

"How could I explain it? It's kind of like knowing you're going to move to another house," he continued. "Have you ever moved? That's really what it's like. No matter how long aways it is, it seems way off in the future, because you can't really imagine leaving your old house and living somewhere else. But you wonder, say, what kind of a neighborhood it will be in, what it will look like from the outside, if there's a porch. You think about going in the front door and walking around, how big the rooms are, what kind of smell the place will have. And especially what your room will be like, what you'll see when you lie on your bed, and look out the window.

"It's not sad. Don't let it make you sad. It's more of something you try to imagine, like what you'll be doing next summer, that's all. The funny thing is, it's going to happen to everyone. I just *know* that it's going to happen to me. You don't know yet that it's going to happen to you. That's the only difference.''

Min could not imagine her own death, the way he said. It was something that only happened to people on *The Guiding Light* and *Love of Life*, or in books, or to her unknown grandmother.

Annie Laurie sat in the kitchen on the chair with the one bad leg, certain she was going to die. This awful sensation, of her own imminent and untimely death, had come to her several times of late, and was so keen that she was momentarily disabled, and must sit down. Right now it was centered in her chest, a feeling of hot, nearly unbearable pressure that throbbed and closed in tighter and tighter, until she could hardly catch her breath. Something is squeezing the very life out of me, *she thought, rocking herself to and fro. It always came when she was at home, luckily, and had time to get herself over to the wobbly chair and collapse backward into it. She tipped it forward so that it was stable on the two front legs, and rested the weight of her torso on her forearms, widespread in front of her on the table. Panting shallowly, saying the names of all her cousins to herself, beginning with the A's*—Ada, Alfred, Alex, Bridget, Barbara, Eveleen—no, Cathleen. Or does she have it with a K? I can't remember—*she waited for it to let her go, let her chest move just a little so she could take a decent breath. As she sat, the things in the room—the streaky window that looked onto the rear yard and their patchy garden, the old clock with its constant somber ticking, the red-and-white-patterned oilcloth to which her cold sweating arms were sticking—all of these things lost their drear, oppressive familiarity, and in the suspended moments between breaths became oddly dear to her. She thought of her eyes closing forever, her panting breath stopping altogether, her head slumping down onto the oilcloth, where her mother would see it, never to move again. She thought of all this, and saw it happen, and a great love moved in her, for every speck of dust on the molding, the faint smell of fried bread coming from over by the stove, the frayed laces in her shoes: all these things shone faintly, they were as her sweet companions.*

John wasn't at the pool the next afternoon. Min idled in the water waiting for him until she couldn't stand the feel of it a second longer—it was a smelly irritating soup, what had she ever liked about it? The serene, vacantly smiling woman at the reception desk would tell her only that "John and Mrs. Winger are no longer with the Institute." Min imagined that the woman's stupid smile said that she, Min, must know as much about this as the woman herself did. What could have happened, that he had gone without leaving her any message, any word of acknowledgment? Could it have been the kissing, did it get him overheated, overwrought, send his body spinning into some kind of crisis? She stared with hatred at the woman's blank face. She wanted to scream *Where has he gone? Did they send him away to die? Is he dead already?* But her lips would not form any of those words, she was suddenly afraid there was some responsibility to be taken and they were only waiting for her to step up and identify herself as the one whose fault it was, whose mother should be told, who should have known better, who ought to take the blame.

The blame for what? For him exploding like an exhausted star? Wheeling himself off the cliff behind the pine trees? For his crazy mother dragging him to some faith healer in Fresno? She had to decide. Say something, or run. But what could she say? She was paralyzed by a hot, queasy feeling that pulsated through her limbs and clogged her throat. She could ask nothing. The rest of the day, the rest of the summer, had suddenly become a closed door, a featureless landscape. Without any conscious thought her feet walked her to her mother's room, her hand opened the door, her mouth began to spill out the words of his name, his illness, the dreams she had, his promise to meet her at the pool that day, her shapeless hot awful fear. Rose turned from the window, where she had been standing, to look at Min—first with incomprehension, then with a dark tightening that spread over her features, drew back her shoulders, and finally propelled her forward, raised her arm, and struck her daughter hard across the face.

"You'd better not be telling me about any boys around here—who do you think you are? Barely eleven years old— what do you think this is? I should've known you couldn't be trusted. Shaving your legs. Drinking coffee. Can't leave you alone for two seconds, can I, with everything I've got on my mind. Oh I could just—"

Rose grabbed a handful of Min's hair and jerked her head painfully sideways, so that Min had to look into her dark shrunken face.

"Never think about anybody but yourself, do you? Never give two hoots about your poor little sister following you around, your parents trying their best to raise you and now me with this thing—how can you think about boys at a time like this? *How can you?* Ask me to help you find him—I'll help you all right, young lady, I'll help you stay locked in that room of yours until we get out of this hellhole. Oh I should've known.

I've had it with you, Miranda. I really have. Your insolence, your moping around—I practically have to break your arm to get you to say two nice words to anybody. Well, this is it. You can expect some mighty big changes when we get home, let me tell you. You'd just better keep your eyes peeled around me from now on, sister, because I'm not going to take one lick of this business from you. *Boys.* You'll be lucky if you get out of the house again before you're eighteen. Now you march your behind out of here before I really haul off and let you have it."

At a loss for days afterward, Min wandered the grounds in the too-bright sunlight, fear thudding in her chest. Nothing was safe. The sun itself was wrong, maliciously radiant, casting a sickly greenish hue over the trees and buildings, the chairs and benches waiting on the lawn, the rotten-ripe avocados that littered the grass. Everything grew too fast here, the lushness was threatening, abnormal, filled with peril, grief, decay.

It wasn't only John—though what on earth could be worse than that? Lying in bed at night she felt a hole in her side, a hollow aching hole when she thought about him not being there anymore, not being able to touch the side of his face again, or hear him say You have nice hair, I like you, I know exactly what you mean. Maybe this was what he meant by dreams coming true. He had ridden off on that horse without a word or a sign to her.

It wasn't only her mother, either—and that was worse than John, really, except in a different way. There she felt something was waiting for her, in some future much less benign than the one John imagined. A thing with a shapeless, billowy body and outstretched arms, like the head nun who used to stand by the curtains at the convent school piano recitals she had played in when she was small, staring at you on the stage through her thick reflecting glasses, her black toe tap-tapping the time signature, her finger crooked at you when you finished. This thing waiting was like the head nun: a dark inevitable stranger in the wings, except try as she did to look at it, to discover who or what it was, she could see no face. Only that dreaded beckoning finger, those long arms reaching out of darkness toward her.

It was that finally, besides everything else, even her own body had turned on her: a few weeks ago, her breasts had unmistakably started to grow. The nipples were a darkening pink and puffed out, the underneath part had gotten hard and sore. It was frightening, humiliating, having these painful swellings which distorted her chest, but weren't really big enough to look like true breasts. She had the feeling that if Rose found out about them, she would somehow be held responsible and punished for growing these things, for allowing something so obviously sexual to take place on the front of her body. *Show-off. Shame on you.* Yet how long would she be able to hide them? Even though she wore her baggiest T-shirts—including one over her bathing suit, telling Rose she didn't want to get a sunburn—she felt like everyone was looking at her, at them, all the time. The Ananda people hadn't been staring at her heart after all: they were trying to see whether she had yet joined the tribe of people who had breasts.

John. Her mother. Breasts.

Pain.

Why didn't she want what she had thought she wanted? She always thought it would be wonderful when she got them, imagined they would sort of appear on her chest overnight, fully formed, the perfect size and shape. She envied the girls at school who had filled out, who had to wear bras that the boys invariably checked you for by trying to snap them from behind in class. "Stacked," the boys called it. "She's really stacked." But what if, like her mother said, the cancer was inside her for years? What if Min had caught it, somehow sucked it from Rose's body when she was a baby, had had it inside herself all these years and now that was what was coming out? She could have cancer herself. Maybe that's why they were sore. Nobody at school ever said anything about theirs being sore; for sure, somebody would have said something like that about it. The right one was definitely bigger than the left one, she checked every morning in the mirror. Lumps were what they felt like, two little hard lumps.

She didn't want lumps. She didn't want lumps or bumps or mounds or titties or knockers or nips or anything that anybody called them. She didn't want to be stacked. She didn't want hair on her arms or under her arms or between her legs, or a bra, or anybody snapping it. She wanted to be as far away from the Ananda Healing Institute as you could humanly get.

When she was little and feeling scared, sometimes she used to hide in the hall closet. The smell and feel of those familiar household articles cosily nested side by side—towels, extra soap, the wicker sewing basket, a bag of scraps—were a comfort to her, gave her the sense that things were always, would always be the same in there: clean-smelling, orderly, helpful. But now she had somehow walked into a larger, darker closet, where nothing felt familiar, where everything she touched was strange, odd-smelling, threatening in shape. The door was lost too, it was no longer behind her where she thought it was, there was no way out of the closet but forward, into that webby clinging darkness, that airless mystery which offered nothing, but was all that remained.

Circle of Light

Nothing had prepared Min for the tangle of feelings that caught at her as she drove toward Wyandotte. Every bit of familiar scenery, every town or riverbank or span of highway she remembered, turned on a light somewhere in the back of her mind, in rooms she had forgotten about, had not entered for years. *Home. Family.* That whole long, messy, waterlogged stretch of life on Huron Street she had tried to leave behind the same way she had left the country. When she first moved to California she'd done a few workshops, like everybody did— body awareness, yoga, a week's worth of group Gestalt at Esalen, that kind of thing—and thought she had gotten her past pretty well out of the way. That was the idea, anyway: to get your personal history more or less wrapped up so you could start living in the Now. *I forgive you. I release you. My life is perfect the way it is.* Moving from Rage to Love: wasn't that what that one weekend was called? Fifteen people in a sunny living room, beating on pillows with red plastic bats.

But when she first crossed the border at White Rock into Canada, there was an old, familiar narrowing, a sensation that her arms and chest were being squeezed together as if she were stuck in a tunnel. And a feeling she couldn't get rid of, that someone was looking over her shoulder, a voice saying *Look out, you're here now, you know, you'd just better watch it. We're keeping an eye on you.* As if the country itself still had some kind of say in her life, in what she was doing, the groceries she bought, the people she talked to. Nobody cared how you acted in California; no one pointed out any double yellow line that divided human behavior right down the middle. There, everyone seemed to flourish on the freedom of having no history, on indifference and grand weather and careless manners. But she had driven around in circles for a half hour in some dusty prairie town, for instance, not wanting to ask anyone where the liquor store was, feeling absurdly self-conscious, criminal almost. She saw reproach in the blank faces of the grain elevators, the shuttered flyspecked windows of the hardware store, the empty café. Later she imagined the sniffing, mouse-faced woman who rang up her purchases thought she was unpatriotic for choosing French and Italian wines, a snob, too hoity-toity to support the budding Canadian wine industry.

"Sounds paranoid, babe." That's what Peter would say. She let him call her that—"babe"—because it seemed to go so naturally with his playfulness, his casual assumption of affection and goodwill. The first time he called her that, she had been teaching him how to eat a mango the way she had learned in Mexico, on a hot dry day in August when the Santa Anas were blowing and making everyone feel crazy.

"Here, look. You take it like this"—she cushioned the mango in the palm of her right hand—"and then start squeezing it down to the end"—her fingers slowly kneaded the fruit as if it were soft, ripe, yielding flesh—"yes, there. Then you bite this little pointed part off the end."

Peter stood transfixed, watching what she was doing, licking his lips as the sweat rolled down his face and neck.

"Now you hold it up to your mouth"—she put the round yellow globe of fruit to his lips—"and start sucking. Go on, suck it. I'll keep squeezing."

Eyes wide and fastened on hers, cheeks burning, Peter's mouth opened and pulled at the mango while she pressed the soft juicy pulp toward his lips. A bit of juice dribbled from the side of his mouth; she wiped it away, and licked her finger. It tasted sweet and salty. She was enjoying this hugely, watching him sucking and swallowing, trying to keep up with her gently pumping fingers. Finally, gasping with pleasure and embarrassment, he pushed her hand away.

"Oh, *babe*," he said huskily. "This has to be the most—I don't believe you—"

She licked at the sides of his mouth, then took his lips in hers and sucked them lightly, playfully, and finally kissed him deeply, tasting his essence, his sweat, and the fruit. He was sweet and sticky and wholly hers.

"Babe," he murmured again, trying to press her against him without smearing himself with mango pulp. "Oh, babe—"

She knew that's what he'd say now, if he were here. "Sounds paranoid to me, babe." Peter thought she was paranoid about a lot of things: nuclear war, meeting deadlines, getting sick, her van blowing up. Maybe she was. Paranoid was not how you were supposed to feel, she knew that. But she couldn't seem to let worry slide right on past her, the way he did. He counted on things taking care of themselves. Peter was what her mother would have called happy-go-lucky, a temperament she had highly prized and wished for her own child.

"Miss Sourpuss. Why can't *you* be more happy-go-lucky?" Rose would say. "Always moping around here. Look at Gina down the street. Smiles at everybody, picks up after herself, has some respect for her parents—are you listening to me, Miranda? Miranda? What are you, DEAF?"

Of course she wasn't deaf. She had merely turned the volume of her surroundings way, way down. So she could see better. Read better: schoolbooks, comics, the *Encyclopedia Britannica*, the side panels of cereal boxes where they listed the ingredients. "BU-TYL-A-TED HY-DROX-AN-I-SOLE," sounding it out as she chewed. Miniature worlds were hers. Anthills. Spiderwebs tucked into the crotches of lawn chairs. The tiny green and red wire network in the back of her transistor. Looking became her occupation, her entertainment, her chief pleasure. It didn't matter that her mother always wanted her to do something else, look at something else, be some other kid. She learned to bring the world inside; she became nearsighted. Peter told her that always watching what was outside herself kept her from fully inhabiting her own life. In fact, he urged her to throw away her glasses and try contacts. "Get a little closer to things. Get rid of your barriers, your suspicion," he said, in his helpful way.

"Paranoid. Is that anything like moping?" she would say

to him. In general, he preferred to keep things upbeat. *Positivity* was what he was helping people learn to have, he said. More positive attitudes about themselves. About life. Min thought that was fine; she could actually see how it worked, to a point. There were just certain things she didn't feel very positive about. Those two radioactive cement breasts sticking up from the earth at San Onofre, for example. Drive-by shootings on the freeway. You couldn't feel positive about everything.

Maybe the difference was that he had been born into a sunny green world and she into a sober, snowbound grey one. He'd grown up in a glass-walled, bougainvillea-shrouded bungalow two blocks from the beach, where Ellie and Jack, his parents, still lived. Of course he called them Ellie and Jack. Ellie Redstone dressed like a real Romanian gypsy and had a small pottery studio behind the house. She embraced Min and kissed her on both cheeks the first time they met, her earrings clanging like tiny gongs. All three of her sons, Peter, Steve, and Gareth, still came and went, bringing laundry, food and friends, sometimes even staying the night in their old rooms.

Peter and his brothers looked and dressed like three guys in a sporting goods catalogue: tanned and sockless, their hair mussed by some invisible breeze, smiling in their bright-colored rugby shirts and scuffed deck shoes, their teeth large and capped-looking. Sportsmen all, regular guys. One of them was forever banging a tennis racket against his knee, waxing down a surfboard, loading shot into a dive vest. People had always assumed Min, a tall gangly bigfooter, to be good at sports; but she had hung back from teams because she was afraid of making mistakes, of having to endure the criticism of the other players. There were always decisions to make in sports; when to run for the ball, which raquet position to use, when to bunt or kick or steal. She was no good at decisions. Neither of her parents played anything, though her father had taught her to swim and pored over the sports pages every night before dinner with almost morbid interest, noting the crippling injuries, the rousting defeats and unexpected trades with a satisfaction she used to find strange in someone who as far as she knew had never tossed a ball further than the end of his own driveway. The Redstone boys genially let her in on the secrets of rip currents, short johns, buddy breathing and long boards, and she had become a decent surfer and budding diver under Peter and Gareth's instruction. She enjoyed this immensely. In the water, no one cared how far down you went, what your form was like, whether you caught a wave. And having grown up without brothers, Min found something illicit, thrilling, almost sexual, about having so many males around. She wondered if Ellie Redstone ever felt that way. It was not the sort of thing she would ever ask her. She could not get over the way the Redstones themselves all *talked* about everything. They sat on the patio, drank gallons of Jack's coffee—meticulously prepared from sacks of Jamaican beans he oven-roasted and ground himself—and discussed their lovers, their breakthroughs in therapy, the state of the arts and their health, laughing, theorizing, kidding one another. She had never been around a family so at ease, so apparently unconflicted; she caught herself stiffening with disbelief as one intimacy after another was casually revealed. Everything was right there, floating on the surface of their talk like the sheen of cream on the coffee, the buttery glaze on the croissants. They might have been golf partners, or college roommates, instead of a family.

Peter's element was the revealed, the plainly spoken, whereas Min had grown used to concealing herself in silence, watchfulness, in that space between lens and subject. He loved vivid, full-blown flowers, over which she would choose a shoot, a bud which promised some fullness not yet seen. Yet what made them different seemed to drive them into each other's arms. They spent hours preparing delectable meals, drinking wine, arguing, explaining themselves. Then usually ended up in bed: laughing, sweating, urging themselves into each other's bodies. Peter was an inventive, tireless lover; Min found a self who did not need to hold back and remain silent, but could move with him eagerly, into vast bright fields of pleasure—"Your basic bliss," he called this—until they were both exhausted, reassured, mystified anew. But they still danced *en pointe* around certain areas of their lives, certain privacies that Min, mostly, needed to maintain. Her ambivalence about the idea of living together, for one thing. Peter was powerfully attractive to her; she loved him, reveled in their time together more than she ever had with a man, itched for him when they were apart, flourished in the warm light of his attention and desire. But she didn't know if she could live with him. The thought of being a *wife* gave her a knot in her stomach. She imagined the gradual erosion of her own interests, her own time, of access to some of the things she loved most in life. It had taken her a long time after she left Wyandotte to build up a self that she trusted, that felt solid and real to her. She wasn't at all sure whether that self was strong enough, integral enough to share someone else's existence—even Peter's, who was so understanding and loved her so much. How did you find something like that out, without the possibility of making a bad mistake?

Her reluctance mystified Peter. Nearly every weekend he would present the idea to her in a new way, as some delicacy she had not yet tasted, a new course in the art of living she might sign up for.

"It doesn't have to be negative. I actually think it would be very positive. Why don't you try to think of it as an opportunity to grow?" he said to her.

"Well, it might be that, Peter. I guess it might. But what if it isn't? What if it's completely the opposite, and everything between us goes bad and we end up hating each other? People botch these things up every day, you know."

"Sure I know. I see them in my office all the time."

"Exactly. So isn't it maybe a little presumptuous to think we'd do it differently?"

He combed all ten fingers slowly through his hair, the way he did when he was trying to be patient with her.

"Nothing says we're doomed to make other people's mistakes, babe."

"Oh I know, I know, jeepers." Sometimes his reasonableness, his therapistic saneness, seemed completely unreasonable to her, left her spoiling for a good fight, or at least a few harsh words. "You make me feel like a lunatic sometimes, you know that? Positive. Negative. What a lot of malarkey. You'd think we were talking physics here. Maybe we are. I certainly can't seem to think about it clearly when you're around. Maybe it's your *magnetic field*."

"Could be. Or maybe it's that you're scared to say yes in case you goof up. Jesus, there are risks everywhere you look. It's like that first time we went scuba diving off the dock.

Remember? Sooner or later you've got to trust things. You can't practice forever. You put on your equipment and check everything out real good and pull your mask down and then you have to get into the water. You have to step off the dock and go under."

"Great example. I was totally paralyzed when I had to do that. I nearly threw up into my regulator. I actually thought I was going to *die*."

"Yeah, you were a little nervous—but you *did* it. And look how much you love diving now."

"Okay, okay. But look at all the things a person has to do to make it totally safe before you go under. I mean, what backup do I have in *this* situation?"

He grabbed her by the shoulder and buzzed her scalp with his knuckles.

"*Me*, you knucklehead. You've got me. Your old dive buddy."

She knew, though, that she had to be able to rely on herself to stay happy—not just Peter. And she needed to be away from him to sort that out. Travel was a comfortable pocket for her to slip into. Unexpected rhythms, the hiddenness of moving through strange places, the doubleheaded sense of moving toward, and leaving behind. On the road you could meet yourself, over and over again, inspecting, clarifying what you saw. You were saved for the moment from routine, failure, dullness, from seeing your face staring back at you out of the same mirror every morning. You could remember how to make choices again—small ones, of little importance perhaps. But choices nevertheless.

She had missed Peter urgently at the beginning of the trip, called a few times—especially after an extra glass of wine—mailed long, probing, passionate letters. But in these last few days—since she crossed the border, actually—his image had been fading, like an old Polaroid, no matter what trick she tried to bring it back to vividness. With every mile closer to her home, he was seeming slightly less real—as was her entire life in California. She was making certain adjustments. Apparently this was her reality now: driving to see her family, taking pictures, feeling guilty in liquor stores, eating in cafés.

Shifting back into the past. Or was she just remembering how to be alone?

The prairies had made her feel powerfully alone. Nothing about them seemed friendly. Or familiar—though she had crossed and recrossed them on any number of trips—except their prairie-ness itself, that flat unmarked endlessness, mile after mile of it rolling past the window, yellow and brown, ungiving, without so much as an interesting rock to look at. Even Mars would have interesting rocks to look at. She listened to some of her tapes half a dozen times, driving all through one night just so Saskatchewan would end sooner. Imagine the crimes all this empty space could drive you to, she had thought, the acts of desperate loneliness, your shouts never coming back to you, simply disappearing into the vastness. Women hanging themselves in barns after they fixed lunch, men walking off into blizzards, never to be heard from again. Children setting fields on fire, pulling the wings off moths. Crimes of the void, of forsaken souls. Was hell other people, then, or no one at all?

Her skin started to prickle when she drove into Ontario. Ontario. Saying it out loud: a rippling, dignified-sounding place to be from. Shortly after dawn one morning she had stopped at a badly carved-up picnic table just off the highway at Kee-watin, to breakfast on peaches, rice cakes, a bit of cream cheese. Her strong coffee. The smell of "up north," that cold, resinous atmosphere, filled her lungs and throat, became part of her meal. She had forgotten the goodness of such clean air, the way it penetrated your cells. That summer her family had driven through this part of the country they'd stopped at a souvenir shop, housed in a rambling two-story log building that reeked of woodsmoke, and filled to its blackened roof with pennants, moccasins, brown plastic Indian dolls, dusty boxes of crumbling saltwater taffy. All the moccasins had that strong smoky smell, as though they had walked through fire. Min used some of her vacation spending money to purchase a small basket with a lid, woven of pine needles. MADE BY LOCAL INDIANS said the paper label on the bottom. The fragrance of the exotic was what she bought that basket for; every time she lifted the lid, this pungent evergreen aroma wafted out, and reminded her of being in a strange place, far from home, of spending her own money on something she had chosen herself.

She touched the names on the map, of places she had never seen. Rat Rapids. Onakawana. North Spirit Lake. Valora. Would you find springs up there, in the barren land left exposed by the trailing hems of glaciers? There would be rock slick with lichens, treacherous muskeg, blackflies, howling noises in the night. Muskrat, sleek otter, deer nibbling the bark from pale young saplings. The bush. A friend from university had worked at a logging camp north of here. The cook had gone mad—"bushed," her friend called it. *He was bushed.* The loggers coming in for breakfast one morning found their fried eggs nailed to the wall, a hundred cold little discs. The crazed cook was never seen again; he simply disappeared, into the Canadian Shield. Something she had imagined when she was a schoolchild as protective, metallic, spread like a magic cloak across the top of her country, keeping out glaciers, Russians, rabid bears. A thing, not a place. Apparently it didn't protect everyone.

But there was none of that around Wyandotte. She drove past small eroded farm towns, accreting nests of lakefront cottages, trampled cornfields, a landscape that appeared safe, revealed, was as shabbily familiar to her as her own running shoes. The lakeshore that flooded one spring and left innumerable wooden rowboats and paddleboats stranded up by the highway, cats shivering in the crotches of maple trees. The Albion Mental Hospital, where she volunteered one summer, its blackened smokestacks conjuring images of concentration camps, still standing on its balding hill, separated from the farms on all sides by bleak expanses of patchy lawn and a chain-link fence. The same stretch of fruit and vegetable stands—her favorite one with the large red plywood tomato perched on its roof like a satellite, faded but still discernible—selling hot buttered corn, heaping bushels of tomatoes, cottage-shaped loaves of homemade bread. She could stop and buy corn and tomatoes, a cucumber, a loaf of the bread to take to her father. But her anxiety was ripening into a feverish excitement that made her want to pee, or turn the van around, or call and blurt out "Dad? Sorry. I'm still in California."

So she didn't stop, didn't buy anything. I don't want him to think I assume he can't look after himself, she decided, that he won't even have the basics in the house. Her father hated to be anticipated, outguessed, subjected to the unexpected. Maybe his own tomatoes would have come in by now. In her teenaged summers she used to live on bacon and tomato sandwiches and corn on the cob, everything heavily salted, dripping and delicious. Corn was three or four dozen for a dollar, then. Would he remember that?

She looked into the rearview mirror, tried to bring a curve to her shaggy eyebrows with a wetted finger, fluffed up her hair in the back. She had put on a white linen shirt and pants this morning, and some big, primitive-looking metal earrings. It pleased her father when she looked good. He thought it was a reflection on him. Already she was falling into the old way of obliging him, without even seeing him. As she got closer to her old neighborhood, she thought, Who knows, I might see someone, recognize a face from high school—though even as this occurred to her, she realized it was unlikely. The town was full of new people who had gone to school somewhere else, whose already twenty-year-old houses stood astride the fields and hummocks she used to run across.

Their house—the house she grew up in, the house her father inhabited by himself now—was in one of the older suburbs of Wyandotte, a middle-sized town richened by several auto-assembly plants and the smaller industries that fed off of them—tool and die companies, scrap-metal yards, stamping plants that took up entire blocks of the city with their hammering, their screeching of metal on metal, their reeking fumes. Though a good-sized river ran past the town, most of the buildings faced away from it, as if from temptation, their stolid red-brick fronts darkened by decades of factory grime. *Downtown*, those red buildings were called—*What the heck, let's grab ourselves a bus downtown*, her mother might say on a Friday, after the baking was finished. Something daring. None of the mothers had cars of their own. Suburban life was routine as prison: wash on Monday, iron Tuesday, clean Wednesday, grocery shop Thursday, bake Friday. There was none of the humming current of the city, nor the tranquillity of the surrounding countryside. Her mother had grown up downtown, in an apartment above a store on a poor street. Years later Min thought that Rose must sometimes have been wild to escape the relentless lawns and folded pillowcases and freshly waxed linoleum for an afternoon. Min went along on those downtown trips, where she was introduced to things she never encountered in her neighborhood: pigeons, submarine sandwiches, alleys. Public bathrooms, which were built under the sidewalks. The smells of ill and unwashed people, of buses and roasting cashews and rich women's perfume.

When Min was a child Wyandotte's air was sulphurous. You could see it hanging above the river on a cold day like a sheer yellow veil. You felt it rasp the back of your throat. It sifted a fine layer of grit onto any clean surface within a matter of hours. Women spent entire maddened, baffled lives wiping this grit from their end tables, rinsing it out of curtains and table-cloths. Older people like her grandfather, when they could finally afford nicer furniture, usually kept their brocade and velveteen couches and occasional chairs under heavy plastic covers, which stuck to the legs of guests—especially grand-children—in the summer, and made alarming squeaking noises when someone tried to move suddenly, or stand up. That was in the fifties, before it occurred to anyone that anything could, or should, be done about the air.

Some of the boys Min went to school with worked in those factories now, boys a few years older than she. Donnie May-hew, Kevin Tofflemire, Randy Kushner, Ricky Renaud: names she had written on her arms, faces of boys she had once dreamed about, longed to touch, stared at through the school windows as they marched around the muddy field in their cadet uniforms. Most of them had taken shop instead of the academic subjects she took, or dropped out after grade ten. It was a sort of joke back then, doing what their fathers had done, calling each other "factory rats," shoving their long hair up under hairnets, get-ting stoned on union-appointed coffeebreaks. Lots of them showed up at work stoned every day. Dave Gilbert, who used to live in the house behind the McCunes and worked a punch press, told Min once he'd been ripped on LSD and put the top of a hamburger bun on in place of a distributor cap. "Pity the guy who drives that sucker off the lot," he said. The foreman was ripped too, never even noticed the bun. **THIRTY YEARS AND OUT** said the buttons on their jackets. A big joke. Thirty years would be no longer than a school year, they'd be over just like that and everyone would be let out for summer, for life, to drive around the country in their RVs, to fish, play rummy, thumb their noses at the other poor sods who still had to work, while their pension checks were mailed to them in Palm Springs. Thirty years of greasing cylinders, attaching hose clamps, tightening bolts. The layoffs started after most of them had leveraged themselves into a three-bedroom tract house, a candy-apple red Mustang, a wife and baby, with maybe another one on the way. Not many managed to keep their jobs. They ended up watching daytime television, looking after the kid while the wife waitressed, lining up at Unemployment for their pogy checks, moving in with their folks or their in-laws after they lost their homes. Evenings, they got drunk on draft beer with their buddies at the Erie Tavern or the Sandhill, and drove the Mustangs into ditches. Rina had gone out with one of them for a while—thank goodness she hadn't gotten pregnant—until he cracked up her car. Some of them finally moved away from Wyandotte, to look for jobs elsewhere.

Min's father had worked for one of the auto companies too, but sitting behind a desk. Between him, his father, and assorted aunts, uncles and cousins, her family had given the company over three hundred and fifty years of service. When her father retired a few years ago, his coworkers gave him a gold-plated top, a memento of the small wooden one he used to spin on his desk while he was working out a problem. His job was to come up with more streamlined techniques for production, more efficient ways for the company to mine its employees' ideas and manual skills, saving the company time, manpower— and, of course, money.

As she was growing up, Min never knew a thing about what her father did at his job. Peter had found this hard to believe, coming from the lush relatedness of his family, where everyone knew everyone else's beeswax. But it was true. Min's father never talked about it or brought home anyone he worked with. Every night her mother asked the same question in her distracted way—"How'd it go at the office?"—and received one of his perfunctory replies: "All right, I guess." "Not too badly." "Same as usual." As though he had no triumphs, irritations, losses. Blankness was perfectly acceptable. Min never saw inside the office where he worked, though at Christmastime the four of them used to drive along the riverfront to look at the lights and her mother would point to a tall brown building and say, "That's where Daddy works, you girls, see that big building?" But he never acknowledged this, never turned his head. His job was an unopened box, a completely hidden part of his life, a slot in time into which he disappeared for nine or ten hours a day.

To Min this had once seemed entirely appropriate, for when she was little she was given to understand that a job was something disgusting; that was what her mother called it when she or Rina shat: "doing a job." How awful for her father, to drive off in the morning and have to do something like that all day—and with other people! Though later she understood the difference, a job was forever something private, slightly shameful, something you didn't talk about. She had never wanted to have a job of her own. *Work* was something different, an important part of your life, something you liked and did because you wanted to, because it had value. It was a long time before she had any real sense of what her father had done for all those years; and even when he explained it to her, he did so with resignation, a slow-moving sadness, as a man would who had served out an unjust prison sentence, and was explaining how he had finally come to accept the failure of justice in the world, the dark suffocation of hope.

"What do you mean, how could I stand it?" he had said, when she asked him—during the period when she was reading Marx and seething with adolescent scorn for capitalism and the bourgeoisie—why and how he had thrown his life away so utterly. "I had to work. I had you."

What she thought of long ago as her father's real work took place in the basement. The man who changed into his soft old grey pants and faded plaid shirt—work clothes, but always clean, pressed and somehow natty-looking—and descended the stairs whistling a dry, unmusical but cheerful tune after dinner, with his cigarettes in his shirt pocket and a coffee cup in his hand: this was Mac, her real father, going down to his real work, something completely different from his job. He made things in his shop in the basement; he was an inventor.

He invented a rolling stainless steel chopper for the nuts Rose used by the bagful in her Christmas baking; soon every housewife on the block wanted Alex to make her one. The McCune lawn was the greenest and lushest in the neighborhood—the kind of neighborhood where a nice lawn was more important than good teeth or a savings account—fed by an invisible watering system of punctured tubing he had devised. Min's first radio evolved from spools and bits of wire found in his cubbyholes. The contraption she remembered loving most was a shoe-buffing machine, which you activated by standing on it. Min and Rina would carry their Sunday shoes downstairs and watch their father painstakingly apply the polish; then one at a time they put on their shoes and stood on the vibrating buffing platform. Neither of the girls cared for well-shined shoes so much as they loved screaming at the rubbing and tickling of the brushes on their feet, through the shoeleather. Then Rina usually ran off, while Min stood in her shiny shoes by the workbench and watched her father, busy at his basement miracles.

The basement was large, and smelled of spiders, damp concrete, and dirt. It ran the full length and width of their house, and for many years consisted simply of a cement floor and concrete-block walls, some round metal poles that Min thought held up their house in some incomprehensible way, the coal shed and furnace. When she was little, a coalman still brought them loads of coal on his truck. It was shoveled into the shed through a high opening concealed by a grey metal door, and lay there in a beautiful black shining heap, which gleamed even in the dark. You opened the cellar door to a blast of freezing air in the wintertime, to get a shovelful of coal and carry it over to the furnace. Min would sometimes tug the door open and take a few little pieces for drawing stick people on the floor, or coloring her fingernails in black. But when her mother was pregnant with Rina, her father decided it was too much to have his wife shoveling coal to keep the house warm while he was at his job, so they had the big green furnace converted to gas. For a while there was talk of a bomb shelter; but when the coal shed was cleaned out her mother had her father put up shelves, where they stored their preserved peaches, pears and jams, tomato sauce and stringbeans, corn relish and quart jars of pickles during the fall and winter. Ever after, though, the shed held the bitter, ashy smell of coal. When Rina got big enough, they played hide-and-seek downstairs, and Min always hid in the cellar in the dark, where it was cold even in summer, knowing that Rina would never get her there because Rina was afraid to so much as touch that door, let alone open it and look inside. It could have been a bomb shelter, for all Rina knew. Once Min told Rina that their parents were going to rent out the bedroom that she and Rina shared, that she was going to live at the Costellos and Rina would have to live in the coal chute, her bed on one of the narrow little canning shelves like Anne Frank, her dolls getting all mildewy and spiders settling into comfortable nests in her hair while she slept. It wasn't so much that she wanted to scare Rina as simply to make her *do* something, as she had been trying to do ever since Rina was a baby: to resist, to fight, to *act*. This time, Rina had swiftly and satisfyingly gotten completely hysterical. "I do *not*, I do *not* have to," she screamed, until Rose came downstairs and walloped Min for lying to her sister and took Rina upstairs for some cookies. Min was made to apologize and tell Rina she had made it all up.

"Just kidding," she smirked.

"I kn-know," Rina hiccupped. But for months afterward she woke up from bad dreams, her pillow soaked with sweat, her pajamas twisted, and gasped that she dreamed she was sleeping in the cold chute, as she called it. By then Min wished she'd never said anything. Rina never seemed to figure out what was pretend and what wasn't.

By the stairs were the tubs, washstand and wringer washer where her mother did the clothes, dragging them over to the tubs from where they fell through the clothes chute from upstairs. In those days, there weren't yet the partitions that later divided the shop and laundry room from the family room and a small sleeping area. The basement was just a wide cold empty space like a skating arena, with the great green furnace standing in the middle, sighing and huffing, the throbbing heart of their house. Min treasured the basement because, except on washdays, her mother never came down there. She could roller skate and ride around the poles on her red wagon, and smash the floor and walls with sticks she brought in from the field, and hit the poles and make them ring, because there was nothing good there, nothing to wreck or save or watch out for. And in the evenings, the basement belonged entirely to her and her father.

"Making something?" she would say to him from where she used to sit on the top step, watching through the railing as he worked in the shop. "The shop" was what she called the shelves and cupboards and rows of tools that had grown up along the backside of the furnace.

"Well—I'm not sure. I won't know if it's something or not 'til I'm done." Modest, he never committed to the reality of anything he made until it was finished, fully functional. He would talk to her from down there, the way he never did upstairs, as though he had changed into someone else when he put on his work clothes. He spoke from a dim, shadowy world, lit only by a bare bulb dangling above his worktable.

"How can you make it if you don't know what it is?"

"Mmmm—it's tricky. See, first you get a kind of an idea, about what might work. So you think about that for a while. Then you think about the parts you might need. Get in there, you—wire doesn't want to go where it's supposed to. Then you get your parts. And after that you have to figure out exactly how they're going to fit together. Then you've gotta try to fit them together. A lot of different ways. There, that's better. Just like this thing here, see, sometimes you find a way that's the right way, and they all go together, real nice. Then maybe you've got something. Or you think you've got something, until you start it up."

"I wish I had something."

Then her mother would pipe up, as if she'd been listening to them all along. Min hardly said anything in the house that her mother didn't hear somehow.

"I'll tell you what you're gonna have, you're gonna have hemorrhoids sitting on the bare steps like that. Get yourself a magazine to sit on. And put a sweater on if you want to sit in that freezing basement, young lady."

"What's hemorrhoids?"

"Something you don't *ever* want to get. On your bum. Now get up here."

She went back up into the kitchen, into the sickening soapy greasy smell of the kitchen after dinner, the humid world where her mother liked to sit with Rina after she did the dishes, and eat a second bowl of Jell-O or canned peaches while Rina mushed around the cold food on the tray of her highchair. Min held her breath while she grabbed her sweater off the doorknob and a couple of *Life* magazines from the coffee table in the living room, and ran back down the short set of steps to the landing, then sat down to watch her father again.

"I want to do something."

"Well, do something then." He was frowning at the pointed end of a tiny brass screw. "Looks like these walls could use a coat of paint."

This was what she had been waiting for him to say. She flew down the stairs, grabbed the big silver bucket, put a stool in front of the washtubs and filled the bucket a third full of cold water, as much as she was able to lift down and carry. Her father handed her the wide soft paintbrush, or maybe the roller, and she took these things over to a corner behind him.

"Can't see anything over here, Mac."

"Here, wait a minute, I'll set you up a light. Hang on."

He would get out the small floodlight they used at Christmastime to shine on the tall spruce tree in front of the house, and set it up on the floor so that it illuminated the wall in front of her. Suddenly the room would become big and bright, the ceiling disappeared, their voices seemed louder, they were in a different world. The walls, which were painted a chalky pale blue, bleached to near-white in the circle of light. Her father faded into the background, busy again at his workbench. Now she was ready to work. She dipped the brush into the water and applied it to the wall, starting as high as her arm could reach, making a broad, smooth careful stroke all the way down, until the cement had leached all the water from the brush. And a beautiful thing happened, a metamorphosis that thrilled her anew each time she came downstairs and applied her brush to the wall. The strip of wall she had painted became a vivid, jewellike, glistening blue, the rich firm blue of the sky above trees in July, the blue of angels' dresses, cellophane wrappers, a bluejay's wing. Bright, wet, miraculous blue. And she had just done this one little strip. Look at all the wall there was left! She would wrap them in this color, this fierce blue that bloomed off the walls into the cold unlovely basement air, that leaped from her brush onto the dead white walls and shouted its beauty back at her.

"How does it look, Mac?"

"Let's see here." A long minute, while he noted what he was connecting to what and set it down. Then as he walked over to stand behind her his shadow got huge, his head grew and disappeared off the top of the wall, he was a giant, putting his gigantic hand on her shoulder.

"Nice. That looks really nice, honey. You're doing great work there."

She glowed, satisfied. It was a game they played, she knew she wasn't really painting, that in a few minutes her first strokes would start to dry and fade back into the nothing color. But it didn't matter. What she had done was beautiful then, that minute, and he thought it was too. She dipped her brush, painted another strip, and another. They blended perfectly. She didn't mind the cold water running down her arm as she stretched up high, soaking the cuff of her sweater. The shadow of her painting arm was enormous and powerful, she was the giant daughter of a giant man, working by his side, moving purposefully in the circle of light, making something radiant and splendid out of tap water.

Was that the man she was coming to see, a giant who praised her for what was essentially a celebration of futility?

"Well, you know, just about the same," her father replied when she'd asked him on the telephone how he was, how things were going. He had called her that spring, something unusual for him. She would usually call him, because the sound of his voice coming from so far away was now unbearably sweet to her: so trusting, as if he was just there, sitting in a chair, doing the best he could not to be lonely, hoping to hear from someone but not counting on it, ready with an explanation why he didn't. He always said he didn't call her because he didn't want to interrupt anything. Men of his generation used the telephone rarely, had to be coaxed into parting with anything but communications of the most urgent nature. And she knew he didn't like asking strangers—her changing parade of roommates—if he could speak with his own daughter, if they would give her a message for him.

"Nothing much changes, around here," he had said. "There's always something to fix, eh? If things had gone differently I might've moved into an apartment and let somebody else do the fixing. What? Oh not really. What would I do with the dog? Ah hah. Tomatoes. Wonder Boy and Beefmaster around the first of June, then I might put in a couple of those Tiny Tims in July. And cukes, like last year, except it never got hot enough for some reason for them to really get off the ground. If it'd been hotter, that's what they say, the dirt has to get real hot for them. I can't figure out how the heck you're supposed to know when the dirt's hot enough."

They were sitting out on the back patio after dinner, swatting mosquitoes and finishing their wine. Or rather, Min was sitting; from twenty feet off her father was sure he saw a caterpillar crawling on one of his plants, and went over to the vegetable bed to track it down. He snipped the caterpillars in half with the shears that hung in a leather sheath from his belt. She had watched him do this yesterday afternoon, when she was harvesting chives for their salad. He gave a little grunt whenever he cut one. Sympathy or satisfaction, she couldn't tell which; she suspected the latter. Their opened bodies oozed bright green fake-looking fluid, greener even than the leaves they had been feasting on. Their separated feet moved feebly, miserably it seemed, trying to cling to the plant.

Fall was making its last mad gasp. The tomato stems were beginning to shrivel and weaken, pumping all their juice into the heavy fruit. The rosebushes, which stood gnarled and human-sized at the edge of the lawn, offered their ultimate, blowzy creations, that looked a little too full, too vivid in the fading light. Circus Parade, Tropicana, Forty-Niner, Mojave. Ma must have planted those nearly twenty years ago, Min thought, smiling to herself. Rose loved garish flowers: flaming orange and yellow roses, fakey blue hydrangeas, those cherry-red zinnias big as dinner plates. Just these roses were left. The leaves were yellowing on the neighboring maples, drying in the cooler air, giving up their scent: sharp, woodsy, sweetish.

Birds came to the yard every night at this hour, as if summoned. In groups of five or six—sparrows mostly, tonight a few sharp-eyed starlings—they descended onto the lawn to enact their jerky parade, staring at Min, her father, then picking at the ground. Step-step-pick, step-step-step-pick. Perhaps it was easier for them to spot the twitching bodies of aphids and sowbugs out of the noon glare, their dark bird shadows flattened behind them now on the grass.

He was wrong about nothing ever changing, she thought. This interest in plants and vegetables, miracle fertilizers, dusts, pellets, and sprays was entirely new to him. Min remembered when he wouldn't touch a tomato, in spite of her mother rapping her knuckles on the dinner table and insisting he was setting a bad example for the girls by picking them out of his salad. "Eyetalian food," he called them, wrinkling up his face. His food was meat and potatoes, white bread, occasionally macaroni. Rina mimicked his dislike, or manufactured one on her own; she never voluntarily ate a raw vegetable until she was in her twenties. When Min used to make clubhouse sandwiches she had to leave the lettuce and tomato off Rina's, and coat her father's with thick layers of bacon grease and mayonnaise. It must have happened a few years ago, maybe when he took early retirement, for there he was, on his knees, tenderly examining each fruit the way he did several times a day, gently holding them in his palms, shielding them from predators, wilt, excessive heat, like a parent fussing over small children playing out of doors: covering, uncovering, wiping off, admonishing against strangers. She had never seen him so solicitous of living things before, except maybe the dog. His plants grew in cages, the laden branches neatly twist-tied every few inches, with little basins spaded up around their feet to retain the water he poured carefully, like a secret ingredient, from an old coffee can.

"What worries me," he had said to her in confidential tones last night before they went to bed, "is an early frost. They could all go just like that." He snapped his fingers in front of her face, fingers she hardly recognized. Gnarled, they were, like her grandfather's had been. Every night while he flossed his teeth he watched the weather, leaning forward on the couch, his brow furrowed, shaking his head and gurgling unintelligible accusations at the weatherman, whose highs and lows and fronts and pressures jostled one another recklessly all over the map, without regard for Alex's tomatoes.

"Have they said anything yet? They should be talking by now, with all the encouragement you give them."

He half turned, grunting, and winked at her, flicking an invisible bug from a leaf. He looked impish: a wood sprite, a garden deva.

"When did that fence go up at Gilberts'?" she asked. The house behind them was still "Gilberts'," even though two other families had lived there since Mr. Gilbert died and Mrs. Gilbert married another man and moved to Florida; it belonged to the original constellation on the street. Except for the Gilberts and one or two other families, the same group of neighbors had lived on this street since Min was a baby. It resembled a long-running sitcom or soap opera, the same people playing their parts year after year. She didn't care about the fence, really. She was trying to weave conversational threads between them, encouraging his talk about the garden, the neighborhood. He had never been talkative; he used to say Rose talked enough for the whole family. Rose used to send Min to him for an opinion the way she sent her to the store for a loaf of bread. Ask your father, she'd say about anything the least bit serious. Min would take a deep breath, then let it all whoosh out with her request. It was never easy, asking him something. Of course, once Alex finally spoke, you found out he *had* noticed, he *did* remember, he *was* concerned. He just liked to make you work for his response. It didn't seem to occur to him now to ask Min anything about herself.

"Last spring," her father said. "Or was it two years ago? No, no, that's right, last spring. Guy who lives there now, Jack Barber his name is, used to be a long-haul trucker. Worked for Smith Transport down on Ottawa Street. Don't know what all happened, but he suddenly lost his nerve."

"What nerve? I don't know what you mean, Mac."

"Wouldn't drive anymore. You know, kind of psycho. His wife—nice gal—says he got up one morning and said he wasn't going back to driving a truck, ever. Period. Now she can't even get him to drive to the corner for a loaf of bread, eh. He won't even sit in the car when *she* drives, for pity's sake. He took the clippers to their dog and shaved half the poor thing's hair off, pruned their bushes back to stumps, cut his food up into teeny pieces before he'd eat it. Then he builds that five-foot fence all the way around the house—oh, it wasn't funny, Min. See those little hearts and things, all that trim? That goes all the way around. Nobody in this neighborhood has ever put up a fence. You know, we all trusted each other, forty some-odd years, let you kids run back and forth, never cared if somebody could see in your yard. Nobody had anything to hide. Course if we'd known what we know now. But no, Jack here's got to live in a fort, eh. Goes around the neighborhood with this here chainsaw all day, looking for wood. You know, if people have an old shed that's falling down, dead tree, whatever—Jack's right there ready to hack it down. I think he scares people half to death with this chainsaw. They let him do it so he'll leave. He cuts the stuff up and hauls it home for this woodpile he's got. Enough wood over there to last him until doomsday. Oh he's a terror with a saw, you wouldn't believe. It's a wonder there's a tree left standing in the neigh-borhood, eh? I've seen him looking over the fence at this apple tree. He'd love to get his hands on it. Maybe I should've let him. Probably pay me a good bit for it—''

He was standing near the patio with his head tipped back, sizing up the branches of the tree spreading above their heads, a tree he planted the year Min was born. It was large, gnarled, fruitless: each year clusters of tentative white blossoms opened, then fluttered uselessly to the patio with the next rain. She felt a shiver of dismay; he wouldn't let some demented ex-trucker with a chainsaw cut down her tree, would he? The yard would be barren without it. *You don't live here anymore, you have no right*, she told herself. So why do I want it all to stay the same? Mac, the yard, the *Readers' Digest Condensed Books* on the bookshelves, the old pink bathmat, the clacking venetian blinds. I want him to dump sugar into his coffee and stir it so fast it slops into the saucer, the way he always has. I want my yearbooks to stay in the bottom drawer of the basement dresser forever. I'm appalled every time I come back here to find that nothing has changed, *but I don't want it to*.

"You wouldn't let him take it down, would you, Mac?"

He didn't answer her. Instead, he lowered himself into a lawn chair and took off his cap, started turning it around and around in his hands. She waited, took a sip of her wine. He's trying to tell me something—

He cleared his throat, pinched the crease in his pants between his thumb and forefinger.

"Honey," he began.

Ah. I knew it, something's wrong. Something is really wrong. He hasn't called me honey since I was little.

"Honey, it isn't—I don't want you to get worked up in any way, there's nothing to get worked up about. There's just this little problem I've been seeing the doctor for . . . "

He's lying. He's never sick. But look at him, stooped over like that. He's sick, he doesn't look right. He could be—dying.

" . . . funny thing is he says I've probably had this darned thing all my life, might have gotten it from my dad or, you know, my mother . . . "

His dead young mother. Annie Laurie. Her grandfather's clawed fingers, his big pale hands hanging at the ends of his sleeves like twisted, useless handkerchiefs. Brain tumor? Cancer? Hopeless?

" . . . neurofibro-something-or-other . . . pain doesn't last. Not really much to do but wait and see where it goes, I guess. Oh, they can cut you open and see what's what, but I don't want . . . They've got every kind of machine over at that hospital now you know, robots and everything. Anyway. Seemed you ought to know—you know, in case . . . "

Why was she stunned, pinned there to her lawn chair like a limbless insect? Everyone's parents aged, started to break down, lose track of things, need help going to the bathroom; you read about it in the Modern Living section of the paper every weekend. But those other people looked crumpled and sunken, overcome with animal fear. Somehow she had not ever thought of illness attaching itself to her father, had not heard pain in his voice on the phone. He and Rina were the same, weren't they? She was the one who was changing. *Mac you never told me.*

"It's not so bad, Min. Old people start to fall apart, that's all. Your dad's getting old."

"OLD? You're barely even sixty." Hot shamed tears welled in her eyes. How could I not know? she thought. I didn't ask. He wouldn't tell me, but I never even thought to ask, I acted like nothing would ever happen here because I didn't want it to.

"Does anything hurt you? Is it something that's going to hurt?"

"Not much. Not yet, anyway. It might even go away, you know? Sometimes these things just heal themselves. Don't even think about it."

"Oh Mac. I feel so bad."

"Don't, Min—see, if I'd have been smart I wouldn't have said anything."

"Of *course* you'd have said something. What do you think this is? How could you not say something. How could you, how could you—"

Wordless again in the face of his denial, his insistence upon the unsaid, the better-left-alone, the past reworked so it wouldn't seem so bad. *How bad is it?*

After she stopped crying, they stayed silent together for a long time. Then she asked, "Does Rina know?"

"Well, I said something to her after I had the first set of tests, but you know your sister, eh, she doesn't like bad news. Hah. Who does? She's got her own problems, you know . . . "

"Mac, tell me. Is it really bad and you're just not telling me? I want to know, I want to talk to your doctor."

He smiled at her, wiping the tears from her face with his thumb, then pushed himself up, out of his chair. He squinted at his cap, gave it a quarter turn and set it carefully back on his head.

"Bad? I don't know what's bad, Min. Maybe if I'd known twenty years ago— No, I don't think it's so bad. I can still look after my tomatoes, give Skipper his bath, do four crosswords a day—my brain still seems to be working, so to speak, though I suppose that could go any day. . . . No. Bad is what your mother went through. That was bad. This isn't bad, really."

"Do you—do you want one of us to move back in here?"

But he pretended not to hear her. Or didn't he hear her? He hadn't heard her when she arrived. She had banged on the front door impatiently—it was locked—then went around to the back, opened the milk chute and reached in to unlatch the door and let herself in, the way she used to when she came home late, or unexpectedly. There had been no sound of greeting in the house, no movement.

"Mac? You home? It's *me*. Where are you?"

"Down here."

She ran down the stairs. He was sitting in the basement, barely visible in the faint twilight that filtered in through the small high windows, sitting in a sagging old chair pulled up next to the furnace, wearing an utterly threadbare cardigan with a raveling elbow.

"Dad?"

No, she thought in that first instant of seeing him. *This is not my father.* She had been preparing herself for the likelihood that he would look older, less vigorous, fatter or thinner than the picture of him she carried in her mind. But not that he would look poorer, shabbier. *Diminished* was the word. Mac McCune, always the best-dressed, best-looking father on the block. When the other fathers all looked like Ernest Borgnine's cousins, her father looked like Gary Cooper, a very tall, thin Gary Cooper, each hair carefully smoothed in place, his beautiful tapering fingernails showing the thinnest white crescents at their tips, the toes of his black shoes lustrous, invincible. He spent up to an hour on his toilette, finally emerging from the steaming bathroom so scrubbed and sleek it was as if he created himself anew each morning from soap and water, razors and combs. And here he was, rumpled, unshaven, in some kind of ratty brown mechanic's overalls and this incomprehensible sweater. It's ludicrous, he looks like a janitor, she thought, or a security guard, sitting down here like this with the dog, guarding a dark empty building. Or someone *playing* a janitor: surely he couldn't seriously look like this? What on earth had come over him?

"Daddy, what are you doing sitting down here in the dark?"

"Well, I gave Skipper a bath and I thought I'd just sit here with him until he dried off. He can't get up those stairs anymore, I have to carry him up and down—don't I, old boy, old fella? Yes sir. So you're here, eh? You look good. Thought we wouldn't see you 'til Thursday."

Her father pushed himself up out of the chair and held out his long arms to her. His hands looked oddly bent at the knuckles, the fingers held shut and straight against the palms, and when he stood up—well, he couldn't be standing all the way up, her giant father, because his back seemed to be bent too, as though something was pulling him from the seat of his pants back toward his chair. Maybe it was a trick of the light in the basement, it was so dim, and clearly he was trying not to disturb Skipper, whose arthritic old tail thumped the carpet, his eyebrows arched hopefully.

But when she embraced him, this bent man with her father's voice, she could feel the way his chest curved inward toward his backbone. Each of his ribs impressed themselves on her as she held him to her chest; she could count them in back, under her fingers. How had so much flesh fallen from his strong body? He held her with those bent hands, still leaning forward as though folding toward the earth. He had an odd, unfamiliar smell, a smell of coldness, extinguished fires, empty rooms, an unwashed smell that was filled, not with bodily odors and secretions, but with futility, indifference, long absence, a smell that bespoke no more reason to wash or prepare. A knot tightened Min's throat. Had he been so long alone and uncared for? She felt as she held him that she was embracing something lost, and sorrowing, a neglected sample of humanity who was washed up, superseded, useless, for whom there was no longer any reason to try, a sample who still inhabited this shell that had been given to him because what was there to do with it but feed it, keep it warm, move it from one sagging chair to another? And none of this had spoken from his letters, his telephone conversations with her, there was never a word that he had come this far down, become such a burden to himself. But she felt it here now in her arms, her own body was alive to his sadness, and it burned her, it was a hot bitter lump in her throat as she tried not to cringe, not to turn away in grief, disbelief.

"Welcome home," he said to her.

Mother of God

The morning Rose Minelli married Alex McCune, a steamy, forehead-mopping August day in 1949, she had a fight with her mother, who was refusing to let her daughter walk down the aisle carrying flowers that clashed with her hair. Earlier that morning, Rose—a stubborn redhead, nearly as stubborn as her mother, Donella—had gone out and cut a dozen or so spikes of zingy orange cannas from the back garden, and was now sitting at the dining-room table with them propped up between her knees, struggling to fasten a floppy silver satin ribbon around their gigantic stems.

"Rose, listen to your mother. I'm telling you nobody carries orange flowers down the aisle. It's not a color for a bride, eh? Your grandmother's gonna have palpitations if she sees orange flowers in church. Bad enough you're not marrying Catholic."

Rose refused to speak Italian with her mother, who she knew lost the force and eloquence of her expression when she had to let the choppy, lusterless English come out of her mouth.

"You hear me?" Donella continued. She was pacing up and down on the living-room rug. "Everybody's gonna think you're not a virgin. Just some cheap East-Side trash with bad taste. How did I ever give birth to a daughter with bad taste? Can somebody tell me that? Look at that dress—oh, my poor heart, you're killing me. A dress like that you could wear out taxi-dancing in some dive, and now you're gonna put orange flowers

90

next to it. Look at that. Mother of God. I wash my hands of this whole thing.''

"Good. Fine, Ma. That's fine. Go wash your hands. It's my wedding, not my first communion, you know. Or a funeral, that I should have big white *mums* everywhere. I hate mums. A wedding, Ma—happy, gay, everything's nice, eh? So I'm gonna have a little fun with my flowers.''

"A redhead should never wear orange so help me God. Haven't I taught you a thing? That color is death to you. Rosie. You look like Halloween.''

"Fine. So I look like Halloween. Alex should know he's marrying into a family of witches anyhow. You want to lend me your broomstick for my honeymoon?''

"You're gonna go noplace nice with a mouth like that.''

"That's not what Alex says.''

"Now you listen to *me*, Miss Smart-Aleck. You're talking to your *mother*, do you hear me? Not one of your bums on the street. Just because you're getting married don't mean your mother don't deserve respect no more.''

Rose carried the cannas, but added six or eight white Madonna lilies to the bunch so her grandmother would see she still respected the Virgin. Her wedding picture shows her buttoned tightly into a shiny, low-cut silver satin dress, standing next to—almost *under*, really, she is nearly a foot and a half shorter—the arm of big-eared, poker-faced Alex McCune, holding a bundle of flower-tipped staves in a manner that suggests she is about to drop off an armload of firewood, or some fenceposts.

This photograph, in a white scrollworked metal frame, hung above her parents' bed while Min was growing up, a silent reminder of their former selves, a picture of two people Min felt she had never met. There was something about the picture—the way the members of the wedding party, the two families, everyone but her father was leaning slightly away from Rose; or maybe the look of distress and foreboding on the face of her grandmother, who was clutching her purse in front of her like a shield—that sent a message to Min from across the years that something, even then, was wrong with the way her mother did things, that people regarded her with caution, as something that might ignite, cause a small disaster.

She ritually scrutinized the picture on Saturdays, when it was her job to dust and polish the bedframes and dressers in all the bedrooms. Her mother's dark eyes watched her from the wall while she worked. To do her mother's dresser, she would spread an old sheet saved for the purpose over the foot of the bed, then take off all the jars of creams, polish removers, perfumes and powders, lipsticks and emery boards, Kleenex and bobby-pin holders, the three-piece silver dresser set with Rose's married initials ROM carved into the backs, and the heavy red leather jewelry box, the centerpiece. Everything had to be wiped off, the silver set rubbed to a shine with a special cloth. Around the edges of the cleared dresser and on the dresser scarf sat the ghostly outlines of the jars and boxes and brushes, a thin film of face powder and dust sifted over the surface.

"Dust ye were and dust ye shall become again," Min would intone to herself in the mirror, with a long dreary face. A Sunday School phrase, which had helped convince her that her parents—her mother especially, for her dresser was the worst—were slowly crumbling away, returning to dust. What she cleaned off their dressers was tiny bits of their skin, nails and hair, far more human detritus than ever littered her own dresser. Wasn't that what her mother was doing with that thick cream every night—trying to keep her skin on? Gluing down her nails with layers of polish, clamping in bobby pins to hold on her hair. Min hoped she herself would die before she started falling apart that way. Even though she resented staying inside on Saturdays to clean, she did a good job on her mother's dresser because she felt sorry for her, sorry for her in her decay. Her mother hardly resembled the glossy young woman in the picture, now. Rose's hair was usually a mess, she only smiled that smile for company, and Min knew there was no way she would ever fit into a dress like that again. After she wiped down and spray-waxed the dresser she put on a starchy fresh dresser-scarf, stood each lipstick on end, made little arrangements of the bottles and jars.

Then, if no one was home, she went through the drawers. She knew this was wrong; her heart pounded like a drum in her ears, and she was always sure she heard the car pulling into the driveway. But no one ever caught her; and didn't her mother go into her own drawers? She hated that, not being able to keep anything secret.

Not that she had a lot to hide. Candy, some notes from school, a tiny bottle of sweet perfume a girl had given her (probably stolen from the Metropolitan Store), a set of yellow barrettes she herself had stolen from someone's pencil case but afterward was afraid to wear. Some red Smarties in a small piece of Kleenex in the back of her pajama drawer, to use for lipstick. When she was in the mood, she took one out, wet it with her tongue, and carefully outlined her lips with the sticky red dye, finally slipping the chocolate into her mouth. She got her stool to stand on so she could look at her face up close in the mirror, trying to say "yes" and "no" without moving her lips very much or wetting them. Then she would lie back on her bed and think about Michael Scott, the most perfect boy in the world. This was when she was eight, a month into third grade.

"It's a damn good thing I was led to that drawer," Min's mother harangued when she found one of Min's caches. She went on rampages every couple of weeks, whenever she felt things around the house were slipping out of her control. Their house was always cleanest when Rose was furious at something. "There's gonna be no secrets in this house, do you understand? I didn't raise you to be a sneak. So you might as well get the idea that you can hide things from your mother right out of your head."

In Rose's top left-hand drawer was more makeup. "Where's my pancake?" her voice might shrill on Saturday night if Min had put her compacts away here, sending Min and Rina off giggling into their pillows. *Her pancake!* Some brown rubber curlers called Spoolies, regular rollers and picks, bank-deposit slips and the envelopes in which Min's father paid her mother. **HOUSE MONEY,** these were addressed, or simply **ROSE— FOOD.** The next drawer down had a rubbery, feet smell, like the insides of Min's galoshes, and held stockings—wadded-up used ones, new ones folded in thin, flat boxes, each pair wrapped up in the thinnest tissue paper. Sometimes Min gently drew one of these upward, to see the mystery of its pressed leg shape. There were garter belts that she slipped on, holding them up on each side of her flat hips like holsters, and girdles she never tried, for she had seen how strenuous it was for Rose to squeeze into one, or get it down to use the toilet. The bottom drawer held some soft sweaters with tiny pearl buttons that her mother never wore—"The Angoras," she called them, like they were a family; a quivery black beaded top Min had seen on her one New Year's Eve; a stack of nearly new leather gloves; and the best thing: a length of fur—minks? martens? fitches?—which was really two or three animal skins sewn together, their backs and tails forming the body of the garment, their little paws limp and dangling, and two small, mean-looking heads coming together at the front, where a plastic springed clasp under each jaw let them bite one another on the nose, the neck, a paw, according to the wearer's fancy. The piece fascinated Min; she longed to take it to school for show and tell, but never dared ask. The eyes had been replaced with beady little rounds of brown glass. The creatures were still in possession of their claws, their stiff whiskers, their tiny pointed ears; you could feel the teeth under the skin of the jaws. Min had searched for soft parts, anuses or stomachs, but they had been covered by a gold satin lining. It was horrible and completely satisfying to find this thing lying coiled in the drawer each time she opened it. Why her mother kept a dead animal in her dresser was a mystery. Min was sure she was the only one who ever took it out of that drawer.

The right-hand top drawer held hairnets, scarves, "junk" jewelry: iridescent starburst pins and earrings, strands of sparkly beads Rose called "my crystals," "my jets," "my pastes," and an assortment of rings, brooches and earrings with missing stones. These ornaments Rose wore to the store, around the house, or put on hurriedly if a caller came to the door. Good jewelry was saved for church, going downtown, or out with Min's father. Good clothes, good jewelry, good behavior, good friends—all of these were in a special category. "We're seeing some of our good friends tonight," Rose would say to Min as she unrolled a new pair of stockings up her freshly shaved legs, and Min understood that these were not the neighbors, or any junky old friends, but special people, saved for good.

Pastel slips and nighties filled the bottom drawer, and Min

always went through it hastily, anticipating the last one, which held the richest, most secret articles. Underpants. Flat pink garments with hooks and eyes, ribs in them the size of her own. Brassieres: yellowish raveling everyday ones, good ones folded in half with the cups pointing straight up, nestled cosily inside one another, and one strange one, with cups that opened out like flaps on a tent. Dress shields, with their rich aromas and convolutions of straps and fasteners. A stack of apparently unopened letters addressed in faded turquoise ink to a "Miss Rosie Minelli," at an address that wasn't Min's house. The stiff yellow envelope with the string tie that had a picture of a rock and all their names typed on the front.

And the mystery thing. It lay inside a cream-colored square plastic container, sort of like one of the pancakes only larger, the lid domed. Min opened the lid very slowly, reverently, for what lay inside seemed so delicate. It was round, almost the size of the palm of her hand. It had a smooth, rolled edge and a dully gleaming ivory rubber surface, made silky by a fine dusting of some unscented powder. She loved the feel of it, its mysterious pearly translucence. Holding it up to the window, she looked through it straight at the sun, a milky orb. She rubbed its softness against her cheek, inhaled its perfect powdery scent, tried it on each side of her chest where her breasts would be. She had no idea what it was, but she knew it must be something very special for her mother to powder it so gently and keep it hidden away in this container in her most private drawer. Once she opened the container and found it empty, and her cheeks flamed, saliva rose in her mouth. She was certain something awful had happened, made worse somehow by her knowing about the thing. But the next time she looked it was resting in its box once again: powdered, serene, and inviting.

From fondling and smelling and looking at her mother's things, Min formed her initial hazy impressions about what women were like. She was fairly sure she didn't want to grow up to be one. A vague idea hovered at the back of her mind that this could, in fact, be avoided: certain processes arrested, choices made, paths taken, in order to divert her body from becoming like her mother's. Rose treated her body with the same energetic annoyance she had for food; it was something to be squeezed, stuffed, plucked, pommelled, and basted, served up for someone else's satisfaction. Every day, the same thing over and over again: starting from scratch. "Here we go, girls—wish me luck!" as she tried to squeeze into her long-leg panty girdle, ripples and rolls appearing in her stubborn, resistant flesh. Min fervently hoped that, with care and good fortune, she herself might somehow turn out more like Miss Nevins, the lady who lived at the corner. She wore pleated slacks and lustrous, silky shirts. Her blond hair swung around her face, perfectly cut; she had none of the swellings and saggings shared by the mothers on the street. Min admired Miss Nevins, and her well-kept grey brick house, very much. She had no husband, no children, no bulges, and seemed perfectly content.

Min wished for a mother who was perfectly content, who would be stirring Ovaltine on the stove when her children came home from school, and would welcome her husband warmly, maybe even with a kiss on the lips. Rose did constant battle with everything: her weight, dust, the milkman, her relatives, the lids on jars. Ice-cube trays. Bacteria. Half the groceries she bought every week rotted at the back of the fridge; she never got around to making a salad before the lettuce leaves were shiny and blackish, the carrots withered, the tomatoes collapsing in her hands.

"Goddamn IGA," she'd mutter when she went to fix dinner. "I don't know why the hell I should pay good money for all this rotten stuff they give you."

Min's father was a tall quiet tower of forbearance in the face of his wife's incessant turmoil, his responses no more than grunts, mumblings, vague shufflings of sound. "Look at him, just sitting there with his nose in that paper of his. How did I ever marry such a stick in the mud, such a bedpost, such a bump on a log?" Rose would holler affectionately at no one in particular, banging her pots and pans. "Try to get him to say two words about anything." But had Alex ever said any two words, she might never have heard him. Because Rose loved to talk. She woke up talking and was the last thing any of them heard at night. There was no place in the house to escape from her voice: no closet, no basement corner. She talked about the neighbors and their kids, movie stars' marriages, recipes, what she'd had for dinner fifteen years ago, what was the right way to wash your neck. "You're all at the sow's ear stage as far as I'm concerned," she was fond of saying to the three of them, to summarize her remarks. "The whole buncha yous. I don't know why I even bother."

MICAL WANTS TO TALK TO YOU AT RECES, said the note given to Min by Donny Mahon, a boy whose lank blond hair was always falling into his eyes. Donny was in the slow group with Michael Scott, and usually had a patchy red sore somewhere on his face. *Impetato face*, some kids called him. He didn't have a best friend and was reduced to being a messenger-boy, a go-between, who kept the machinery of other children's friendships working. Min would die if she were a slow. The Racers, they were called. Her own group, The Popeyes, was at the top of the class and had smart-looking pink readers. The Popeyes regarded The Racers as being mutants, outcasts, lisping stuttering remnants of the human race. Yet in spite of being a Racer, Michael was one of the most sought-after boys in class. Tall and husky, he had already failed second grade once, and his classmates slunk around after him and did his bidding worshipfully. He had three older brothers, one in prison and two who should be, people said, and acted like he knew things other kids didn't. Min and her girlfriends consistently voted him the cutest boy in school—"A living doll," she wrote carefully next to his name in her seven-year diary, in her new, cursive script. Michael had never been known to pay any attention to girls. Cootie bags, he called them.

But the next morning he shuffled over to her when recess started.

"Wanna go watch me play War?" He was cracking his knuckles one at a time with a sickening *pop*, looking down at the tarmac.

Min's face went scarlet. He's actually *speaking* to me, she thought. It was a crowning moment in her existence.

"I guess so—hey, wait a minute, where do you guys play?" she hollered after him as he took off running. *As if she didn't know.* She ran after him into the bare stony field behind the school, her jacket flapping, and sat on a rock to watch a dozen or so boys flail at one another with baseball bats, broken hockey sticks, and whiplike twigs wrenched from the nearby trees. Half of them had their jackets on backward so the others could tell which side they were on. Hooliganism, her mother would call this. Min was thinking that none of them could compare to Michael, that no one even came close, when he suddenly dropped to his knees, then rolled over into a motionless slump on the ground. NO! He's been killed! she thought, and rushed to his side.

"Michael. Michael, are you okay? Are you dead or something?" She hadn't seen him get hit especially hard, but he appeared not to be breathing. Finally one eye opened halfway.

"I guess—I'll live," he croaked. And his face contorted with pain.

"Oh god. What's *wrong*? Do you want me to get the teacher? The bell's ringing, we're going to be late—"

All at once he leaped to his feet, laughing hoarsely in her stricken face.

"Don't be stupid. It's *pretend*. Don't you know anything? You pretend that you get wounded." He was slapping the mud off his pants as they ran toward the teacher, a black figure with upraised arms in the distance.

"Cripes I'm an idiot, but you *scared* me," she panted. "Can I play tomorrow?" I will gladly cut off my leg, she thought, if that's what it takes to play War by Michael's side.

"Don't be a spaz. Girls can't play. Run faster, come on."

Min brooded all the way home from school, her newly bestowed joy already muddled by frustration. What did he want from her? Why did he send that note if he thought she was such a spaz? How would she ever get to talk to him if he was at War every recess? He lived way in the opposite direction from her so they could never walk home together; he barely made it to school before the morning bell. How would he ever find out how much she loved him? She could never trust Donny with a love letter. Anything to do with boys was confusing and seemed to take a lot of work. It was hard to figure out what they wanted, how they thought. Every night when she lay in bed she went over Michael in loving detail. Black hair in a grown-out brush cut, blue blue eyes and long lashes, her favorite plaid shirt that he wore every Friday, the pleasing rasp of his voice. She adored everything about Michael Scott. Michael, Michael, Michael. She wanted to marry him, and rub his brush cut every night before they went to sleep. Min Scott. Perfect, the perfect name. Michael and Min Scott, it would say on their mailbox. Mr. & Mrs. M. Scott.

She woke up before it was light the next morning, from a dream that Michael had fallen into a deep hole in a corner of the schoolyard. He was yelling for help when she happened to walk by. She ran home and got the fur thing from her mother's dresser, then ran back and lowered it down the hole to him like a rope. He was kicking a lot of big, twisting snakes off his ankles as she pulled him up to safety. When she awoke she was disappointed there had been no kiss; but she had an idea. For the next hour she tiptoed around the house assembling what she needed. She was looking for something in the medicine cabinet when her father got up, and came into the bathroom to start getting ready for work. He was always up before anyone else, and left the table set for the girls' breakfast. Rose had a terrible time getting out of bed in the morning, and sometimes barely made it before Min and Rina left for school. She was a nighthawk, she said.

"Hi, honey. Have a good sleep?" Her father picked up his toothbrush and shook some toothpowder into the palm of his hand. He didn't ask Min what she was doing. He never asked her what she was doing; he seemed to believe she was in charge of her life in the same way he was, the way he assumed everybody was.

She ran the eighteen blocks to school that morning; it was Friday, Plaid Shirt Day. At recess she gave the boys a headstart, then made her way after them, waiting on the same rock until Michael flopped down on his back again. Triumphant, she quickly tied a white handkerchief around her forehead and ran over to him, her red plastic nurse's kit banging against her leg.

"Hey, what are you—"

"Please be quiet. I'm an Army nurse. You have to save your strength—you just fainted, you know. I'd better take your temperature. Open your mouth."

As she popped the plastic thermometer under his tongue, she thought, Oh god, here I am looking right into Michael Scott's *mouth.* The stethoscope was next.

"Okay, I'll have to undo your shirt to check your heart. Now don't move."

A few of the boys came charging around them, sending bits of grass and dirt flying, yelling incoherently at one another while they looked at Michael on the ground.

Now I'm touching his bare chest, Min thought. I am really going to die. His flesh was whiter than her own, his chest smooth as a feather.

"Hmmm. Your heart's going way too fast. This could really be serious. Don't try to talk—your temperature won't turn out right. I think your arm's broken, don't you?"

Michael nodded, winced convincingly as she jiggled his elbow.

"Yeah, good thing I brought a sling." Two other boys had fallen to the ground nearby. One of them was rolling his head from side to side, moaning loudly.

"Nurse. Nurse!" Stupid Donny Mahon, yelling at her. "Over here, quick! I think this guy's dead."

What a moron. Min gave him an icy stare.

"You have a really bad temperature," she said to Michael in her most serious voice. "Here, you better take this pill." A red Smartie disappeared into Michael's perfect mouth.

"I think—I might need two."

"Well, okay. Two."

Min's romance blossomed. It was late October, the air felt colder and clearer each morning, and fallen leaves crunched and swirled under their feet as they ran in the field. A new girl with curly blond hair, Ellen Morrow, was assigned the seat next to Min, who hardly noticed. She wrote eleven Michael Notes in two weeks, received two back, and did a prodigious amount of bandaging, slinging and medicating. Almost all her allowance went for supplies. Getting him to keep liking her—well, maybe he had never said he did, but she was pretty sure—took all her time and resources, but she didn't care: she had never felt happier, and was starting to wonder how she might buy him a Christmas present without her mother finding out. He was painting next to Ellen Morrow on the Thanksgiving mural; Min figured it was because he felt sorry for her being new, embarrassed that the other boys might suspect the depth of his love for Min. Then Donny handed her a note:

MIN PINFACE
I'M TIRD OF WAR WITH YOU. DONT SPEKE TO ME AT RECES.   PERIOD.

                                        M. SCOTT

Pinface. No "Michael," no X's and O's. Min felt like someone had given her a rock to swallow. Michael wouldn't look up from his work at her. He hated her, he had never liked her, he just wanted somebody to come and watch him die every recess. She didn't know how she was going to live until 3:30. Donny had probably told the whole world. It was probably that little pig-nosed blond sitting next to her. Just sitting there, pretending to copy her work off the board, pretending not to notice that Min's life had just been permanently ruined. How could he even look at someone with a nose turned up that far? Min wondered how you would go about poisoning someone's lunch.

It was time for something serious. She started working on her note as soon as she got home.

M.
   YOU ARE SO CREUL. I STILL LOVE YOU BUT YOU HAVE RUINT IT. I WILL NEVER BE IN WAR EVER, DON'T WORRY
                                        M. MCCUNE
P.S. DON'T LET MORON MAHON SEE THIS

He should know how much he's hurt my feelings, she thought. He should suffer too. She opened her mouth and carefully let three large drops of spit fall on the page, so he'd think she'd been crying. Now for the love ceremony.

It was Rose's bowling night. Rina had been put to bed early with a stomach ache, and their father was stretched out in the flickering darkness of the rec room watching the new TV. She got the flashlight from the hall closet, thoughtfully applied a coat of Smartie lipstick, then went into her mother's room to get the round thing. It was the most powerful object she could think of. The container glowed dimly in the darkness, felt almost warm in her hand. Inside her closet, she shoved all the shoes to one side and set up her atlas as an altar: flashlight, both her Michael Notes and the note she'd just written to him, her mother's thing, an envelope with her first ringlet in it. She wasn't sure about the ringlet, but she didn't have anything of Michael's or any of his hair. She squeezed in next to the altar and shut the door as far as she could.

The smells of dust, winter clothing, and the soles of shoes made her remember hiding on her parents when she was little. Feeling exhilarated, feverish and almost sick hearing them— "Where's Min? Where could she have gotten to? I guess we'll have to have dinner without her. Min, Min!"—as they came closer and closer to finding her, then bursting out into the cool air, the bright light—"Oh *there* you are!"—screaming with pleasure and release. Opening the case ceremoniously, she set the round thing in the center of the altar with the hair beside it, and fanned the notes out around them. Then she held the flashlight under her chin and turned it on.

"Mother of God," she began. An expression of Rose's, this sounded much more forceful than "Dear Jesus." *Baby Jesus*, they called him at church; she needed to apply to a deity with more authority than some baby. "Mother of God, I am asking you to make Michael Scott be in love with me again. I'm asking you for—"

Suddenly the door flew open, smashing the flashlight against her bottom teeth.

"*What* in the name of Christmas is going on in here? Min? What have you—oh! Where did you get this? You little— answer me. WHERE DID YOU GET THIS?"

It felt like her mother was yanking her ear off.

"Ow! I don't know, I just found it."

"A splitting headache, and I have to come home to a scene like this, some little liar who's been in my room. I cannot believe my eyes. And lipstick yet! What business do you have wearing lipstick? Get out of that closet this minute!"

Rose snatched the round thing and held it up to the bedroom light. In spite of her fear and pain Min was amazed. That was exactly what *she* did! Maybe it had something to do with light, with the sun.

"You're gonna get the back of my hand for this, young lady,

believe you me. I'm getting that father of yours up here this minute too. Alex! Get up here! Laid out like a corpse in front of that TV while your daughter's doing black magic right over your fat head!''

Rose got mad quite a bit, but when she was really mad, she gave off a burning, organic smell, like something that had boiled over on the stove. Min knew she was really in for it.

Her father trudged upstairs and stood in the hallway, nodding while her mother enumerated the charges against his daughter: going into their room, rummaging in her mother's drawers, wearing lipstick (she hadn't had a chance to explain it was only Smarties), taking the Thing out of the drawer. Making Rose's headache a million times worse.

Say something so she won't go get the belt, Dad, Min thought with all her might. Say I didn't really mean to do anything bad. Say I was probably doing some kind of school experiment in the closet. Say I had no intention of hurting her Thing.

But he simply stood with his hands buried in his pants pockets, shifting his weight from one foot to the other, nervous, uncomfortable. The look he gave Min said, Why did you have to get me into this? She knew that it was hopeless, he would never help her, never had, never spoke up and said, Give the girl a chance to explain, or, No, Rose, I think you might be wrong on this one. He was merely another dweller in her mother's universe, like her and Rina. *What your mother says goes.* He wouldn't hit Min, but he would be a silent accomplice. He would hand Rose his belt.

He cleared his throat. You could barely hear his voice.

''Well, Min, you know you're not supposed to—I don't know why you—you heard your mother. You'd better go wait in our room.''

It was really bad when you were sent to Rose's room to contemplate your doom instead of getting whacked right on the spot. It meant she was going to figure out some particularly awful punishment. Maybe the belt, or a cruel deprivation of some sort. She might hang one of her bras around Min's neck for going into her drawers, the way they did to Buster when he chewed up her father's shoe. Or worse: a public confession of her act. Her mother would make her stand in front of the whole class and read Michael's notes out loud, tell what she'd done and how she'd been found out, while she herself stood at the back of the room wearing her good jewelry and a sickening smile on her face. She was capable of doing something like that.

Rina started crying from her bed. What's *her* problem, Min thought, I'm the one who's going to be tortured. Her lip was bleeding from being knocked by the flashlight. She stared glumly up at the wedding picture, trying to read mercy in the features of any of the people. It seemed to her she could see a love of punishment written on her mother's face tonight, secreted in the folds of her gown, buried in her massive bouquet, a dark malignant blossom ready to burst forth out of the frame. Her father's face was a blank, a perfect blank.

Mother of God, she whispered to herself. Dear Mother of God.

The Junkyard

Min lay in her old bed, thinking about her father and mother, surrounded by blankness: the old, bad kind of blankness that used to move in and settle down on you while you waited for something to happen—something you thought might be awful.

Years ago, it appeared to her that adults waited for specifics. When they put the sidewalks in. When the driveway gets paved. When Daddy gets paid on Friday. When the coalman/the sheenyman/the breadman comes. It was children who weren't provided with details; they were left to cope with the barrenness of waiting itself. Wait until we're all finished eating. Wait until you start school. Wait until church is over. Wait until you digest your lunch. Wait until you get married. A waiting that was shapeless, dense, invisible. An endless game of frozen tag your parents made you play, that could end in punishment. *Wait until your father gets home.* Then long minutes of nothing but despair, of feeling you could mess your pants, you were so sick with worry. The mothers in her neighborhood had all been masters of that particular torture. *You're really going to get it after dinner. See if Santa brings* you *anything this year.*

Punishment of all kinds was a grand theme in those days, in these houses. It fit perfectly into the landscape. Not the brutal, unimaginable kinds of abuse you started hearing about a few years ago—cigarette burns, electrical cords, starvation—but the old-fashioned garden-variety kind, just corporal enough to keep children on the edge, let them know who was boss. Some child was always getting walloped, whacked, slapped, spanked, swatted, straightened out or licked. The streets echoed with promises. *I'll lick you good. I'll really give you something to cry about. I'll teach you a lesson you'll never forget. I'll show you what back talk gets you.* Each mother had a specialty, the same way she cooked her family's ethnic dish at Christmas and Easter. Mrs. Costello always said, *I'm going to crown you, my dear*, which sounded like it could be something kind of nice, but you knew from the twisted smile on her face that it wasn't. The German lady, Mrs. Snecken-something, hit her kids red on the backs of the legs with a big wooden spoon. Another neighbor was an accomplished pincher; she knew how to grab a hard pinchful of cheek and shake her hand so that Sally or Randy's head would lob around the pinch slowly, like a water-filled balloon. Min's mother favored what she called *the back of my hand*—a stinging knuckle-hard blow delivered to an unexpected body part, a part that Min hadn't thought to cover with her own hands—though she frequently announced that her sister's kids got the razor strap and she was just about ready to get one of those herself if things kept on the way they were going.

There was no one here punishing her now. But she felt herself cupped in the great rough hand of Fate: prodded, examined, put to the test. Fate must be female, she thought, with absolute brute power over life and death, deciding for you the way your mother used to. *This is for your own good.* Of course, I shouldn't be thinking like this. I should think positively—right, Peter? I should be doing affirmations. *My father is in perfect, radiant health. There is no death. The universe is unfolding exactly as it should.* Except these brainless, hopeful formulas never worked for her, any more than the ones she had once been taught in church. *Believe and thou shalt be saved. The kingdom of God is at hand. Goodness and mercy shall follow me all the days of my life.* Surely the world was more complex and unbelievable than that. The gods she knew were not only wise and lovely but lame, jealous, vengeful. Their necks were as susceptible to the embrace, the necklace of Necessity as everyone else's. Now they had her suspended, her and her father.

*   *   *

She never slept well in this house. Not for all the years she was growing up, not now, when she came to visit, not ever. She lay awake twisting from side to side, bathed in sweat despite the central air conditioning, fighting waves of remorse, anger, dread. How could he be sick all of a sudden like this? In the back of her mind she had expected that they would be spared this, their house passed over, after what happened to her mother. Mac would live on and on, die peacefully in his sleep when he passed one hundred.

She wondered if the house itself could be poisonous, something terribly wrong with its foundation, a toxic substance leaching slowly out of the paint on the walls. Had it been built on the site of an abattoir, a morgue, a cesspool of radioactive wastes? But it was built not much more than thirty years ago, the third house on a street with board sidewalks in what was one of the earliest suburbs of Wyandotte, which in pictures of that time looked like a huge parking lot, a landing strip for spaceships: flat, treeless, utterly bare. The McCunes were the first and only family to live in this house. They filled it with their own quarrels, desires, lies, pain, fantasies, cruelties. It was a brick and wood scrapbook, a catalog of four lives lived within twelve hundred square feet and a full basement. It was small, cramped, and had ever seemed so to Min. To some children the houses they grow up in have an aspect of unnatural largeness; they are full of looming objects, vast shiny stretches of floor, replete with private corners, places to hide, to lose yourself. But Min's home had always been too crowded, with things and people bumping into one another, vying for space. Mac used to read her a story about a Mr. and Mrs. Vinegar, who kept house in a vinegar bottle with a cork in the end of it. The bottle was packed tight with their tiny things, and Min could see the little husband and wife going around in circles, trying to put their teeny-weeny socks into drawers, stacking their teacups, tidying their books, the way Rose was always after her to do.

Yet she used to like going to bed at night, in spite of not sleeping. She could be alone there, at least, and her first bed was roomy, big enough to roll over in completely, twice, and end up on your back again. In bed you could do things you weren't supposed to do: pick your scabs, whisper swear words, lie on the edge of the mattress and let spit drool out of your mouth onto the green scatter rug. Lying alone in the darkness she came to life, her senses sharpened, she was aware of a self, a being that was her, which disappeared in the morning by the time she woke up. Her junkyard self.

The junkyard. The demesne of her comfort and happiness, from the time she was very young, before she learned all the words with which she would later tell herself the memory. At first there was only the outline of the darkened room and her own small shape lying in it. In the bed. Soothed and complete, because in that place created out of her mind she was safe, she knew for certain who she was, with no other hands upon her, no lumbering bodies in her way. She enacted a drama there nightly, a silent ritual in which she performed the only function: she was the Mother. Chubby, babbling, still a milky creature herself, she was already attending to, caring for another. It was her earliest memory: not of being a baby girl, but a mother.

She lay in the big bed, a white cold empty expanse. Her crib cage was gone, that sweet varnished wood tattooed with her tiny toothmarks, the mattress scented faintly with her pee, the lamb on the end panel standing in the attic now, waiting to welcome another child to bed at night. Staccato eruptions of laughter, puzzling muted sobs, mock arguments: faint sounds of the radio coiled down the hallway from the living room. Her mother's words, like big bunches of bright flowers, asking her father a question; his board-flat response. Cigarette odors, the coffee they drank while they were listening with salt and sugar and Carnation milk in it, no sugar in her mother's *because as I said, there wasn't any during the war and I just got used to drinking it bitter*. The wooden creaking coughing night-sounds and smells of her house. In through the window, through the tiny squares of screen, trotted the sound of feet going down the sidewalk to the corner. To pick up a loaf of bread, a quart of milk. Then the train rattled across the tracks at the Dougall Avenue crossing. No little girl waving from the front seat of her car at this hour to the man standing out on the porch of the caboose. A teenager roared his car very fast, up, down, around the block, looking for a girl to sit next to him on the broad seat, to feel his hard thigh. The roaring, that smell of cigarettes and exhaust which seared through her nose and into her ears, the old-cat-stale-kitchen smell from the house next door: everything was louder, penetrating in the dark.

And she in her pajamas, under the sheet and blanket with her doll. Smooth rubber bald spots on the head, the ever-fresh scent of doll hair, the cosy flannel baby undershirt with the side-ties that she was dressed in. Tara, are you sleeping? Tara, that doll was named. Tara like tar. The sound had leapt out of her mouth one day, from nowhere, the way night leaped out of the afternoon, the way having to pee suddenly flooded you when you stepped on a cold floor in the morning. Straight out of nowhere, a place with nothing in it, no top or sides, just empty empty air. Lying on her back, smelling Tara's head, she started to sink into the junkyard. She saw and felt herself as if from above and a little to the left—not from a great height, just about the height of the bedroom ceiling. Maybe the room started to sway a little when this first happened. Then her bed was in the junkyard—a vast field, heaped with rubbish and dirty piles of snow, like the one they passed on the drive to her grandfather's house—and had become an iron bed with grey metal ends curving cold as ice. *Her junkyard bed*. All around the bed was strewn the derelict leavings of a city— ruined automobiles, rubbishy couches, rusted stoves, springs, frames, raspings—all of it the no-color of old, useless metal.

When the small iron bed and the piles of junk were placed exactly, when she saw each bit as it always was, the grey nowhere sky opened and the snow began to fall. Pursing her lips she blew hollowly, to make the wind sounds that gathered around the windows in winter. *Whoooooo, ooohhhoooooo*. She was the only human thing there. Tara she knew was not human, but a baby—something sort of human. She pressed Tara tightly in her arms, very close to her heart, and began to croon, a consonantless croon of gentle circlings and child's breath and blanket-wrappings, of don't worries, I'm holding you, I'll keep you warm, hushushushush. Tara must be pressed to her body, pulled inside the pajama top and the rubber skin held along her own length—or she would die. This was a certainty, even though she did not know death yet, except as a sensation of coldness, a bird stiff on a sidewalk: something which could never be warmed. This was the task, the reason she was there: to keep Tara warm. Tara's head must not come above the covers; a puff of space was made under the sheet, to let her breathe. From time to time she blew her own hot breath down there to warm the top of the doll's head, the visible bunched roots of her dark red hair.

The sounds of the street and the living room would fade. The bed glowed with warmth, a safe luminous island in a sea of ruin. She was sated with contentment, feeding on her world, the twilit sanctuary she had made against the darkness, and on the love she felt for her doll. She was at once above the bed and in it, surveying herself from that corner below the sky, looking down on the junkyard. On the child keeping the baby warm, in the midst of the howling wind and vast mountains of metal, under the silent, constantly falling snow.

The Day They Found Out

Roaring. She woke up from the dream lying on her back in a sweat, making a loud roaring noise, like a lion. She started up from her pillow, her mouth wide open and dry, her head thrown back. Outlines of objects were beginning to appear in the weak dawn light creeping through the slats of the venetian blinds. It was nearly a minute before she recognized her surroundings, her old bedroom, the pastel picture of a child saying her prayers still hanging on the wall above her bed.

Her hands shook. A full, damp outline of her body was pressed into the bottom sheet, like an angel in the snow. She expected her father to come rushing upstairs from the basement any second. But apparently he hadn't heard her. Or wasn't I really making that sound? she thought, putting her fingers to her throat. Yet her ears were still ringing from the noise: it must have been real. She sipped some water from the bottle by the bed, disoriented, half in the dream, afraid.

She had been sitting at a table in an outdoor restaurant with some friends, the kind of Mediterranean garden setting you found at restaurants on the coast. A woman was going from table to table, doing readings of some kind. She offered Min a bowl filled with pebbles. Min reached down to the bottom and pulled up a scarab, of some kind of bluish-grey stone. The back of it was divided in half, the right half a smooth flat surface, the left half a tiny dark cave. Somehow she entered the cave, and found a very old woman, in long robes with a

111

veiled face, sitting on a rock. The woman extended an arm, and started to speak.

She rubbed her face and eyes. She didn't want to wake up. She wanted to go back into that cave, where the woman might still be waiting. Something familiar about her, though she hadn't been able to see her face— Why did she always wake up before the main event, the secrets of the universe just about to be revealed? She knew people who took classes in dreams, who said you could get so good at dreaming that the dream would turn out however you wanted it to. *Make Your Unconscious Work For You!* If she could just have seen that face. But sleep was leaving her body, leaving in its place a feeling of something heavy, inescapable. Echoes of her father's words last night. If only she had been dreaming that, and when she got up everything would be fine, the way it always was, Mac sectioning a grapefruit for her in the kitchen, pouring them some coffee, listening to the news on the radio. Even his silence would be welcome, if it meant that nothing was wrong. That everything would be fine.

Didn't you hear me, Mac? I was roaring.

In the morning she moved around in a fog of uncertainty, disorder, disbelief. Suddenly her life felt profoundly *unmanageable*. The perpetual, spontaneous disruption of her work, the anxious no-money times between jobs, occasional bouts of numbness that came after a relationship had bottomed out— all of those things had happened to her, yes. And she had managed. She never let herself go off the edge, or succumb to any single disaster. She found ways to gather her forces, to work again, to court forgetting. But that morning her life felt like a jumbled disordered room; someone had come into it last night and trashed it, upended the furniture, pulled everything out of the filing cabinets and tossed it into the air. She felt sick in her stomach, felt a sick person's lassitude, helplessness, lack of direction. What was the point of eating breakfast, reading the paper, going over her notes? Not a single thing I do will make any difference, she thought. They can pretend otherwise, but they're kidding themselves. There is death in this house, I can smell it now.

The lies death brought with it were unbearable to her. She had always thought of her family as specializing in lies, the way some families formed gospel singing groups or started a business together. Rose's spontaneous, inventive lies, Mac's talent for denial, the rewriting of history. It was happening already. Look at the way he refused to discuss his illness.

"I'm not going to talk myself into a sickbed, so don't you start," he said to her firmly over the grapefruit.

He whistled at the table, filling in the last few squares of his crossword puzzle. He grinned obliviously at her bleak face and tapped her nose with the end of his pencil. She hid in the hall closet and called her sister on the phone.

"I know, I know, what do you want me to do about it?" Rina said irritably. "He won't listen. Might as well bang your head against a wall."

Rina was busy, would call back later. Her father went outside to wash and wax the car. She called his doctor. It seemed that a tumor pressing on a spinal nerve was causing loss of coordination in her father's extremities, the contraction in his hands, occasional dizzy spells. The tumor did not seem to be growing. Mr. McCune refused to consider surgery or radiation unless his condition worsened significantly. There was a possibility— he did not say how great—of more tumors, especially along the cranial nerves. They could affect motor and sensory functions. Nothing to do, in light of the patient's refusal of treatment, but wait and see if other symptoms developed.

Sensory functions? Is he going to be blind then? Deaf? Crippled? She did her best to keep from screaming into the stupid black receiver.

We have no way of knowing that at this time, the doctor said.

She thought then of Peter's warm hands. His extraordinary hands, the first thing she'd noticed about him: long, nimble, tapering fingers, palms with a span broad enough to cradle her entire head, to encircle her waist when he moved her above him, up and down, up and down. She wanted to hide her face in them. She called him.

"God, I'm sorry to hear that, babe. It must be awfully hard for you."

"It's *impossible*. I don't know what to do with my face. I

can't look at him without wanting to burst into tears. I know I should be able to be more adult about it, but I feel so out of—I mean I walked into this out of the clear blue and now it's like the only thing that's happening, all I can think of. Oh, Peter. I don't know what to say. Tell me you're still there, at least, everything's still there—''

There was a short silence. Min could feel her pulse thumping in her temples.

"Sure. I'm still here. You know. So what's your dad say about it?''

"Nothing. As usual. He's acting completely normal. Normal for him. That's his specialty, pretending nothing's wrong.''

"Sounds like he can't really face what's happening. Sometimes that's one of the stages you go through with illness—''

"Who knows? How the hell can you know what he's going through when you can't get him to say two consecutive words about anything except his tomato plants? He doesn't act like he's even living in that body, Peter. All this could be happening to somebody else.''

"Have you thought about getting him to see a therapist?''

Min suppressed a sudden urge to laugh hysterically.

"Brother. You have no idea where I am, have you? People in Wyandotte don't see therapists. They don't *process* things here. They don't talk about stages. They'd think you were some kind of wacko for even suggesting such a thing.''

He sounded a little defensive then, distant. After she hung up she could have kicked herself; she wanted to erase the whole conversation and start over. She knew he was trying to be helpful, to give her information. But what was the use of therapy talk in the face of reality, of disease and death sitting across from you at breakfast, spooning up grapefruit? All that stuff was fine, as long as you were dealing with the past tense. Well. He was just doing the best he could from so far away. She was too hard on him. Too picky.

She tidied the kitchen, picked up her father's papers, idly rearranged the plants and china figurines on the living-room tables. Figurines of women with impossibly tiny feet wearing ball gowns, children in lederhosen feeding birds, mugs in the shape of men's heads, with bulbous-nosed, ruddy, alcoholic-looking faces. No one had table decorations like this where she lived. They would joke about these things. People there decorated rooms with masks, dried grasses, huge old grain and storage *pithoi*. She had photographed a couple in Newport Beach once for a magazine, sitting in their vast living room surrounded by a host of these empty, expensive containers, by virtual fields of pampas grass. The house was completely beige, seemingly purged of anything domestic or undecorative, a neutral material landscape of empty jars and dead plants. She had worked to find any expression, any passion in the couple; there seemed to be nothing alive in them except pride in their possessions, their acres of perfectly mown lawns. She tried to imagine these Toby mugs on their coffee table. Those jars in her father's living room.

She wandered outside, sat down on the top step of the front porch. The sun was bright—far too bright, it seemed, for the end of fall in these latitudes. For waxing a car. Skipper heard her movements, and hobbled slowly across the driveway in her direction. Arthritic, nearly blind, afflicted with some flaking, rotting skin disease which gave him a bad smell, he was a creature straight out of Job. Everyone in the neighborhood knew and looked out for him; he tended to wander into the street, unaware of approaching vehicles, confused about which way to run when their horns started honking. He had been hit a few times lately by impatient, irate drivers. Her father was as tender with Skipper as if he were a newborn baby, carrying him around, brushing him, buying special shampoos and lotions for his eroding skin.

"Good boy, Skip," she said. She patted his head, and couldn't help smelling her hand. "Now go lie down. Go on."

The dog waited for a moment, making sure this was all she had to give, then settled his body down on the grass, hindquarters first, then front legs, one at a time—a painful, complicated process.

Is this what it all comes to? she wondered, her head aching. Decrepitude, bad smells, having to be carried up and down the stairs? *Is* slipping inexorably into *was*? All her parents' years of effort, making do, creating a life for themselves in a bleak suburb—creating her and Rina, planting shrubs, waxing the car, baking tuna casseroles, putting up with strange new neighbors and thin polluted air, with no certainty, no expectation of joy? What made it—not even *all* of it, but *any* of it—worth-while? Where was joy? Or beauty? "We had you," her father would say. "We had you girls." Is that where you were sup-posed to find happiness, the food for your spirit, in your family? But look at her family: shriveled up to something dry, painful, her mother gone, her father ill, probably dying, she and her sister barely able to carry on a conversation over the telephone.

Bad is what your mother went through. That was bad.

She remembered clearly the day they found out about her mother. *The day they found out.* As though she had murdered someone, done something in her pants. That was how people talked about it in those days, like the person had deliberately gone out and done something, endangered themselves on pur-pose.

Min and Rina used to walk home from school for lunch every day—or skip, or chase each other—arriving just before noon, when *Search for Tomorrow* came on. Rose prepared their food absently, absorbed in the story of Joanne Vincente's family—Patty's horrible car accident and subsequent paralysis, the frustration of Joanne's mother coming to live with them, the next-door neighbor's sleazy affairs, one right after the other. Min would have been only slightly surprised to see any of the Vincentes walk in their front door (Patty, of course, would have been in a wheelchair); they were almost like relatives. Once Rose had handed Min a bowl with a whole unpeeled banana in it, half sunk in milk; she had been listening so carefully to Patty's doctor she had forgotten to peel and slice it, and put on the brown sugar. That was the kind of thing the girls ate for lunch—bananas in milk, sour cream and cottage cheese mashed together, bread-and-sugar sandwiches. Bland, white food. Cream of mushroom soup, on a wintry day. Min would heat the soup, because Rose couldn't see the set from in front of the stove.

Rose was usually too preoccupied to eat any lunch herself.

"How's school?" she'd say during an Anacin or Tide com-mercial, scrabbling her fingers nervously through her daugh-ters' hair, forgetting she'd already asked.

"Fine."

"Okay."

"Don't forget your dishes."

"We won't."

"We won't."

Then she was back in front of the set, inhaling another cigarette, sitting spread-legged on the footstool with her elbows on her knees, meditating, eager for some fresh disaster.

The day they found out, Min and Rina saw their father's turquoise Mercury parked in the driveway when they walked home at noon. They stopped talking as soon as the car came into view, mutually subdued at the sight. Fathers never came home until after five o'clock. Only mothers and children lived in the suburbs in the daytime, except for the occasional milkman, mailman, Fuller Brush man. The men who worked shifts at the plant were snoring in their bedrooms with the blinds down, their wives tiptoeing around the house, saving the vacuuming for later. Any other man on the streets in the middle of the afternoon was a burglar, a child molester, someone up to no good, a bum. That car in the driveway was bad news.

"We're home."

No reply. The blank face of the television staring out at the living room. Their father—a shock—sitting on the couch in his dark-blue suit holding his head in his hands, his fedora resting on the cushion beside him. He wasn't moving, he didn't look up. Didn't say anything to the girls.

The girls walked down the hall as one body to their mother's bedroom. She was standing in front of her dresser, staring at her face in the mirror with a flushed, angry look, as if the woman she saw there had just slapped her, insulted her.

"Ma? What's wrong?" Strangeness boomed in Min's ears from the walls of the room, from all of them being home in the daytime. She was afraid to speak, to find out the answer.

"Nothing's wrong." Still looking at that woman in the mirror. "Your father just took me to the doctor's this morning, that's all."

"Mumma, are you having a baby?" Rina's face lit up, radiant with hope. Two of her friends had babies to play with; she had asked for one at Christmas.

"Shut up, Rina. She's not fat enough to have a baby. I didn't mean you're fat, Ma," Min added quickly.

"Don't say shut up to your sister. No, Rina, I'm not having a baby," Rose said, speaking to her reflection. "I'm having cancer." She spoke the words thoughtfully, as if assessing whether what she was saying could be true.

"What's cancer?" Rina piped up, ready to be interested, to have something explained to her.

"Cancer—well, honey, cancer is when they tell you you have—it's when they have to—" Rose stopped short. Alex was standing in the doorway behind the girls, his face a pale stricken apparition in the mirror. His wife turned slowly to face him.

"What are you going to tell them, Rose? What are you going to tell the girls?"

His voice was breaking. He was staring at his wife as though he had never seen her before, as though she had just grown out of the floor. Staring not at her face, but at her body—the body he had caressed and watched and slept beside contentedly for more than a dozen years—at something neither his daughters nor his wife could see, a thing that seemed to fill him with dismay, and dread. And Rose—big billowy Rose—seemed to recede, to diminish, to shrink under his look, giving Min the impression that life's juices were already leaving her cells, draining off into thin air, because that word had been spoken: *cancer*.

For once, Rose had nothing to say.

And Min could feel that some alien presence had come into the house and was here in the room with them, some cold damp rubbery thing *that terrified her parents*. This was worse than her sense of the thing itself: the smell of their fear, a thin acrid burning high up in her nose, a whining piercing smell like a child's scream heard from a distance. The smell was what frightened her.

That word, and the awful hush around it, drove a wedge of silence and strangeness between her parents. Lies started to buzz around the house like flies in hot weather.

"No, honey, you look fine. Really. Great. That hat looks just great on you."

"Nothing happened, Ma. Honest. Not a single thing. I'd tell you if something happened."

"No, it's not like it's real *sore* or anything, uh-uh, you can just feel a little something up in there. No, he says to come back in next week. I know, her daughter told me about it when I saw her at the IGA Thursday. Yeah, it sounded terrible. Well I don't think it's anything like *that*, no. They'd have told me for sure.''

Alex pushed his chair away from the table and left the room while Rose was talking on the phone. He always left the room now if she were discussing it with someone, describing a symptom or sensation; he acted as unnerved and embarrassed as if she were displaying her private parts. Every time Rose passed him, he made a barely perceptible movement away from her, a kind of cringing, as if her illness was visible, palpable, contagious. He sealed himself off at his job more than ever before, into something called ''putting in overtime''; he didn't get home until nine or ten at night, then collapsed bonelessly into an easy chair in front of the downstairs television. Min noticed he no longer cared what he was watching. He forked a cold supper into his mouth while his eyes dully followed the flickering display; he seemed to have faint hope of seeing anything that would help. He often slept on the living-room couch now; when Min got up for school he would be folding up the covers and stuffing them back into the linen closet, and she pretended not to notice, so as to save him the awkwardness of explaining himself. She felt sorry for her father, for poor old Mac; of the two parents, he was the one who acted most afflicted. Rose mediated between Alex and the rest of the world; it was she who decided where they went, what they would eat, who they saw on weekends. She was the libidinous pulsing red heart of their pairedness, the body to his brain. Her cancer threw him back on his own resources like a bachelor, a sailor lost at sea.

As for Rose, except for that first afternoon when Min had seen her in the act and attitude of shrinking, having a serious illness actually seemed to give her new life and vigor. She stirred the very air about her with briskness, determination, an almost radiant sense of purpose. She had something to do, something toward which to direct her boundless energy.

''We're going to lick this thing,'' she said to the girls after a second round of tests had confirmed the diagnosis. She talked about her cancer like it was a family problem, a cold going around, something they all had to fight. The three of them were doing the ironing downstairs—Rina sprinkling and rolling the clothes, Rose shoving the iron this way and that, Min putting shirts on hangers, folding pillowcases and tablecloths.

"I want you girls to know there isn't anything a person can't do once they set their mind to it. If that old Doctor Mason thinks Rose McCune is just going to lay down on a table and let him slice her wide open, why, he's got another thing coming. Rina, stop that sniveling, for pity's sake, you're enough to depress anybody."

Rina hiccuped, dampening the laundry as much with tears as with the sprinkling bottle. She cried now whenever Rose talked about doctors, tests, hospitals. Someone at school had told her cancer meant you slowly turned all black, and then died. She was nervously waiting to see if this would happen to her mother, and in the meantime was terrified by the bruises that darkened her own small legs every few days. Min didn't know what to tell Rina about the school story; maybe bruises *were* a form of cancer, for all she knew. They were both afraid to ask.

"You girlses great-grandmother, my grandmother, lived to be eighty-seven and she had lumps all over the place, you know. She had a knob this side of her pointer finger, the size of a thimble, she used it to test how hot things were, milk and soup and things. It was really handy. Now I'm not saying we haven't got any *lump*. We've got one all right—a lump is a lump. You can feel it as plain as the nose on your face. I'm not denying it. But heaven knows you can't let a little *lump* ruin your whole life, now can you?"

"N-n-nnno," Rina hiccuped.

"Come on, Rina, don't be such a baby," Min said crossly, yanking a dampened doily from her sister's hands. She wished her mother would quit saying *we*. Bad enough they had to talk about lumps all day.

"And it's just here on the one side, just in this one little spot," Rose continued. "Now when they opened up Edie Costello's mother they said she had them everywhere, like bunches of grapes hanging all over her insides. Imagine."

Min was trying not to listen. She didn't want to hear any more about it, about this thing that had crowded into the house with them like an ugly cousin, that gave off a bad smell and whispered at her from the dark corners and closets and drawers, that threatened to turn her life upside down and shake it out, the way her mother emptied pants pockets for the wash. Mac had the right attitude—don't keep dragging it out in front of everybody, don't get all worked up about it, don't *talk* about it all the time. She tried sending her mother this message, with her eyes shut, her hands smoothing and smoothing the warm, flat, orderly laundry. *Don't talk about it. Don't talk about it.*

But when she opened her eyes, to her horror Rose was pulling up the loose shirt she had worn since coming home from having the tests at the hospital and exposing one breast to her daughters—*the* breast, the one with *it*. It hung on her ribs sadly, its pale nipple puckering, a dark bloody line slicing it diagonally near her armpit, a mottled blackish bruise the size of a hand imprinted there. Rina stood open-mouthed, transfixed in midsob, the sprinkler motionless in her hand. Min heard Rose's voice following her—*not so bad, honey, biopsy, incision, little scar*—as she ran out of the room with her hands over her ears. Blood pounding in her head, she mounted the steps blindly, leaping, running, scrambling as fast as she could away from that bruised blue bag of flesh and the terrible message it contained, the brooding round malignant bud of all their futures.

Relations

"When I heard you were coming I figured we'd both let him have it at once," Rina said. "The guy never lets me touch a thing in here. He doesn't trust me."

"Come on, Rina."

"Seriously. The way he acts you'd think it was like a shrine or something."

Min stretched her legs out slowly in front of her; they had grown stiff from kneeling in her mother's closet, where she was opening shoeboxes, one after another, and sorting their contents into piles: shoes, papers, junk.

"A shrine to what?" she asked her sister.

Rina shrugged, picking at her lower lip. Her lips were always dry, flaking. Min told her it was not enough B vitamins; that, and licking them too much.

"Hardheadedness. I don't know."

Min shook her head.

"Dad's not the shrine type."

Rina had tied an orange chiffon scarf around her head, with a giant bow by her left ear. She jumped up from the bed to study the bow's effect in the mirror over the dresser.

"Well, you'd know. You're the expert on him, aren't you? Our out-of-town expert. Keep this or get rid of it, what do you think?"

Rina enjoyed needling Min now. After Min left home, Rina's devotion had turned to scorn, her childish insecurity to a definite knack for picking at things, little cracks or protrusions in human character. Min's she claimed by birthright. A sister was here to be pestered, solicited, complained to—always with impunity—someone born to put up with the myriad forms of cosy tribal abuse.

"Keep it, it looks good on you," Min said. "He's got to be overwhelmed by all this stuff, right? He doesn't know where to start, so he doesn't do anything."

Rina's blue eyes widened in disbelief.

"Overwhelmed? Are you kidding me? After twenty years?"

"I think some things don't ever get any easier, Rina."

After several days of careful persuasion, their father had reluctantly agreed to let them clean out Rose's room this weekend. The bedroom had become an overstuffed, unused closet, a storage area for the family's past. It had once been both parents' bedroom; but Alex had removed himself to a sofabed in the basement some years ago, where Skipper lay stinking and snuffling beside him all night. His few clothes were scattered throughout the house. Min felt awkward, watched somehow, as she picked through the worn purses, canceled passbooks, bottles of hardened nail polish, dried up ballpoints. But Rina tackled everything with unleashed, greedy energy, pulling on her mother's old undergarments, rayon dresses, hats and costume jewelry without inhibition. Rina had always loved to dress up, show off, make people laugh. Her flamboyance balanced Min's reserve, brightened the corners of their house. And though Min found her brashness today somewhat annoying, lacking the kind of respect or at least decorum she felt ought to be observed in this situation, she was grateful for Rina's ease, because she herself recoiled from the touching and evaluating of so many intimate artifacts, the slither of nylon taffeta on her skin, the faint, ever so faint, smell of her mother rising out of the drawers like a voice on an old recording: haunting, imperfect, lacking the means of transmission, the proper surface to make it really real. She was better able to deal with paper history—the snapshots, stacks of Mother's Day cards and valentines and undecipherable crayon drawings, warranties and operating instructions for long-defunct appliances, report cards, records of vaccinations, infant formulas, overdue books, prescriptions: papers that taken in sum spelled wife, mother, that totted up the daily rounds and rites and worries adding up to an existence, a lifetime, and were ultimately useless, of no historical significance or value. She was at a loss to account for scores of faded jellybeans and stiff caramels rattling around in the bottoms of several boxes, and experienced a sharp, queer stab in the chest when she finally decided that all that was worth keeping, besides the pictures (even though Rina squinted and shrugged at dozens of them and finally handed them back saying "But what *good* are they?"), was a handful of unrusted, perfectly usable paperclips.

Rina pulled off the scarf and leaned her face up close to the mirror.

"Maybe we should move this chester drawers out, too."

"Chest. Chest-of-drawers."

Rina had a cavalier, experimental approach to English, formed early in life.

"Whatever." She shrugged, then took a step back, lowered her chin, and squinted at her reflection.

"Like what do you think of my face, *really*?" she asked.

From being a chronic scab-picker as a child, Rina had grown into a relentless self-examiner, a porer over film and fashion magazines, ever in search of a new look for herself. Min admired her sister's diligence and versatility in this area, her talent at slinging on a cheap belt and a good shade of lipstick, and looking like a million bucks. Rina had figured out how to follow the Five-Steps-to-Beautiful Skin, remove unsightly warts and wens, tone and trim her calves, blow-dry her hair to perfection. "Quite a showboater, that Rina," Mac would say, shaking his head admiringly. Min herself had never quite found a look, nor really known where to begin the search. "Try this," Rina would say to her, pulling her hair back behind one ear with a comb, expertly knotting a silk scarf at her throat. "It'll pull your whole look together." And it would, though Min would have been at a complete loss to reproduce the same effect on her own.

"What do you mean, Sis?"

"I mean, like, do you think I look like Mom, or what?"

Min considered this.

"Mmmm, not really. Your head, your face is smaller,

your eyes are different—you know, you've got the red hair and everything, but I'd say that's about it. Ma's face was a lot heavier. Especially later on. You've got a great face, Rina, you know that. People would kill themselves to have a face like yours. I don't know why you're even asking me.''

"Because you have an opinion about everything. Because you're my sister and you'd tell me, you know, if you thought there was something weird about me."

This wasn't strictly true. Min thought there were a few things about Rina that were a little weird—what she ate, for example, a no-protein diet that as far as Min could tell consisted of pretzels, chocolate bars, and gin and tonic (and left her skin flawless)—that she didn't mention. It was still hard for her to believe, sometimes, given Rina's petite, small-limbed body, her golden-red hair and hazel eyes, and her own nearly six-foot frame, smoky blue eyes and dark hair—and beyond that, simply the way each of them thought, the way they lived, their utterly divergent values, their memories of growing up together as dissimilar as if they'd been raised in two different houses by other parents—that they were even related. Even though Rina was only five years younger, she seemed of another generation completely, another world of beings. Maybe because she had never traveled, had stayed in Wyandotte, still loyal to several girlfriends from high school. "Where else could I ever find a Volcano pizza?'' Rina would ask. She went with her friends—a select group of hopeful, perennially-self-improving-and-never-quite-making-it young women—to the Volcano for pizza, and later to a movie, every Friday night, then wandered around the mall on the weekend, picking up a blouse, a new lipstick, some shoelaces with hearts on them. She meandered from one job she didn't like to another: waitress, cashier, part-timer at the post office, waiting for life to offer her something more interesting, something with promise. Her good looks overwhelmed the rest of her life, brought her just enough attention to keep her unhappy. She had great natural grace; Min used to try to encourage her to go out for gymnastics, dance, anything that might fan that spark. But that sort of discipline never appealed to Rina. She had flitted, birdlike, toward whatever seemed attractive to her, then flitted off again. It was only now, at twenty-eight, that the lure of her desultory existence was starting to wear thin. Min could see that. Rina was sharper now; some of her humor had taken a bitter edge. She sounded, at times, like Rose, Rose in her darker, guttering moments. For the summer Rina had been employed by a company that cleaned swimming pools. She said she hated it, the sun was giving her more freckles than she could cover up, the chlorine burned her hands, she was tired of hosing up other people's scum.

"Rina."

"Mmmmmm?"

"What are we going to do about Dad?"

"Why? He been talking to you about it or something?"

"He's sick, Rina. Something could happen here, and he'd—he'd be helpless."

"He's not that bad."

"Yet."

Rina lifted her skirt and looked critically at her knees.

"He might not get bad for ages, the doctor says. Or ever. It's a nerve thing, the nerves in his brain are getting lumpy or whatever. It doesn't like, all go at once."

"I can't stand the thought of something happening to him all of a—"

Rina dropped her skirt and wheeled around, her eyes blazing at Min.

"Something happening? Are you kidding me? Something can happen every day of a person's life! He could stick his knife in the toaster one morning and ZAP! What are you talking about? He could have been run over by a bus the day you moved out of here. What are you going to do about it? Move back to Wyandotte? HA! No way. You're just raining one of your guilt trips on me so I'll come over here and pour the milk on his Bran Buds every morning, while you're tanning your ass in some foreign country—"

"Rina—"

"Don't you say a single thing to me about Dad, Min. I don't want to hear about it. *Helpless.* I lived here like a frigging nun with him for five years, watering the African violets while you sent us postcards, while you—while you *barbecued shrimp* in your condo—"

"You know I don't live in a condo."

"How would I know where you live, you've never even asked me down there."

"Oh baloney. I sent you a *written invitation* to come that Easter, but you—"

"Right, like the one time in my entire life I already had some plans you sent me an invitation."

"So that was my fault."

"Just face it. You don't like having me around. Remember how I used to pretend that we'd go on trips together when we grew up? I always thought that would be the coolest thing, going somewhere with you. But you never took me to one single place. You've been around the world practically and I haven't been any farther than the West End Mall. I used to *beg* Ma to get you to take me to the park with you guys—"

"Break my heart, Rina, for pity's sake, that was twenty years ago—"

"Twenty-three."

"What do you do, lie awake at night and count all the times somebody's been mean to you? You could go anywhere you want. You're not chained up. And what does this have to do with Dad? I was talking about Dad."

"I'm just saying. You expect me to always be here, to look after him—"

"I do not. I have never once asked you to look after him. He's perfectly able to look after himself. At least, so far."

"What about all this stuff then? If you think I'm keeping it—"

"You don't have to keep any of it. Let's just throw it all out."

Rina paused. She looked shocked, dubious.

"Really?"

"I mean it."

"But Dad—"

"Dad's got other things to worry about."

"Well but don't you want to take any of it back with you?"

"What would I do with a bunch of underwear from the forties, Rina? Get real. I have my bedroom and my studio. My share of the basement is full of camera equipment."

"What basement? I didn't know they had basements in California."

"We do. My one squirrelly roommate, this born-again vegetarian rebounder—"

"What's a rebounder?"

"Somebody who's heavily into jumping up and down on a mini-trampoline. He says it reorganizes his molecules. Anyhow he wants to build an earthquake shelter down there."

"Sounds like the worst place to be in an earthquake."

"We've been trying to tell him that."

"Just like Jeff."

"Jeff?"

"Yeah, Jeff." Rina sighed, working back a stray cuticle with her thumbnail. "My former fantasy lover. Remember? I wrote you about him. Tall. You don't. The one who lived with me before I threw him out. Anyways Jeff says when they start dropping bombs they'll drop them here first, because of the factories on the river. Every weekend he'd drag home these like, huge sacks of rice and pinto beans and flour and pile them up all over the apartment. For survival. I mean, the guy couldn't humanly cook a pinto bean if his life depended on it."

"So you threw him out?"

"Oh, partly it was that pinto bean stuff, and partly that he just sat around and drank up his pogy checks. Beer companies must make a shitload of money off unemployment in my opinion. I paid for everything. I mean talk about not motivated. It was like he was waiting for an atom bomb. Like, he was actually looking *forward* to it."

"While he lived off of you. A typical Wyandotte hoser. I don't know what's worse, these burned-out sponging rednecks around here or the airheads in California who want to help you get in touch with your feminine."

"Your *feminine*? Your feminine *what*? Are you kidding me?"

"Uh uh, a guy actually offered once. At a workshop. To help me."

Rina giggled. "D'you ask him how he was going to do it?"

"He was so bizarre I didn't want to know. So do you know what you're going to do with your money?"

"Uncle Louis's money?" Their mother's childless brother, whom they had not heard from in many years, had died the previous winter, and unexpectedly left the money he had saved from fifty years of working for the gas company to his two nieces. Min still wondered at this peculiar line of progression: her uncle's character, the Old World meanness and thrift that made him deny his own wife a new dress for the last six years of her life on the grounds that she might not live long enough to get sufficient wear out of it, was to finance her own travels halfway around the globe, support her while she worked on her book. Causality seemed to be of less interest to Rina.

"Dunno. Been thinking I might buy a new car, or take a trip somewhere. Or like, buy a car and then take a trip in it. I've never had a new car."

"They depreciate, you know. As soon as you drive them off the lot."

"Well, what doesn't? You sound just like Dad. I mean god, my entire *childhood* was depreciated—getting your old clothes, the next-door kids' toys, that crappy blue bicycle with those bent training wheels. Hell. I'd like to depreciate something myself for a change. Not some American piece of junk, either."

"Really? God. Dad would kill you for driving a foreign car. Nobody in our family's ever driven a foreign car."

"So? Is it my fault they're idiots? I'm going to get myself one of those Japanese cars. Or maybe a German one. Something that really *goes*. That does something for my *image*. Cars are like an important statement, you know."

"Yeah? Who are you going to make this statement to?"

"What do you mean, *who*? People. The people who live here. You know. My friends. God, Min. You haven't lived in a real town for so long you forget what's important to people."

During the summer before Min started school, an unnameable presence had begun to gather in her house: shadowy, voiceless, slowly ripening. Her mother was distracted, even more unpredictable than usual, her already large body spreading in a frightening way. On the rare occasions when Min could persuade her to read a story, she held the book too far away, perched out on her belly where Min could hardly see the pictures. Min was afraid to sit next to her, afraid of being crushed, smothered in the crack of the couch when her mother shifted sideways.

The feeling lifted a little when Rose went away, though there was an oddness: because Min's world had never been without Rose's presence before, and because her father stayed home from work to look after her. For the first time they were entirely alone here together, days and nights on end. Her father was unexpectedly tender, let her have dessert every night, even folded his endless legs underneath him to sit on her rug and play doll tea party all one long sunny morning. This was something entirely new: a father to play with, who laughed and acted silly. One afternoon he took her to a dark smoky place filled with men playing cards. Min was frightened, and curious. All the men had funny names—Boot Man, Dinny Dineen, Old Stub Clancy, Fat Bromley—and knew her father. Instead of Alex they called him Mac, and her, Little Mac.

"Hey, Little Mac, how'd ya like a swig offa my beer? Here, taste it, go on," Fat Bromley offered. Fat was huge and round; his pants came up under his arms like Humpty Dumpty's.

Min had accepted the damp brown bottle politely, took a sniff of the little hole. Her father and the other men were watching her.

"No, thank you," she said, handing it back to Fat. "It smells like throwup."

All the men roared.

"Ah, Fat, you big pig, offering the little lady something like that. Aren't you ashamed of yourself?" hollered the man called Dinny.

Fat hung his head. "I'm so sorry, Miss. I'd like to make it up to you if I could. Will you marry me?"

Was he pulling her leg? Her father's face gave no answer.

"No, thank you," she said a second time, shaking her head. "I don't love you."

"Oh Fat," they all hooted. "Oh Fat, I love you, I'll marry you, ha ha ha."

That night, while she was undressing under the covers for bed, her father said, "When Ma comes home, she's going to be bringing someone with her."

"Who, Mac?" She liked this new name for him. "Who's she bringing?"

"Your sister."

Was he joking?

"What sister? You know I don't have any sister."

"As a matter of fact, though, you do. I saw her at the hospital just yesterday, while you were at Mrs. Costello's. You have a little sister who looks a bit like you did when you were a baby."

This was astonishing. Should she believe him?

"If I have a sister what's wrong with her, then? Why is she in the hospital instead of here?"

"Well see, that's where she was born. Mumma went to the hospital to get her."

Min was silently enraged. Doom settled over her again like an old blanket. Why hadn't they told her about this sister? Why would her mother go all the way to a hospital to get a baby when everybody else's came right to their houses? The Costellos' did. The German people's did. She tried to picture this faceless baby, a little rubber thing, while her father read to her from *Myths and Enchantment Tales*. She went to sleep thinking of beautiful goddesses and sea monsters, golden chariots with piles of tiny babies in them, and herself with a great set of white feather wings strapped to her arms, soaring over the sea, the wings growing heavier and heavier until she could flap them no longer and called to Mac for help as she was falling, falling toward the churning grey waters below.

Sure enough, when Alex brought Rose home the next day— a somehow smaller, quieter Rose, who hugged and kissed Min absently, with a dreamy look on her face—she placed a bundle, like a carefully wrapped teacup, in the middle of their bed. Tightly swaddled, the new baby looked to Min like a little grub, a limbless torso with a gigantic head. While her parents whispered in the living room, she blew air in its face, tickled its eyelashes, gave a few experimental pokes, and then a good nudge, to see if it would roll all the way off the bed. *Roll, roll, roll your boat, gently down the stream—*

Almost off, when her mother came in and saw her. Saw them.

"Min!" she gasped. "What are you *doing*, you nearly—"

Rose snatched the bundle into her white arms while Min tried to disappear in the side folds of the bedspread.

"Come over here." Rose's face gentled as soon as she touched that blanket roll. "Look, Regina is your *sister*, she's a human, not a toy. You could *hurt* her by pushing her off the bed."

"I wasn't pushing."

"You could *kill* her. You're a big girl now, you're her big sister. It's your job to help me look after her and make sure nothing ever happens to her. You have to be like a grown-up, Mumma's helper. Do you understand?"

Min stared at the baby. It had a red wrinkled face that she found disgusting, and was starting to cry. No sister of mine. Rose was calling it Regina. What a name! Her name ought to be Rina, a better name for such a wrinkly whiny thing. Rina Hyena.

Everything worsened. The crib was set up in Min's room, and her playhouse and people moved to the basement. Rina lay in the crib most of the time, crying or sleeping or staring at the ceiling, except for when Rose was holding her.

"Why don't you let her *go?*" Min would ask, irritated no end by all the fussing and cooing and *mauling*. They were always telling her not to maul things. "Put her on the floor. Let's see what she does." Her father laughed at this, and rubbed his knuckles across the top of her head, which hurt, but which she allowed now because they were friends.

"Knucklehead. She's not a frog, you know. She can't do anything yet. Right, Rose?"

"Mmmmm." Rose was licking her thumb and rubbing some crusty stuff off the baby's forehead.

Mac gave Rose a moony look—had she forgotten all about him, then, too?—and waited for her to say something. But all she did was rub Rina's big old head. Min had no interest in this staring, helpless baby, in smelly diapers, mush food, little clothes that stank of throwup, the bleating noises it made that kept her awake half the night. Let her mother have it. She had found something better, bigger, infinitely more satisfying: her father. Her new father, the kind and attentive Mac. She felt the two of them were allies now, ever since that hospital-baby business, allies against what she privately called The

Stinkbombs: Rose and Rina. Those two could go right back to the hospital for all she cared. She and Mac ate supper together while The Stinkbombs "nursed." He let her light his cigarette with the bullet lighter when he finished eating. On Saturdays the two of them washed the car, cut the grass and hosed down the driveway. Sometimes she got to steer from between his legs when he drove. Mac was funny. He bought her comics and read them out loud so they could laugh at the jokes together.

Mac. He was all she needed.

Min and Rina made dinner together for the three of them; garlic bread, macaroni and cheese, Neapolitan ice cream with chocolate sauce for dessert. Their father beamed, clearly tickled to be eating with his girls again like in the old days.

"Why don't you dry and I'll wash and Dad can read his paper?" Min suggested when Rina started to clear the table.

"No, you guys go talk. I'll clean up. There's a dishwasher here now he never even uses. Then I've got to split, we're giving Denise a baby shower and I'm supposed to put up streamers and bake a patch of chocolate-chip cookies."

"Batch. You mean Denise *Yaworsky*? *Little* Denise?"

"Min, little Denise's belly is like, the size of a television set."

"Huh. See you then."

"Yeah, see you."

Min had been trying to include Rina more when she talked to their father. When Min and Alex slipped into discussing the book review page, or free trade agreements, or the hostage thing, Rina went into a sulk, and at breakfast yesterday accused them of deliberately ignoring the fact that she was sitting there at the table with them. Min remembered her mother doing the same thing, whenever her father tried to shift the dinner-table topic from the neighbors, or their children, or who had been at the supermarket that day and what they had had in their cart. "Let them talk their snob talk, then," Rose would say pointedly to Rina, making Min feel shamed for her father. "Who even wants to listen to it?"

She gave Rina a one-armed hug before she left the kitchen,

and Rina kissed her on the lips—too wetly, but a kiss was a kiss, and she let it dry there without wiping it. Strange, how when she was away her connection with her sister faded nearly to a remembrance, how she could forget her own love, and the store that Rina set by their relationship. Or used to. Min had looked out for Rina through the extremities of Rose's illness, and for years afterward, when she had yearned, unknowingly, for some kind of mothering herself. For a time after she left home she had shunned Rina's longing, almost loverlike attempts at contact, feeling—rightly or wrongly—that in order to prepare new ground for herself she needed to leave Mac and Rina firmly behind her, uproot certain shoots, though they were still tender, and growing. She had never been able to establish any middle ground with her family; they were an all-or-nothing proposition. That had cost her, and her sister too. Rina would not stand for being set aside, or forgotten. They were on delicate footing.

But hadn't they always been, all of them? You said something simple, trivial even, to someone in your family. And your words stood out blackly against the enormous backdrop of shared life: the weight, the form, the pressure of all the details of that life that had piled up over the years, unspoken and insistent, hidden and yet manifest in the very act of you saying those words, and not some others, to that person. They could not see you as detached from them, as having any other life than the one they knew. What you said arose inevitably from your common history, like steam coiling above a bubbling pot of soup. How could any of it be separated from the rest? That was what you were up against.

"Who's this, Mac?"

Min was sitting on the living-room floor, sorting through mementos she had pulled out of the hall closet. There were floppy scrapbooks stuffed with school pictures, clippings, yellowed restaurant napkins; stacks of unhung photographs, the glass smudgy, grating in cheap wooden frames; heaps of letters and unmounted snapshots overflowing from old candy boxes; little pastel-covered booklets, a dozen black-and-whites comb-bound in each, her mother's treasures from the fifties.

"Let's see." He put down the newspaper and took the picture from her carefully, holding it in front of him with an outstretched arm and squinting. Too vain to wear his glasses.

"Mmmmm. That's Fat Bromley there on the left—remember old Fat?—right before we enlisted. But who's that with—oh I know, that's—what the heck was his name, quiet little guy, shot himself in the foot on the boat going overseas—"

"Really?" squealed Rina from the sink. "How gross."

"—kind of a—Mailer? Mayley? *Mayfield*. Jack Mayfield. That's who that is. Jack Mayfield." He said the name firmly two or three times, to reroot the man's identity.

"What did they do to him?" Rina asked. The varieties and details of punishment had always been particular interests of hers.

"What the heck could they do? Turned around and sent him back home. Can't fight a war on one foot."

"I'll bet a lot of guys freaked at the last minute, didn't they?" Min said.

"Oh jeepers, we were all scared to death, what do you think? Seventeen, eighteen years old, never been more than a hundred miles away from home before, sick as dogs on that boat—'course if any of us had known then what we knew later on . . ."

Min had loved to look at old photographs ever since she could remember. A richness hung about those books and boxes and relics—so many of the people unknown to her, dead, nameless, unremembered—something that awakened and fed a part of her imagination, her sense of who she was, and her family, where they fit into certain small corners of the human tapestry. Perhaps her love for photography was nothing more than a simple, inevitable extension of this: the first way she had learned to make sense of her life.

The pictures of her parents' families used to seem almost sacred to her—sepia-and-ivory-toned portraits, mounted on stiff black paper by little scrolled corner holders, all kept together in a heavy brown leather album—because of their age, their foreignness, the great seriousness and formality of the people they presented. She had scarcely believed she was connected to those people; in her mind it was like being related to Jesus, or Mary. She and Rina had been named after two particularly wrinkled specimens, her mother's great-grandmothers: Miranda and Regina.

Now as she turned over one picture after the other, she realized a thought, or several thoughts, was embedded in each of them, that had occurred to her the first time she saw them. *He's a good man. She loves that little baby. These people must be crazy.* Whole stories built up around the vast stretches of time inhering in each photograph, time that belonged to these people, which they had already claimed, or were anticipating with a confidence you saw in their eyes, the set of their shoulders, the way they held their children. Life is ours, their faces said. This stony ungiving soil, my gold necklace, our stiff clothes and dirty-cheeked children. It has been given to us and we give it to you in your witnessing of it. Open-handed, full of faith. How could she have forgotten them, and the hope they proffered? Or any of this? This faded house. The pink and red roses trailing across the carpet, whose dusty woollen shapes she used to trace with her finger for hours. The urgent secrets she and Rina had passed back and forth in bed, as if they were the lone, doomed survivors of a shipwreck lying on a plank, talking through the night to save their lives. It was all here: the rose bushes, the mothballs up in the vestibule closet, ancient cooking smells, the same gummy jars of Vaseline and iodine that had been under the bathroom sink for years. As if she were visiting the museum of her lost self, moving among things that had served as containers for her thoughts and feelings, had been animate, precious, utterly necessary.

What she didn't understand was: except for the photographs, how she could have used them up, devitalized them? She might as well have been going through someone else's things, the way she and Rina had sorted Rose's possessions. Was forgetfulness the opposite of caring, then, as Rina insisted? The antipode of remembrance? Or was it something completely different, something Peter would declare positive, movement in a new direction, a clean bill of health? What about the great spaces she had felt open up inside when she moved to California, leaving all this behind, letting it sink like a rock tossed over your shoulder into a lake? Peter says our bodies remember, she thought. But they must want to forget sometimes, too, to give up heaviness and darkness for some new, ungoverned, scarcely imagined state of being. Perhaps they even lie, make things up to deceive us, so they can carry us off to places our minds cannot conceive of, our moral eyes might not approve of, our souls wait in dread—or maybe glee—of. Isn't that what happened with Peter? I didn't think I wanted to be with a man. All that stickiness and heat and hunger. But my body went dashing off toward him like a big gangly puppy, snorting and snuffling around in joy and confusion, while the rest of me stood there, stupidly holding the leash, not knowing whether to follow. Was that remembering—some atavistic desire for relatedness, the complications of love—or was it pure forgetting: of everything I had been urging myself toward, the living of an uncomplicated life, simple and straight as the letter *I*, without reference to another?

There were a great many pictures of her Minelli relatives, scattered throughout northern Italy—*Poorer than dirt*, was how Rose used to describe them. Blurry figures in white shirts with the sleeves rolled, or dusty black dresses, standing in farmyards, their arms hanging down at their sides, momentarily paralyzed by the camera, their hands gripping—what? Tools? Rocks? Chunks of bread? Because of their poverty, their threadbare clothing and swarthy complexions, Min used to think they were something like the Flintstones: a much hardier, more primitive race of people than her father's.

There were fewer pictures of the McCunes; her grandfather was the only McCune she'd ever known, besides her father. They huddled in photographers' studios in Dublin in front of murals that strangely suggested Italy, a lush Italy: flower-laden trellises, ancient vine-covered walls. The women in these pictures looked cornered, desperate, their fingers tightly interlaced, or furling the hem of a blouse. Their men's faces were blank, unmoved. She thought they must have been pretending they were somewhere else, where there was no camera, no eye pinning them in that peculiar way to that present, that stiff suit of clothes, that lying Mediterranean backdrop.

The pictures from the thirties and forties were glamorous;

the people in them, including her parents, looked as though they had just stepped out of the movies. The women's hair was rolled, waved, pinned differently in every picture, catching the light in a way that seemed consciously willed, purposeful. They had large white teeth, darkly stained lips, and arranged their legs carefully for the camera: knee and ankle bent, knee slid forward to slim and elongate the line of the thighs. Min had practised that stance herself many times, in front of the hall mirror. They wore gay dresses with puffy short sleeves and twirling skirts, dark narrow suits with elaborate fur collars, bathing suits with discreet front panels. Hats, and alligator purses. In the early pictures the women stood beside men in uniforms, sometimes one woman between two men, their delight in their own allure irrepressible. The men looked serious, they held cigarettes like tools or weapons, ready to strike, to defend these females. *There is nothin' like a dame—Nothin' in the world*.

And because the men suddenly disappeared from pages and pages, leaving groups of women with linked arms and sadder, braver smiles, Min had assumed that was what war was, something between men and women, the men going off somewhere to fight for these dark-lipped women, for their pearly teeth and long, stockinged legs, for their right to carry little alligator purses, to sit in convertibles with all that wavy hair lifting gently in the wind. That was why her father told her stories that circled around the war—led to blue-smoke-filled nightclubs, blistered limbs, powdered milk and wretched tinned meat, sadistic officers, waist-high mud—because the real thing about war, what was at the sulphur-smelling heart of it, was something you could not tell anyone else; it was the raw, sticky, private stuff of broken sleep, of him shouting from his bed and waking them all up in the middle of the night, of a mortar shell screaming through the air toward you with the voice of a woman, your sweetheart, your wife, your name on it as it tore into your chest, it was everything you never wanted your child to hear about. Her father's mind and memory, forever blasted wide open by Dieppe and North Africa and Italy, by everything he had seen, his best friend blown to bits, death touching him on the arm, kissing him on the mouth—wasn't that all, in some way, for her mother? And for her and her sister, born out of that cold sweat, that nightmare of blankness? Wasn't it all for women?

And her mother, who seldom had the patience to sit and read to her from storybooks—"Oh geez, we've heard about those stupid bears a hundred times. You know that story, why don't you go read it to yourself? I've got to get this supper on the table"—could sift through photographs for hours, telling Min their stories: who was in the picture, who she married, what their first car looked like, whether they were tall or short. And if she herself had been here, who was holding the camera, what everyone had to eat on the picnic, what color their dresses and hats were. The story that remained untold was the one about why she married Min's father, instead of the guy whose arm was around her in this picture, or that one. How you made that final, crucial choice, how you knew that *he* was the one—this was the bit of information she had longed to add to what she had gleaned from her friends, from *The Canadian Mother and Child*, from the books she read in secret, from the photographs: the clue that might make sense of the rest of it, that would demonstrate, finally, how a woman's life finally fell into place and everything *fit*. It was the last puzzle piece she had sought here, the one that Rose had kept hidden in her pocket, and never shared.

Min loved Rose most at those times; she was at her softest and wittiest, cracking jokes, lighting one cigarette from the tip of another and squinting through her smoke at the past. She felt her mother was letting her in on something adult, privileged by taboo, that was just between the two of them. She was careful not to ask too many questions, lest she break the spell around them. It was the closest she ever came to an initiation.

From those stories of her mother's, Min gathered that making and living your life was a kind of creative act, one that had to be built carefully from the bottom up, like a layer cake, by taking a series of small, ordinary steps: buying a convertible, wearing a nice Italian suit, marrying the right husband or wife, teaching your kids how to swim in the lake. In life, everything was related to everything else. Getting the right wife could depend on the convertible, or the suit, on whether you were tall or short, even something as simple as if it rained on your first date. You could never know for sure what it would be.

Those pictures became her storybooks, the people in them the gods of her childhood, their lives allegories of moral choice and action, of fatal necessity, their obsessions, errors, wounds, and peculiar behavior far more important than Sleeping Beauty's rescue or Goldilocks's discovery, because—ever unknown to them—they belonged to her and she to them: they were relations.

"See this guy here with the hat on?" her mother would say, pulling a small snapshot with pinked edges from somewhere in the pile spread around them on the floor. "This is your Uncle Louis, the day he got married. You never saw a better-looking guy in your life than Louis, believe you me. Look at that head of hair. All us girls wished we had his hair. Ma sent his measurements over to a friend of her father's in the old country, and he made Louis's wedding suit. See that suit he's wearing? That suit came all the way here from Italy. Before the war. What a suit that was. Nobody hardly looked at the bride—'course she wasn't much to look at, nice girl, but kind of plain, you know, not what you'd call a real looker—but they sure couldn't take their eyes off your Uncle Louis in that suit of his."

Min would take the picture and study it, looking not so much at the suit or Louis's head of hair, but for the shadow of what she looked for in all the family pictures: the shadow of herself. If this was her uncle, if this was a picture of a particular time in his life, there could be a hint of her in the picture, couldn't there?—a certain slant of a cheekbone, a glint in the eye, a curling of the fingers indicating that she would someday exist, that possibly in the back of even Uncle Louis's mind there was a glimmer, a faint outline in the shape of a small, dark-haired girl, a fuzzy, squarish place with the word *niece* on it. That was the reason she sat so patiently and listened, watched her mother shake her head, chew her lips, even cry as they turned the pictures over one by one: sooner or later, if she listened carefully and waited, the stories would surely get around to her, to the immanence, the shining fact of her own existence in the world. The one of the tall blond man, for instance, his white buck shoes braced against a rock so he can lean forward and wrap his big arms around the compact, fresh-faced woman who was her mother: now what if her mother had married that man—Don was his name—what would Min have turned out like? Would she have been herself, or someone else? Would she have been slim and blond and smiling, as Don's daughter, or short, swarthy, dejected? Would he have loved her even more than Mac did, bought her more clothes, more presents? Would she live in a bigger house, in a different city, or in some kind of shack? Would she have a brother, or six brothers, or no one at all, instead of Rina? All this, her entire life, could have been different, depending on the man in the picture, maybe depending on something as silly as his shoes, whether her mother had liked white buck shoes or not. Maybe that was why her mother cried over some of the pictures. Maybe she had picked the wrong man, sat on the wrong rocks, worn her hair the wrong way, and now she was sorry.

After Rina left, and Min handed the brown-covered photograph to her father—the one she had treasured and kept hidden for years, perhaps just so she could present it to him like this, then sit back while he finally told her a story, any story, about her grandmother, about her great unforgettable beauty, or talent, or pluck—and watched him open it like a telegram delivered unexpectedly from the past, it was some time, a long, slow-moving passage of time, before she really heard what he was saying to her, comprehended that he was not taking one of his usual long walks around reality, telling her what would have happened if things had gone differently, or looked up, or turned the corner, if so-and-so had only known better, or been able to see past the nose on his face. He was simply and unaccountably handing her his version of what had happened, like a sandwich on a plate. A fact.

Wasn't that what she'd always wanted—facts? Truth? A solid chunk of the real, instead of uneasy evasions, concocted boneless plots, what she'd heard all her life, or made up for herself, in order to account for the way things had gone. There'd always been plenty of useless facts to go around. The engine specifications on every car her father had ever owned. The amount Mr. Costello paid for the fur coat he gave his wife for having their fourth baby. The number of times the word "love" appears in the New Testament. Facts she didn't care about. The rest of it, the bedrock, the matrix their lives sprang from—what happened in sex, how much money her father earned, where people went when they died, why her mother and father had married each other—all that had been mostly hidden from her, stuffed way down in her parents' private conversations, the way her mother's sanitary napkins were wrapped tightly as Christmas presents and carefully tucked beneath the ordinary trash. Privileged information, that children from other families might be allowed to possess, but not her and Rina.

In the days to come, fact took on a new meaning for her. She looked at it from different angles, the way she examined negatives in the darkroom, manipulated light and shadow so as to effect a clearer contrast between rock and water, cheek and hand, making the world more, or less, real to the eye. Sometimes a dark face could absorb too much light, leaving just a head-shaped hole, or an outline without meaning or differentiation, as if the person had somehow been sucked out of the picture. In the same way, her father's words became shadows: cutout shapes of something that had inexplicably disappeared.

"The thing was," he said, bending his elbows down onto his knees and staring at his contracted hands as if they'd been stuck onto his wrists by mistake, "back then they didn't know what to do with people like that. There weren't psychiatrists or social workers or any of that. When things got bad enough you sent the person to a hospital, that had the—you know, facilities and whatnot."

Min remembered the facilities at the Albion Mental Hospital quite clearly, from her summer there as a candy striper. Massive grey chimneys chuffing smoke continuously, which she imagined arose from some basement crematory where men in white coats disposed of broken useless bodies, day and night. Gridlike shadows slanting across the floors, falling from the iron bars that crisscrossed the high, dirt-streaked windows. A garishly lit TV room filled with bobbing, dribbling, horrific creatures in wheelchairs. A man with an enormous head he seemed barely able to balance atop his neck, and a shiny red lower lip hanging like a piece of raw beef down onto his chest. A red-haired girl—a woman? a child? You never knew how old those people might be, a nurse had pointed out a couple of thirty-year-olds the length of a yardstick, lying stiffly in their cribs—with lengths of rags knotted around her waist, securing her to a barred window, where she strained and screamed like a gull. Screams, which ran toward you from endless hallways whenever one of the heavy doors swung open; high, mesmerizing, unearthly screams. The sickening smell of the gruel she and Sandy McGregor were supposed to feed the ones who could sit up, a smell which, mixed with those of urine and disinfectant, made you gag. Made you want to never eat again.

She and Sandy and two other girls visited that monstrous surreal world every other Saturday, until her father happened to talk to Mrs. McGregor and found out where they were going. Min was half relieved when he forbade her to go there again, telling her she would have to quit candy stripers unless they'd send her to the pediatric ward or the gift shop at St. Joseph's hospital downtown. Though she dreaded going to Albion, it held a sick fascination for her. Since her mother died, there had been something haunted and unresolved in her about institutions: what happened in them, what they did to you there, how you went in the door of a big old brick building whole and came out broken, cut up, crudely patched together. That had happened to Rose, who had never been bossed by anyone in her life, as far as Min knew.

Now her father was telling her it had happened to her grandmother. She had been locked up somewhere in one of those dingy impervious buildings. Had lived there for years, her hair uncombed, her fingernails clawing and ragged. Had been fed that nauseating grey mush by someone with a large spoon, maybe someone as queasy and appalled as Min had been. Had screamed down a long hallway. Only she—unlike Rose—had not come back out.

He rummaged around in the bottom of one of the boxes and pulled up a thin, yellowed foolscap notebook.

"Only thing I've got of hers," he said, and handed it to her.

BOOK OF LIFE was printed in large crooked letters on the cover. It was a scrapbook, filled with pictures cut out from magazines. Pictures of families sitting around tables eating dinner, women in aprons peeling apples for pies, children running across fields. Pages covered with tiny, individually glued-in onions, chairs, hairbrushes, dogs, brooms. **Have give BIRTH to a HORSE this A.M.**, one page was headed. **Electrocution HAIRS. The PEACE of it. They will TAKE your LIFE.** So this had been her grandmother's photograph album.

"Found it in with my Dad's stuff after he died. Not sure why he kept it."

"Did you ever show it to Ma?"

"No."

"Mac. You still haven't said what was wrong with her."

"I don't think I ever knew, really. Maybe nobody did. My dad never talked about it. I remember hearing once—who was it said? Maybe our housekeeper, old Mrs. Steele—that she'd gone, my mother had gone after him with a butcher knife. Now I'm not at all sure where I heard that, or even if I heard it. That she used to sleep with a butcher knife under her pillow. I could've made it up. It seems to me I used to make things up, about why she was gone and what she did. Like I must have known, eh, that she wasn't dead. But that was what I was told, that she died."

"Did she try to hurt you, do you think?"

"Oh no, no, I don't think it was anything like that. No. It seemed she had me and never really got better from—you know, the birth and whatnot, and my dad was working the night shift and he didn't know what to do, I guess, and the doctor said she ought to be put in the hospital, and that was that."

"But god, Mac, she never came *out*. She died in there. People go into those hospitals, and get therapy or something, and go home. Don't they? I mean, it sounds like it was maybe just postpartum depression or something. That happens to lots of women. Why didn't they ever let her out? She doesn't look crazy in the picture. She doesn't look the least bit crazy to me."

"Well. People don't always look like what they are, do they?"

*   *   *

Annie Laurie lies in her bed, her tongue thick and pulpy in her mouth. Through the fog all around her she hears the other women in their beds, crying out like animals trapped by fire in a barn, horses and pigs and cows

Sunday afternoon. Annie Laurie sits on a plastic chair by the streaky window in the dayroom, picking at some tiny white threads in her dress. The look of her own arms surprises her, soft and pale as suet. Can't even hold a spoon can ye missus, yer like a great big baby

They gather Annie Laurie in and strap her down like a sail on the table again. Every time like that first time, that thing tearing the spine out of her—

For all Min knew, she might have seen her there. Fed her. He had gone to see her, yes. Once.

A rainy fall day just before his regiment was shipped overseas. A tall nervous boy in a dark-green uniform, holding a bunch of the garden's last flowers tied up in a cone of waxed paper. Almost an hour he waited on a bench in the hallway, trying not to hear the high-pitched wails pealing through the dank sultry air, lonely as sirens. Finally a nurse showed him to the small, high-ceilinged room with peeling green paint and no windows, where a rail-thin woman sat on a cot against one wall. She didn't look anything like what he had expected; her hair had gone dark, her skin hung yellow and puckery as a plucked chicken's, though he counted backward and was sure she couldn't be more than forty. Her eyes were large, staring, glassy: she looked at him with horror, as though he had just risen from the dead. She snatched the flowers from him and laughed shrilly, plucking the petals off one by one. Would he like to hear about her two naughty boys, Johnny and Jackie, who must be spanked for their dirty trousers and sent to their room? Naughty, naughty boys, never minded did they? She reached under the bed and pulled up a tattered shoebox. Holding it in her lap, she took out objects one by one and set them on the bed beside her. A filthy hairbrush, its handle black with tarnish. An empty mint tin with a hinged lid and three buttons inside. Something grey and crumbling that gave off a faint smell, and could have been an ancient crust of bread. A picture of the Virgin Mary, parting her pale-blue robes to expose a plump, dripping heart. But she had been Protestant; his father had been an Orangeman. Why would she have this? He reached toward the picture. Suddenly she shrieked and leaped off the bed, letting the box fall. Her skinny fingers raked the bodice of her strained, shapeless dress. Petals showered the floor. She swatted the air in front of his face like she was trying to kill a moth. Mother, he tried to say, but the word would not rise to his lips. She was mad. Mad as a hatter, nutty as a fruitcake, crazy as a loon.

He fled the room. By the nurses' station he combed his hair back from his sweating forehead, fumbled in his pockets for a few dollars to leave with them. Maybe they would buy her a new dress. And how did Mrs. McKenzie seem to him today? a round-faced nurse asked him kindly. Mrs. McCune, he said. I was visiting my mother, Mrs. McCune. Oh no, she insisted. The dark-haired woman across the hall? That was Mrs. McKenzie. There must have been some mistake. Mrs. McCune has been off ward all afternoon for treatment. Shall I go downstairs and bring her up to see you? No. Shall I get your flowers back? No, no. I don't want any of it back.

"I can't believe Ma told me all those years she was dead. Why didn't you tell us? It was your own mother. I mean, it's like something out of a book. Why weren't we told?"

Her father lifted his head, and his eyes blazed at her.

"Because I didn't want you to know, that's why. It wasn't any of your business. People didn't go around talking about every little thing then, the way they do now, somebody on television dying to show you the crack in their rump every time you turn around. Why should we tell you? Why should the whole world know? People hear things like that, somebody at school tells you it runs in families or something, and next thing you know you could be walking around wondering if you're going to go off your own rocker. She had problems, they put her in the hospital. That was that. Some things don't turn out the way you want. I didn't particularly want to grow up the way I did, my dad making me do all the housework, wash out his clothes, scrub the floors every Saturday while the other kids were playing ball and whatnot. Black his shoes every night or get beat. I didn't think any of that was so hot. But that's the way things turned out. You kids now think life is just getting whatever you want, like calling up for a pizza—"

"Oh, Dad—"

"Don't oh Dad me. Living your own life—my god, nobody we knew ever lived their own life. You went to school, you worked, you joined the army, if you were lucky you came back and got a job—if you hadn't lost your mind, or had your legs shot off, or didn't shake too badly. There were some things— I had problems of my own after the war, you know. It wasn't any piece of cake. Your mother looked after me and earned a salary to boot and drove us to the store to get the groceries and never said two hoots about any of it."

Looked after him? What did he mean? All she could think of were the stories they told in school about men who had come back from the war and spent the rest of their lives in the army hospital in London, immersed up to their necks in vats of oil because all their skin had come off—during a gas attack, was it? Mustard gas? She used to imagine being an army nurse who cared for these men, topping off their oil, stirring them in their vats the way bones-in-their-noses cannibals in cartoons stirred the missionaries: lovingly, with lazy anticipation and goodwill. She had not understood how something as insubstantial, as invisible as gas could do that to you, melt your skin right off. But that would have been the first war: her grandfather's war. Him sitting erectly on a glossy horse, in his cavalry uniform. She had not known of anything ever happening to her father, save for an unnamed event that left a pale scar, like the thinnest white bracelet, on his wrist. *These are the men whose minds the Dead have ravished.*

"I didn't know. You never talked about any of it."

"Well, some things a person doesn't want his kids to hear about. Doesn't mean they didn't happen. What good would it have done you? You want to hear about it? I saw a thousand men wiped out in one day. Just like that. Guys with so much equipment strapped to their backs they landed in the water and sank like stones. The water blood-red, fifty feet out from shore. Never had a chance, never had a shot at any of it. Guys trying to get to a medic, holding in their guts with their arms. Hughie Fitzgerald, marching right in front of me, gets his head blasted off—right off his body—and his legs keep walking, three, four steps, before he keels over. I had his brains splattered all over my face. You want to hear about that? About us trying to dig a hole in the pouring rain to bury what was left of poor old Fitzgerald? You want to hear about guys screaming in those stinking trenches all night? Crying like babies? No. A person doesn't come back home and talk about that. What would you say? You don't say anything. You just keep your mouth shut and go to work every morning and hope to god you never see or hear anything like that for the rest of your life.''

What he was able to tell her, then, as pools of darkness deepened in the corners of the room, the lamp casting its faint circle around them, was far less than she wanted to know, more than she had a right to ask. His pieced-together recollection of his childhood, like a dark heavy quilt patched from somber used woollen goods, with only a few spots of color, of lighter material. Years of suspense, of waiting for a glimpse of a presence hovering at the margins of his memory, years that subsided into the dullness of routine and useless chores.

Listening to him, watching the shadows move on his face, Min could see that her parents had had full existences before they came together to live in this house, to bear and raise their children: full in sadder, more profound ways than her own life had ever been. And they had continued to live those lives, far beneath what she had been able to perceive or understand, like the dartings and slitherings of fish in murky waters, whose restless movements send scarcely a quiver to the upper surfaces, whose heavy silver bodies remain unseen. Their hidden griefs, their privacies, had more to do with shame than falsehood, with unexamined pain than deception. And probably with hope: that whatever damage they had sustained, whatever they had failed to get out of life was not absolutely going to be handed down to their children, along with curly hair or a squint. After all, that was one of the reasons they had had children at all: to make something soft and new and fresh as snow, that had no idea of bereavement, insanity, or want, that would in fact reverse the past and set the world back on the right track again. *Just whistle while you work, when there's a shine on your shoes, no they can't take that away from me—*

She had known all that, of course, had grasped it dimly, bit by bit, after the ironic surface of adolescence began to splinter, allowing her to see her parents as two regular people, Alex and Rose, who had not been a great deal different from anyone else: worried about the car payments, undressing in the dark, wanting the best for their children. She didn't hate them for not giving her the truth about life, for not going along with full disclosure, California-style. If anything, she regretted that she had not been able to love them more, to grasp their fragile, bumbling, unsuspecting humanness, simply because she hadn't known. She had never really known who they were.

You never told us.

You never told us and I never told you. Ah Ma, we broke each other's hearts, didn't we? You went away and left me here stranded, before I found out what I needed from you, before there was time to get over our wars and tell you—what? What would I have told you? That it seared me to the bone to watch you die. To stand there in the doorway every morning, knowing there was nothing any of us could do to ease your wretched pain. You didn't want me around, you screamed and cursed and even threw that glass at me, that shattered against the door. I couldn't help, couldn't do anything right. You were utterly alone with it, in a dark private room I couldn't enter, where it ate away at you, bit by bit, leaving just your rage, and finally nothing, not even your shadow.

She would have to find out what she could on her own, for herself. She would write to her McCune relations. Mac must have an address somewhere, his father had gone back overseas to see them. Maybe she would go see herself, if any of them were still around. She was headed for Europe, after all.

When Mac went to bed, she put away all the pictures and albums, turned off the porch light and the lamp. Then she went into Rose's room. From all the cleaning out she and Rina had done, the room had regained its original contours. In the moonlight it appeared black and white: pale walls, dark bedspread and dressers. As it had seemed on the nights when she awakened from a bad dream, or with an earache, and walked across the hall from her own room, opened this door into a room completely different from the one that was there in the daytime: a cold shadowy place of dark shapes and strange animal smells, the sound of two people breathing, a clock ticking.

She walked over to look at the portrait of her parents on their wedding day, the silvery light picking out her mother's face like an image in a dream: strange, yet completely familiar.

"So," she whispered to Rose.

The Age Of Light

Min spent an evening examining negatives and sorting through a preliminary set of prints to send to her editor. It had been unexpectedly easy for her to work here. Pauline, her oldest friend in Wyandotte, taught an extension class in the university art department, and offered Min a lab key so she could use the darkroom facilities. She accepted it gratefully, and had spent several days developing film from her trip and printing contacts. There were no distractions here in the lab at night, or in the tiny adjacent office: occasionally the *ssshh-ssshh* of a janitor sweeping down the hall. There was nothing to look at either, except a broom closet full of solutions and paper, a metal desk and chair, a Mr. Coffee machine, last year's Audubon calendar hanging on one wall. Min could almost pretend she was back in school, writing a book report, finishing a term paper.

Work was a familiar prophylaxis against uncertainty, the darkroom ever a reliable haven. She felt she had slipped into a kind of limbo here in Wyandotte, a crevasse stretching between her past and her future. It was as though she had come home and found another family, a different father than the one who inhabited her memory. She couldn't leave yet. What if he suddenly got worse, or fell down the stairs carrying Skipper, or couldn't get up from bed one morning? He might need help, even hospitalization. Rina seemed unwilling to acknowledge that anything like that might happen. She didn't care to look beyond the surfaces of things, seldom asked questions, pre-

151

ferring not to take a chance on the discomfort, even pain, that more information might bring. Min didn't know whether to grab her by the shoulders and shake her, or leave her alone. Maybe the changes in Mac had happened too gradually for Rina to see. Maybe she couldn't face the possibility of losing him. Of being without a father, and a mother. *Rina doesn't like bad news*.

Rina had been eight when Rose died. Rose had had one, then the other breast removed. Then a hysterectomy, to shut down the flow of estrogen that was pumping cancer through her bones. Then chemotherapy. Her hair fell out, her eyebrows, her eyelashes. Angry red patches surfaced on her pasty skin. Fifty pounds of her disappeared in six months. She acquired a raspy, barking voice. In Min's eyes she became a radical kind of man/woman, crosshatched with dark-red scars and hanging, puckery skin, her body a war zone, a topographical map of sorrows. She ranted at all of them—her family, the doctors, neighbors who came timidly to the back door. *This meat tastes terrible   The sheets stink   Don't give me your crappy Bible booklets, those licorice all-sorts, this ugly bedjacket   Get out   Get out   Get out*. She tore open her nightgown in front of her daughters one morning in a rage, and Rina fled trembling from the sight, from that unwanted vision of the center of her mother so raked and empty, as if giant birds had been feeding on her, stripping her flesh of its human markings.

With Min, Rose was critical, impatient, only occasionally tender. Tenderness had been burned out of her, cut away. Min's very presence seemed to annoy her; she could not keep from correcting her posture, her manners, even her recollections of things. In Rose's opinion Min was growing far too tall, and had the unmistakable look of the McCunes about her—the dark masses of hair, long awkward limbs, deep watchful blue eyes. Yet she insisted that Min come in to see her every day, to deliver a report on the household.

"What are you staring at?" Rose would crab when Min entered the room. "Quit gawking and light me a cigarette." Some days Rose was too weak to even shake a Sweet Cap out of the pack by the bed, and much as the taste nauseated her, Min would awkwardly light one up and take the first couple of puffs, then sit on the edge of the bed picking flakes of tobacco off the end of her tongue while Rose inhaled and watched her smoke coil up toward the ceiling.

"How's your sister doing? You been keeping an eye on her?" Never a word about how *she* might be doing. Her mother seemed to have given up on her, except for the nagging. The way she asked after Rina you'd have thought the kid lived somewhere else.

"Yeah, Ma."

"If anything happens to that kid . . ." Rose would say darkly, narrowing her eyes at Min, as if to say she could expect a visit from the beyond should she screw up in any way.

"What's that thing you've got on?"

"Nothing. Just a shirt Evie Markham lent me."

"Hmf. Must think you're really something going around with a top like that on and your boobs sticking out halfway to China. Don't let me catch you wearing it to school."

"No."

But it had been a long time since Rose had been up to catching her at anything.

Though she could not name exactly what it was, Min sensed that her mother resented the way she *was*, the way she had acquired breast, hips, a waistline, the fact that she was growing toward womanhood while Rose was having it yanked from her, along with any claim she had to life itself. And she began to feel a sweaty, exposed sense of shame in Rose's presence, as though she *had* done something indecent and conceited by metamorphosing like this. So she slouched, wore her father's baggy shirts, left for school early so she could change into her miniskirt, do her hair and put on blusher in the girls' bathroom. There was no room for the person she had become to live in the same house with Rose.

Then one day Rose turned her face to the wall, her fire suddenly burned out, blackened. She was quiet, showed no interest in anything. Day and night blurred; she slept all afternoon, then stared at the wall in the darkness. Min was relieved, though she felt guilty about it. It was like some demon had left the house, but Rose was still there in the bed. Min felt she had witnessed awful, private things, things she would rather not have seen, and counted her mother's back as a sign, an end to them. But Rina, in the darkness of their bedroom, confessed between sobs that she had been sneaking into Rose's room while her mother rested, taking stale chocolates from the box next to her bed. She had longed for, counted on being punished, at least yelled at.

"Mumma ha-hasn't noticed," she hiccupped. Her invitation had been ignored; that bothered her the most.

Though the last year of Rose's life had been a long bad dream of surgeries, painful partial recoveries, fitful sleep, bad smells, rambling drug-soaked monologues, still she was with them: they continued to be a family. A sweetish, cloying smell emanated from her sickroom all summer, wafted through the doorway by the oscillating fan next to her bed. It got into the furniture and rugs, became as familiar as her perfume had once been. Her pain and rage gave a shape to their days, filled the rooms with unmistakable sounds and a rasping, toxic energy. When she finally died, one stormy night in her sleep, some essential element of family died with her. It was not the way it would have been if one of the girls had finally gone away to school, or gotten married and moved to another town, and those still at home could feel her absence as temporary, a change in the group's form but not its essence. Time on Huron Street was halted, suspended: the very tables and chairs seemed to wait for Rose to come back, as if they did not know how to be tables and chairs without her there to dust and arrange them. Everything had to shift to accommodate her permanent, indelible missingness: the sense which, vague at first, gradually enlarged to a certainty that they would never hear her hollering in the kitchen again, that this was it, this was who the McCunes were now, three people marking time in an unfamiliar, make-shift relationship to one another, trying to figure out how to get dinner on the table, how to act at Christmas, how to send the most basic messages back and forth in order to carry on the simple business of living, given that space, that dark gap of Rose's deadness yawning like a pulled tooth, upsetting the whole process of assimilation. As a family, a coherent social unit, they had come undone. They were at a loss to know why they were there together in that house at all.

And love. They had all depended on the love that had flooded toward them from Rose when she was well, the warm if over-heated current they swam in, greedy and heedless as pet fish.

All three of them, Mac included, were childish in that way, thinking that love meant receiving it. Only Rose—in her potent, abandoned, burst-dam style—had known how to let it flow out of her. Sometimes fitful, overwhelming, causing more irritation than pleasure, but there, nevertheless.

Rina articulated the burden of what Rose would never do, see, be, feel, think, disapprove of, laugh at, buy, want, eat.

"Mumma will never see me dressed up for Field Day."

"We'll never get our pictures taken in the park at Easter with Ma again."

"Mumma would of liked this show but she'll never get to watch it now, will she?"

She meticulously cataloged what her mother would forever miss, and the ways in which she would forever miss her mother, achieving thereby a thoroughgoing comprehension of Rose's deadness, and of what it meant to ordinary life—to *her* life. A home without a mother was something unheard of. What did you do with your dirty clothes? Where would the groceries come from? How would you know when to go to bed?

"What's for supper?" Rina would ask her father with tears in her eyes, looking up at him for some kind of leadership, a firm decision that would help her make some sense out of the ruin of her life. But in the early days Alex was of little help. He would look at her blankly, rubbing his forehead from side to side with the palm of his hand, as if this might coax an answer from his useless brain.

"I don't know, honey. I just don't know. I haven't really thought about supper," he would say. It seemed to be a terrible strain for him to consider something like a meal. As though food were a part of what he was mourning, a whole lost female realm of comfort. Not recognizing that he had one—albeit a young, undeveloped, incapable one—there with him still. Then Min would have to intervene. She could not bear it, the way he simply didn't see them anymore, the way he abandoned her and Rina in his grief, his enduring sadness, which marked his face like a dark blurry tattoo. Especially Rina, who had sobbed in the back seat all the way to the graveyard, her little saucer hat shoved sideways, her white cotton gloves damp with snot. *I'm too little, you guys, I'm too little for this.*

"Don't worry about it, Rina. There's stuff in the fridge. We'll make some supper."

And they would eat macaroni and cheese again in front of the television, the screen making up the missing fourth presence among them. They ate a lot of starchy, cheesy food, which made them all sleepy almost as soon as it left their plates. Min could not see the point of cooking. Why not squeeze a tube of something into your mouth, if the whole idea was just to get full? Later Alex started to bring home take-out food. Rina thought the paper cups and plastic utensils very elegant; she loved throwing them into the trash, and could hardly wait for the other two to finish eating so she could do this, with great élan.

One night the three of them had dinner at the Chinese restaurant and then went to an old movie, *The Inn of the Sixth Happiness*, at the drive-in. Min and Rina sat in the back seat, Min covering Rina's eyes at the beginning so she wouldn't see the shadow of a person's head being chopped off. Rina's own head started lolling on Min's shoulder halfway through the movie, though every few minutes she would jolt herself upright and exclaim brightly, "I'm awake!"

Min could hardly take her eyes off Ingrid Bergman. Her selfless concern for the children's safety, the pure luminous goodness gleaming from her sad eyes, from every bone in her face: she seemed some kind of ideal female being. The kind that made Min feel sweaty, grubby, scrawny, inadequate, the same way the nuns at St. Mary's used to, with their stiff ironed smell and bleached pale skin. *You'll never be this good*, those kinds of faces said. When the movie was over Alex and Min just sat there, looking at the empty screen, while the cars around them came to life and snaked slowly toward the exit. Rina's head lay heavy in Min's lap. Finally he started up the engine, and pulled away from their stall with his usual lurch, forgetting that the speaker was still mounted to the passenger window. Rina woke with a scream as the window shattered and glass fell into the car, littering the empty seat where Rose used to sit. Alex jerked the car to a halt and sat there without a word, staring at the glass glittering on the seat next to him. A thought rippled like a deadly current between the girls: *He doesn't know what to do*.

With Rose gone, Min had a sense of a great emptiness, which began in the basement and spiraled upward to fill every room of the house, a cold whooshing of air that seemed to have lifted the roof off, sucked the form out of their lives. She could feel the possibilities in this: the wide open spaces of release and movement, a delicious anomie, a new stage on which to act out her own life. The space that terrified Rina meant release to her. Release, stained inevitably with guilt, because her mother had had to die for her to feel it. Her first awful, unspeakable thought when she heard Rose was dead, was: *I'm free*.

In the first months after she died, Min tried to imagine her mother in different situations, which would now never happen because she was dead. What kind of grandmother she would have been, for instance. *Grandmother Rose* sounded responsible, firmly contoured: it had a definite weight to it. Or maybe Grandma Rose would have been thinner, the way some women got when they were exonerated of all the shopping, baking, peeling, squishing together of countless meat loaves for their families, when they could finally get back to themselves, more or less. Smoking—oh, she'd still have to smoke. Min couldn't see that going. She'd crook her grandchild, whoever that might be, into one arm and prop a bottle into its mouth, a cigarette slanting from the corner of her mouth while she squinted through the smoke at her stories on TV. She'd be wearing some oddball outfit: tight slacks, maybe a beaded cardigan sweater, fuzzy bedroom slippers. Clip-on earrings.

She would still read to everyone out loud from the newspaper after dinner, only she'd need bifocals to see it. She used to do that every night before she started the dishes, in a jeering voice, as if she couldn't get over the world still being as stupid and unbelievable as it was the day before.

" 'Household hint: Cut your old brassieres in half and strap a cup under each knee the next time you're down on all fours to scrub the floor.' Jeepers. Who do they think they're kidding?"

"Oh, Ma." That was all you could say to her.

Then she would read her horoscope for the next day, frowning, picking a bit of tobacco from her lip, and cut it out with the blunt-tipped children's scissors from the junk drawer and tape it up on the fridge.

SCORPIO: Get out of your slump by doing needed repairs around house. Seek out new friends, ideas in P.M. A change in finances may be unexpected.

"The thing is," she'd say about those horoscopes, "the thing is, maybe they're not true, maybe like a lot of people say they couldn't possibly be true. But what if they are? You tell me exactly what I have to lose. So what if I cancel bowling and clean the house and fix the pull on the silverware drawer? I'm just that far ahead, aren't I? All right. So if *you* don't believe it, if you don't buy one of those lottery tickets at the IGA because you don't think Mercury or Saturn or whatever can change your finances, and then the next guy comes up to the counter and buys a quart of milk and the winning ticket, I'd say you're the loser. Wouldn't you?"

By then she would have quit sending out Christmas cards, calling it useless. She'd pay less and less attention to her garden, proud only of the ragged volunteers—nasturtiums, lily of the valley, the odd scraggly little tomato seedling—because they didn't have to be planted or cared for in any way. "Look at that," she would mutter, jabbing a finger into your arm, then pointing to something that looked for all the world like a common weed. "You see that? Came up all by itself." The old roses, the dahlias and peonies would all be gone, having become more trouble than they were worth. Same as the Christmas cards. Knock yourself out and nobody even notices.

Min's friend Pauline had three little children now; her life was a vortex of tiny socks, crayons, towels, mashed banana, assorted plastic parts. Min remembered playing house with her under the trees in the Gauthiers' backyard, shelling maple keys and stirring up dirt and water in a cup for their pretend suppers. They still wrote, though Pauline's letters had grown less frequent with each birth. When they talked now it was quick, darting, a rush to get at the nub of each other's lives before someone started crying or needed their bum wiped. In a single breathless sentence Pauline asked Min about her father and Rina, her relationship with Peter, about getting married.

"Jeez, Paul," Min had said, jiggling the baby while Pauline thrashed around in her bag looking for the lab key. She groped for a way to explain how she had thought of Peter since she'd been in Wyandotte. Except for their telephone conversations, he was becoming almost a dream lover, a fantasy. No one here knew him; her family seemed to ignore his existence. She was having trouble bringing her two worlds together: the world of everyday life back in Malibu, and this world, so much out of the past, yet so much with her, so *real*.

"You know how I am. I just never could figure out all that. I can't even stand that word 'relationship' anymore. It sounds so whiny and *gummy* to me, like something that sticks to the sole of your shoe—so miserable and futile. That's what every- body has now in California, relationships. Nothing spontaneous or fun—I mean, you don't fool around anymore the way we did before AIDS and herpes and whatnot. You wouldn't dare. People check each other out like they're buying a house or something. 'Sharing' is a big word. 'Would you share your life with me?' Like it's a pizza. You know how I've always hated to share. I mean, I can see it works for some people, like you and Gerry. But for me—hell. I just don't know. I'm not sure I can see the advantages. I wish things could just stay the way they are."

Pauline took the baby, who was beginning to cry, and quickly shifted her breast into its mouth.

"Nothing stays the way it is for very long, Min, if it's growing. Personally I think you've got this fantasy going that you're suddenly going to *lose* something—forget how to use a camera, I guess, or fall into some black hole and wake up in a stucco bungalow with an apron on. Or whatever. Some real either/or, black or white situation. But you might not lose anything. Really. You might actually gain something. Some- thing that's really nice."

"You think?" Min asked doubtfully.

"Yeah. I mean, sure, no guarantees or anything. But I think you love this guy even more than you think you do. And you want your work too, and you'll keep working, no question, it won't disappear. It's not there to hide behind, though. And it isn't everything, either. So your mom was a tyrant and your dad was no help at all. So what? Everybody's got some kind of screwups in their family. You can't really blame anybody for it.''

She shifted the baby onto her shoulder and tried to thump a burp out of him.

''That's life—I mean people screw up, life goes on, things work out. I never could have had a baby if I thought about all the ways I could screw up. And look at this little unit here. Huh? Look at you. You don't even know your mother's screwing up, do you? You have no idea.''

Their conversation echoed in Min's mind as she made one print after another, watched the images of the past months coalesce on paper. Was it true she used her camera as a shield, used work partly to ward off some other, fuller life—a home, people to love, some common destination? Or was life really more like what you found in California, a matter of picking a workshop to find out what there was to yourself? Pauline had signed up for Marriage and Family, a twenty-four-hour-a-day marathon where you never got to take a shit by yourself. And she, for what? Transience? Uncertainty? Looking for hopeful signs and visions? A rootless wandering in search of texts, topics, any small light-filled squares of reality she might be given. The working out, moment by moment, of her intention, her relationship to what she saw.

There was a way in which her work still felt embryonic, fragile, something that actually needed her attention and care, the way Pauline's children needed hers. It had taken her a long time to discover the camera, and more years of failure and frustration learning what she was capable of doing with it. She had done all kinds of commercial work—photographing fruit salads, shopping malls, running shoes, anything that paid—in order to buy film and materials for the pictures she preferred to take. It was true that the world had opened into freedom after Rose died. But it had been a pathless freedom, for years afterward. Her mother had left her without a sign, any word or indication as to how she should proceed. Thus empty-handed, with her father for a long time wrecked by grief, her sister as forlorn and useless as any child could be, Min had to make up a world for the three of them, hiding away her own dreams and uncertainties the way she used to hide secret things at the back of her drawer. There were no sports or school clubs after four o'clock, because she had to buy groceries, fix dinner, help Rina with her homework, iron a shirt for her father. She and Rina begged Alex not to hire anyone to help out, to let them fend for themselves. So they had. The house grew dustier, dimmer, certain rooms—the living and dining rooms, Rose's bedroom—becoming uninhabited, as the three of them wore useful, familiar pathways to the back door, the bathroom, the TV room downstairs, where they ate on metal trays, unable to face sitting at a table looking at one another the way they once had. They lived like animals in winter, in a small stuffy space, cosy in their own skins and debris. The age of darkness, was how she thought now of that time in her life. A long, lightless tunnel.

When she finally left, it was with the urgency of someone saving herself from drowning. She did it as decently as she could—though it seemed Rina would never forgive her for it—and headed south, stopping here and there for a few weeks, a month, waitressing for travel money, using up the provinces and states one by one and finally wandering into Mexico, still without any clear idea what she could make of her life. But she was driven—after all those years of macaroni dinners in the basement, nights of listening to Rina cry herself to sleep, of walking to music practice before the sun came up, with a frigid gritty wind blowing in her face—by an instinct, an unwordable longing, for strong sunlight, a different kind of space to move in, new ground under her feet. A beginning, in a clement place. And though she had known no one, gone as an alien with no papers or prospects, she had felt at home from her first day in California. Blessed, even, by the caressing air, the yellow hills, the great sweeping arm of the sea. And by the light, that shimmering white presence that gave to every blade of grass, every improbable blossom, the cleanly etched clarity of a gem. The light shone clear through her; life suddenly seemed smooth and lucent as a sheet of glass.

She could finally *see* things, in this light. For all those years her family had tried to get her to see things in their light: something she had never been able to do. Here her limbs felt wonderfully weightless without sweaters and boots, her chest expanded as she took in the fragrant air of the canyons and hillsides. The summer she had suffered there with Rose dying was gradually reversed. Life in California was rampant, delirious; something was always growing, flowering, drooping with fruit, matting underfoot. The coastal air reeked of chlorophyll, of salt spray and excessive fertility. There was no season given over wholly to death and inwardness, no time to dwell on things.

She found a job easily, and friends, a place to live. While she was house-sitting a canyon cottage for some friends one summer she happened to take a photography class at a small nearby college, and discovered in the camera a tool that finally made sense to her, that fit the curve of her palm, something she might use to dig herself out of the uncertainty remaining in her about work. She had always drawn, and studied painting at university. But she had never soared with it. Facing an empty sheet of paper or a canvas and making up something from scratch felt too risky, too involving, messy. But the camera was generous; it offered a starting point, something her imagination could fasten on, extrapolate. Certain decisions had already been made by the objects themselves. Even the language of photography bespoke taking action in a forward direction: *Develop. Solution. Process. Enlargement.* She read and studied everything she could on photography, and in order to learn more apprenticed herself to a man who had a studio in Santa Monica, and paid her a few dollars an hour in the evenings to help him in his darkroom. That had led to other jobs, more money, a green card, a small studio of her own.

But most importantly, it began to open up an airy, illuminated, confident place within her, where what she saw—her own vision—was at last valid, useful, even beautiful. A place of choice, rather than compulsion. She grew into that space like a plant taken out of a closet. She had a sense, finally, of participating in *time*, through her developing ability to fix something—a certain arrangement of light and shadow—for an instant. An image could be observed, weighed in her mind, recorded. It could speak. It could say: tree: farmyard: wall. And she had a part in that. Her work was moving her to a wholly new sense of purpose and understanding, to pride, and even an awkward liking for herself. To an awakened love for and sense of belonging to the natural world: to the raw vibrant energy of hills and sky and ocean that surged around her, the baked cliffs fuzzy with golden yarrow and chaparral, the summer air thick with sage and jasmine, droopy-legged bees dragging themselves from flower to flower. To the perfect blue line of the horizon, the rimose canyons falling away to the sea. The age of light.

Being a good photographer was the most difficult thing she had ever attempted. For a long time she made photographs that disappointed her, which showed so much more of what she hadn't noticed than of what she had, as if there had been something invisible in the air between the tree and her lens, say, that kept her from getting a "true" picture. In time she came to realize there was no such thing as a true picture, a pure vision, that vision had as much to do with her intent as viewer as with the nature of the object itself. The objective world was already *there*: stuffed, charged, vibrating with meaning. So she had to discover, each time she picked up her camera, how to do less and less. Make herself blank as a sheet of paper. Wait. That was hardest: the sheer effort of doing nothing, of being patient. Waiting for the light to move, for the building or the leaf to adjust itself in her field of vision, so that her hands and eyes lined up with it and she could feel some bond, some kinship or understanding. Then allowing the image to give itself, reveal its *mana*, and being perfectly ready with her camera to receive it. When it worked, and that confluence was happening, the light seemed to stream into her and a frisson ran through her body as the shutter clicked.

Images for photographs came to her in her sleep, while she stood in a checkout line, or absently scrubbed her nails. They seemed to inhabit a particular place, a kind of inner chamber, out of which they emerged in their own time and leaned toward her—in close-up, the way people sometimes step up to a home movie camera, filling half the screen with their noses, the pores in their skin gaping like small craters on flesh-colored moons.

Only recently had she begun to photograph people. They had crept slowly, one by one, into her work, as if emerging from some underbrush, primitive and voiceless, uninvited but making no demands. That human presence was melting something in her, an icy crust that had once kept her critical, brittle, unsure of herself. *Everything doesn't have to be hard*, she kept telling herself. *You can enjoy this*.

So though she had not intended to photograph families at these hot springs, yet that was what bloomed up at her from the solution: the faces of families. One batch was actually pictures of pictures she had found in the lobby at a springs in British Columbia. Several scratched sepia photographs of Indians sitting in the hot pools, gazing through the steam into the boxes held by the white fools. Even the children looked solemn, burdened, unjoyful, as if anticipating a great decline. Everyone's skin appeared lustrously smooth, their bodies sturdy and beautiful. They stared back at her out of time, gathered together closely as the fingers of a fist. More than anything, they looked *of* one another, greater than family: a tribe. She imagined their laughter, bitter laughter that would smell of smoke, of tears and burning hair. There was no way you could comfort people like this. They had come out of a rock that cleaved in two, giving way to the water. Their pictures had hung on the wall near the cashier, oddly captionless; they had not been given their names, ages or histories. As though they had been framed that way by white people's desire to make their own "discovery" of the springs more picturesque, more substantial. For white people had discovered the place; there could be no doubt of that, if you read the brochures.

And pictures of those white people, their faces pale as bits of bread thrown against the dark surface of the water. Their hair was dusty, from riding through the mountains in open cars. Some of them wore bathing costumes; others stood fully clothed beside the pool, ready to hand the bathers towels, or perhaps cigars. They looked overfed, prosperous, somewhat embarrassed at being seen wet and uncovered, but good sports about it. Perhaps they found the water a little too hot, the rocks dangerously slippery with algae. None of them were children. Mostly they were looking forward to eating the large lunches cooling in the hampers strapped to their automobiles. She imagined there were certain parts of the pool they would not swim in, perhaps because they thought they smelled Indians there: to them a smell of newly cured leather, of elder smoke, of small furred animals with pointed teeth.

Of course, as she looked at the pictures she was seeing them a certain way. Of course. She saw them with her mind and heart, as well as her eyes: in the context of history, place, her own sympathies. The same context that informed the photographs she made herself.

She thought the best pictures were some she had taken in Guatemala, when she was sick with what the natives called *intestina*. At first she thought it was the sight of all the soldiers at the border that made her ill: young boys in fatigues, grinning like thieves, grabbing at their crotches, poking the noses of their machine guns into her bags, along the panels in the van, then shooting thick white puffs of insecticide everywhere. She had cached much of her equipment stateside and had no more with her than any tourist might carry, so as to avoid suspicion. Some Canadian friends who lived down here had warned her about the border, the civil patrols everywhere, the places where it was still not safe to travel; but the experience of it left a cold chill in her belly all the same.

Then she grew dizzier and weaker, her drive into the country became a long hazy feverish dream. Thick clouds clung to the peaks; the van disappeared in them, then emerged into brilliant sunlight, screeching birds, goats scrambling across the winding roadway. People were walking everywhere in the mountains, tiny brown people in bright clothes who sometimes stopped, waved, smiled toothily as she drove slowly past them. She remembered reading somewhere that in earlier times local peasants had been commandeered to carry the wives of the landowners on their backs. A man lurched by the roadside with an old woman in a wooden chair strapped to his back; the woman's face was nut-brown, deeply wrinkled, serene, shaded by the red-and-white blanket folded on her head. Other people had bundles of sticks, leaves or plants anchored onto them by woven bands stretched across their foreheads; she even saw a scruffy brown dog weaving along the road wearing a billboard. A few women held their babies up in the air as she passed—was it for them to see Min, or her to see them? There was little vehicular traffic to prevent her from stopping; the business of this part of the world was conducted on bare feet. A few shots, then, of moon-faced infants, completely swaddled, startled to find themselves suspended in midair, with nothing but blue sky behind them.

She had stopped at a marketplace and bought some rice, warm tortillas, and a packet of herbs for tea. A small wrinkled old man was selling the herbs, heaped in little piles on a white sheet spread out on the pavement in front of him. They were identified by cardboard signs bearing drawings of various body parts and organs. The picture on the pile she bought from fairly resembled a stomach hanging above some gnarled, unhappy-looking intestines. The people in the square stared at her. Maybe she looked as horrible as she felt. Maybe she was the tallest person in the country.

Sick and weak, she camped a few nights on a gravel beach next to a cold, deep blue mountain lake. There was not a tree or bush or any kind of plant the whole length of that beach. The afternoons were scorching. A parade of child-sized women came by every day at siesta time, trying to sell rugs, wooden animals, scraps of embroidered cloth. *"No, gracias,"* Min would say, shaking her head. *"No lo quiero."* The bundles of goods they lugged up and down the beach looked impossibly heavy. Some of the women had infants strapped to their backs besides. They would put the bundle down, shake out the top blanket, hold it up and stare at you. If you shook your head they would shake the blanket sharply and continue to hold it there, as if you must not have really looked at it the first time. They refused her offers of water with dignity, but allowed her to pay them for taking their pictures. They were dauntless, coming to the van every afternoon and unfolding the same blanket, holding it there silently for an interminable length of time in the searing sunlight before packing up the whole works and trudging across the gravel to the few *turistas* who sat further off, sipping sodas and looking at the water.

Back on the main highway a few days later, she was passed by increasing numbers of military trucks and Jeeps, and decided to avoid Guatemala City. At a roadblock she was stopped by soldiers older and rougher-looking than the ones at the border. "American lady," they shouted at her, as they jerked up the floormats and shoved their rifles behind the seats. "No, no, *Canadiense*," she protested, flapping her big blue passport at them. There wasn't much she could do about her California plates. Still quivering from fever, she tried to look unconcerned and cheerful. She could not remember why she had come here.

Other vehicles began to pile up behind her; finally a soldier thumped her door and jerked his head sideways, and she was moving again.

The country around her felt compressed, ill, about to explode from its own bowels, until she left the main road to the city and traveled smaller routes. The hot springs town she had been looking for sat in the middle of a rolling, fertile-looking valley in the western part of the country. A huge field with a wall around it, which looked far too big to be anyone's private garden, occupied the center of town. Roosters were crowing; the sun felt warm and the air peaceful. She saw no soldiers here, and parked the van. As usual, she was the only person out for a walk; everyone else was busy, purposive—even the children. Each person on foot was carrying something: a bundle of wood, a pail of water, a child or a chicken.

She approached two men loading boxes into the back of a pickup truck, who looked as if they might speak Spanish.

"Por favor," she asked. "¿Dónde está el balneario?"

"Balneario, sí, sí—arriba," the shorter one said, pointing to a large plain cement building that stood at the top of a nearby hill. A stream ran down alongside the building and forked off into irrigation ditches below.

She walked up the hill and photographed the bathhouse, the huge town garden, some women washing clothes in the warm stream. One of them, chattering excitedly at her in Quiché, deftly slipped the child on her back out of his layers of wrappings, into the water, then held him aloft, dripping and smiling, for Min to take his picture. So many cheerful, fat-faced children, displayed to her everywhere like edible things freshly plucked from the earth.

It was nearly dark when she joined the small groups of people outside the bathhouse. She asked a young girl how to get in, where to buy a ticket, but the girl only smiled at her and nodded her head; she didn't understand. It was the same with the second and third persons she asked. She could see nothing that looked like a ticket booth. Finally a man separated himself from one of the groups and took her arm, murmuring softly to her in Quiché, and pointed to a man standing by a wall, pulling bits of paper out of his hatband and handing them to two little girls. The ticket seller. Relieved, she thanked him, and went over to buy her ticket. The ticket seller, at least, understood her Spanish.

When her turn came he gestured her inside, down a long hallway to the little cubicle that was to be hers. There were several toilets on one side of the hall; the rest of the cubicles were private bathing rooms. No electricity: the hallway was dark, illuminated only by the soft glow coming from the rooms where some families had set their kerosene lamps. A few open doorways revealed groups of a dozen or more—old people, teenagers, babies lying on the heaps of clothing on the floor. The building was honeycombed with these little rooms, abuzz with human voices echoing off the cement walls. She managed to get the ticket seller to ask one family if she could photograph them. They paused, hushed by the request, and stood soberly in front of her, the women smoothing their skirts. Everyone leaned in toward the center, as if trying to see what was inside the black hole of her lens. To a person, their faces looked calm, expectant, as if they understood what life would serve them and it was only a matter of waiting for the dishes to be brought, one course at a time. Soft ripples of laughter erupted behind her as she walked away. The ticket man stood in the doorway of her room and stared at her, until she thanked him firmly, pressed another coin into his hand, and closed the wooden door.

She ran water into the tub, which was built against the wall at one end of the room. The only other article here was a rough wooden bench placed along a side wall. A single faucet—no cold to temper the near-scalding water that gushed into the tub, sending metallic-scented clouds of steam billowing up to the ceiling. A woman was laughing in the next room, laughing and talking with someone in a low, caressing voice. Min sat on the edge of the tub and undid the buttons on her shirt, let her boots and socks fall to the floor. Her naked foot tested the water—much too hot. She would have to wait. Idly she scratched her back, rubbed her hands over her breasts and shoulders. Her skin quivered, still sensitive from her sickness and lingering fever. Maybe this hot water would soak the germs out. How good to be here tonight, in a place that felt warm and safe. A small window high above, just below the ceiling, let a square panel of moonlight fall across the nearby bench.

She looked at that scrap of silvery light playing across the wood, etching each of the fibers, and heard the woman next door laugh again. A sudden wave of nostalgia emptied her chest. It was a perfect bit of light to be shining on someone, a person, lighting up hair and skin, playing across the planes of a face. If someone were here with her. If she weren't in this room alone, a solitary woman about to step into a bath, thousands of miles from home, surrounded by people who didn't speak a word of her language, to whom she was nothing, a momentary curiosity, a woman alone with a camera and a sick stomach.

But she had wanted to come here alone, in spite of the danger and isolation, even though Peter had initially suggested taking time off work and joining her.

"My contract at Rainbow Bridge doesn't start until November," he'd said. Besides seeing private clients, he was a counselor at a halfway house for disturbed adolescents—runaways, druggies, the flotsam of east Los Angeles. Keeping his finger on the pulse of the city, he called it. "I've got that trunk filled with clothes that I order from L. L. Bean every year and never get to wear. Down booties, thermal underwear, waders—yeah, I've got waders. Camp stools, mess kits, dehydrated food— even a tent warmer."

"I'm not taking a tent," Min said evenly, trying to control the apprehension rising in her at the idea of him coming along. Why was he saying this? He knew she had been dreaming about this trip for years, planning it for months and months. It was not a vacation, a trip you took with someone else; it was a trip to be taken alone, a kind of test you took to find out if you could accomplish something really big on your own.

"You never know when something like that might come in handy, though. The van might get a flat late at night and suddenly you're freezing and surrounded by bears. Or say you're having coffee in a really *cold* little café somewhere—"

"Peter. Hey. I couldn't do it with you. I mean I could, but it wouldn't be the same trip. And I thought we agreed we could use some time to think about things. Away from each other."

"I know. But something could happen—"

"Something could happen at the corner. I could get creamed

on the Santa Monica Freeway, right? I'll be fine. I'll call and write and be really careful."

"It's because I love you, you know. Not because I think you're lame or anything. Will you at least take a can of mace?"

"If it'll make you feel better. Can't take it to Canada, though. Come on. Hey, you hate Mexican food, you'd have a rotten time."

He smiled and hugged her, but the blue of his eyes deepened, the way the ocean did under a clouded sky. Deep down, he really didn't understand why she was doing this, why they couldn't just talk about things until she felt better. He didn't want to let her go for so long, and so far away. But she had gone anyway. And tonight she felt sorry—not because of the work, or the travel, or the border guards, or any of that, but because of how she left, the way she always did such a lousy job of explaining things to him. Maybe it was asking too much of someone, going off like this and putting everything on hold and expecting him to be patient and understanding and agreeable. But Peter *was* that way. She had not felt until tonight how much she risked losing if he got tired of waiting for her, not realized until she was away from him how much she had grown used to experiencing the world with him as companion, fellow traveler. How many times a day had she thought: Oh, Peter would love this. What would Peter think about *that*? He had become embedded in her very seeing. And his body, his physical presence, she missed sometimes as acutely as a severed limb. She thought longingly of sex with him. When she had camped on the beach, all her clammy, fevered dreams were of Peter, of his lithe hips and curling blond chest hairs, of their legs and arms tangled together, the sheets soaked with sweat, their damp hair smelling of each other's juices. She had been greedy for that ever since their first night together, that wet urgent union. Every time it was different, the two of them creating an intricate, surprising, male-female event together, which was blissful for her, an elaborate spin into the void.

She did not completely understand what she was meant to learn from being with him. It had been her hope that she would discover it by going away, folding back up into herself. In all her other relationships with men, she had come to a point— and sometimes it was years later, when she could barely recall the shape of the man's face, the way his hands had felt on her body—when a light bulb suddenly went on, and she was able to perceive some process that had been at work, a reason why she and that particular person had been so important to each other for that time they were together. With the Spaniard, for example, that first trip to Europe, she had had a sense of peering through some ancient wooden doorway, looking out onto an old, ancestral, blood-steeped scene. She absorbed Spain's language and customs directly through him, through his poetic melancholy, his reverence for her womb and menstrual blood, the invariable, essential maleness that was as much a fact about him as the color of his eyes, or his lengthy name, and of which he was exceedingly proud, would never consider undergoing therapy, for example, to scrutinize or adapt. Spain was matrix, *madre* to him: she had given him birth, and would sustain him for all his years—invisibly, completely—as surely as Gibraltar guarded the Mediterranean. His complete identification with his country was a revelation to Min.

So far, she had not been able to work out any explanation for Peter, for the way he unnerved her, made her happy, hungry, eager, embarrassed at her own voracity. At times she felt caught up in a kind of adolescent delirium of pleasure, of precisely the kind she had never experienced as a teenager because of having been such an old person back then. California seemed to have been created for just this sort of euphoria, that had you wearing shorts in January, kissing in the street, singing at the top of your lungs as you barreled down some eight-lane freeway with all the windows down. It was a permanent vacation from obligation, adulthood, consequences, the future.

But she was here now, feeling like the odd woman out on the planet. All the people in this building were performing old simple rituals: washing their children's bodies, rinsing one another's hair, lighting lamps, bundling the laundry. They had homes, gardens, pigs and chickens, a place to come for their bathing. And she had her freedom: this splendid liberty she prized so highly she had thought she would give up almost anything to keep it. The right to wander, to move lightly through the world, to stop and go according to her own will. Was she kidding herself, was all of that a myth? Was she missing something? Was this what she was afraid of with Peter, of simply becoming family with him? Of going back over that old painful territory and participating again? Creating something serious, perhaps unalterable. Family was not a joyful word to her. Years with a sick mother, a silent father, a needy sister had reduced family to a manifestation of necessity, of inevitability, which she stayed away from, the way you stayed indoors after getting a bad sunburn, because it hurt, all that penetrating heat, even the idea of letting it touch you hurt. Maybe I don't know how to open up my insides, she thought, to let anything grow. I'm afraid to let him see me in there, to see how young it is, how small. *How still.* I'm not sure I even want anyone in there. What's the point of it, of all that mess and grief and rawness you get when you let somebody come so far inside? I don't know if I can do that, without dying somehow. I know how to keep moving, make a living, I can tune my own car if I have to. I can watch, and wait. I can hide in this water where no one sees me.

A man's voice next door. He was singing the woman a song. Min slipped her body into the hot deep water, and closed her eyes.

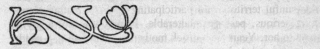

Don't Cross Over the Line

The train station was located in what looked like the middle of nowhere: a maze of tracks and utility poles set in flat, scrubby, windblown fields, some low industrial-looking buildings hovering off in the distance. Min and Rina got off in this nowhere because they were afraid to miss their stop, because they thought this might be their stop: they didn't understand German and four or five signs already had read "Weisbaden-something." Rina nearly toppled out of the car behind her heavy bags.

"Like, you think this is it?" she said uncertainly. They were supposed to transfer here to another train.

"I hope so. I think so. I don't know," Min replied, rubbing her eyes. "Maybe we'll find a schedule somewhere." She was trying to pretend there was still a possibility that this was the right station, for Rina's sake. No one else was here.

Rina hoisted all her bags, a first-time traveler unable to leave a thing at home in case they didn't have it in Europe. She lurched behind Min to the end of the platform, up some stairs, down a long corridor that crossed over the tracks to a building on the other side. There they walked down more stairs and found themselves on an identical platform to the first one, looking across the tracks to where they had originally stood. They walked up the stairs again, and for some minutes stood hopefully in front of a torn, undecipherable poster that was

173

probably a schedule. Then they walked back through the corridor to the first platform.

They had flown to Frankfurt together because after much deliberation about her father's condition, Min had decided to continue her trip—visiting springs in Germany, Italy, France, and England—and after no deliberation whatsoever, Rina announced she wanted to join her. Min had reluctantly come around to saying yes to her sister, watching the remnants of her trip alone, her great adventure, slide like water through her fingers. Being in Wyandotte had changed everything. It had become clear to her from the way her father acted that it would mean a great deal, not only to Rina, but to him, to see the two of them do something together like family, like real sisters. And by then she was confused about what she owed them. Ought she agree to it, if it would make them so happy? It was absurd and impossible, she told herself, but she felt an urge to alleviate Mac's old sadness, make up for some of his pain.

Then there was Rina. Saying that she wanted to come was an indirect offer from Rina to create something new, shared, and in so doing, try to set aside their past. While Min was still thinking about it, Rina worked herself into a real state. She quit the pool job, bought an eight-piece matched set of brown vinyl luggage, got a haircut, manicure and facial, went down to the Triple A and brought home an armload of glossy brochures. Min was secretly worried about traveling with her, about the fact that in most ways, she hardly knew her sister at all. What would they talk about? They had no *present* with one another, except for their father.

Actually, when you came right down to it, the three of them had nothing much to work with. They pulled what little content there was in their conversations out of that web of feelings spun so long ago, which still netted them together. When she was with Mac and Rina, Min could feel that she began to lose track of herself, of what she did, who she was. Though she tried to bring what she thought of as her real self, her *current* self, into conversations, it was clear that Mac didn't give two hoots about hot springs. Nor could Rina understand what her sister did. She didn't think taking pictures was any kind of real work—certainly it wasn't something a person should be paid money for. I guess we'll just have to sort it out, one day at a time, Min thought. At least Rina came right out and said what she wanted, without whining or insinuation. Min liked her for that. Her family's wishes had been too long unspoken, running across the bottoms of conversations for years, like subtitles, to which no one paid any attention. She was determined to pay attention, now.

Rina arranged to pick up her new car in Germany, to be Min's personal chauffeur, as she put it, around the Continent. Then, two days before they left, Min finally received a reply to an enquiry she'd mailed to some of her father's family in Ireland, asking if she might visit them.

"What does it *say*?" Rina asked.

Alex was listening, though he pretended to be concentrating on a crossword puzzle. He had never met these relatives of his, but as a boy had written many letters to them for his father.

"It says they've cut the hay, they're enjoying some fine weather just at the moment, and would welcome a visit from any of their relations."

"Their *relations*!"

Alex beamed at them, as if to say he'd secretly known all along it would work out. His daughters had asked him to accompany them for part of the trip, to meet them somewhere. It would do him a world of good, they said, not really knowing what they meant. But he had declined, in his gruff way.

"Saw all that during the war. Can't say as I want to see it again," he said.

"Then you just sit tight here, you and Skipper," Rina said briskly. "We'll be back for Christmas. At least I will."

Min had called Peter and her roommates, wired money for her rent, asked about her mail and her plants. She was surprised at how irked Peter sounded at the idea of Rina going with her to Europe.

"What sister? I didn't even remember you had a sister. You never talk about her."

"We haven't really been in touch a whole lot in the past few years. She definitely exists, though."

"What's she like?"

"Rina? Let's see, what *is* she like. Not much like me, I don't think. Talkative, kind of funny. Bitchy sense of humor. Pretty naïve. Basically soft-hearted, but doesn't want you to think so. Really attractive—small, reddish hair, perfect skin, knockout figure.''

"You get along?"

"We're trying. I don't think she quite trusts me, actually. She's still checking me out."

"I just don't understand, you know you told me how much shooting you had to do, how busy you'd be, work work work, and now you two will be cruising the Continent in a new car, soaking at spas, eating pastry—"

"Come on, Peter. You sound jealous."

"Hell, wouldn't you be? What if I up and said to you, 'Oh by the way, Gareth and I are going to be off in the South Pacific for a couple of months, I've got some things I want to check out over there.'"

"Listen. I didn't know how to say no to her. In fact I didn't even invite her to come. I'm freaked out by the whole idea myself. My sister's not the easiest person in the world to be with. But this whole thing of our past together is just sitting here in pieces, like an old radio that somebody took apart, and I'm trying, I'm really trying to figure out how to put it back together again. So it works. I don't know. My dad and Rina, this house, my mother's stuff—I've got a hell of a lot of sorting and fixing to do here. You're in it too, you know—it's all heaped in together. It *is* work, Peter, it really is. I don't want to be away from you forever, I don't want to screw things up between us. I'm thinking about us a lot. A *lot*. I missed you more this week than I can even begin to tell you."

"Have you?"

"Really. But it's not time to come back yet. Going away with Rina—maybe it's a really lousy idea, maybe it'll help, I don't know. I've got so many things to talk to you about, so much is going on."

"Yeah?" His voice sounded husky, full of evening and shadows, closer than her ear. "I've got a few things I want to tell you about, too. Like what I'd do to you if you were here right now."

"Tell me."

And she stood in the hall closet with the telephone cord wrapped around the door, Rina and her father reading their magazines ten feet away in the living room, while Peter's voice undressed her, nibbled at her breasts, breathed softly on her neck, stroked the long length of her thighs, urged her to wetness. Then she hung up, and emerged into the light as if from a time capsule, her skin pulsing, her disorientation complete. What was she doing *here*?

She went out and parked the van at the front of the driveway, where her father stood three mornings later, waving good-bye as the taxi drove his daughters to the airport.

"I should have taken some pictures of him," Min said, looking back at his brave, bent form.

"He's not going anywhere," Rina said.

There was no train in sight. The two of them stood trancedly still, in a haze of fatigue and hunger after the long flight. A piece of paper blew up and wrapped itself around Min's suitcase. The wind sweeping across the platform was bitingly cold, and smelled of snow, ashes, damp newspaper. Rina finally put down her bags and unzipped one of them to extract a cardigan. Min figured Rina had brought enough luggage for five people.

"How do I know what I'll feel like wearing?" she'd asked, when Min suggested she take fewer clothes. "I might *need* this."

"Chocolate?" Rina said, offering a bar she'd pulled from some pocket.

"No thanks. Look, Rina," Min said. She nodded toward a woman sitting on a bench about a hundred feet away. How could they have missed seeing her? Suddenly Min felt renewed hope, a sense of purpose.

"Maybe she speaks English. I'll see if she knows anything about the trains."

The woman was wearing jeans, a bulky jacket, thick black gloves. Her hair was cropped short, she had a powerful, clamped-looking jaw, and leaned forward on one leg, tapping her boot. Min would not have been surprised to see a big bunch of keys hanging from her belt; she was like someone in one of those women's bars in Westwood, waiting for a lover to show up, her energy coiled like the springs under a jacked-up truck.

"Excuse me, do you know when the next train is coming? We're not sure where we are."

The woman jerked her head in Min's direction.

"You from United States."

"No, Canada."

"Ah, you from Canada."

"Yes. I mean I live in the United States, but we came from Canada. On the plane today."

The woman bounded heavily to her feet and walked over so she could talk right into Min's face. Her breath smelled of onions. Her brawny arms made semicircles in the air.

"You from United States. I am Russian. I come here from Australia. I live Australia two, maybe three years, I don't like, is too hot, no? So I am in Germany. Here is too cold."

"Yes, it is very cold."

"I think very bad my English, no, I say such bad English at you."

"No, not at all—"

The woman spoke in a gruff, agitated manner, moving closer and closer to Min, circling her arms like oars, like she was trying to levitate. Her gestures made Min nervous. But she had committed herself, and felt so exhausted and disoriented, so thankful to find a person who spoke English and might be able to tell her where they were and how to get the right train, that she nodded and smiled brightly, while she took tiny steps backward.

"Your girlfriend?" the woman said, charging toward Rina, who waved at them. "Ah, sister. Nice. Your beautiful sister."

The Russian woman completely ignored Min's anxious questions about the train. She seemed distracted, indignant, and began to bang her gloved hands together in front of her. She told Min and Rina that she was in Germany because she had fallen in love with a German.

"He invite me here. I come. I stay at his house. I find he have other woman."

She said it "voomin," and bashed her hands together, knitting her heavy brows.

"This voomin is a Turk. You know Turks? They care for nothing, believe me. Nothing. This voomin wash my jeans, my bikini—you know what that is?" she glared at Rina, pointing in the direction of her crotch.

"Sure. I think so," Rina said. Rina was open-mouthed, fascinated; this was her first European Experience.

"You know nothing. The Turks will eat shit, just like that. I say I will just kill her. I know a gun. I am Russian. We don't eat shit for nobody. My bikini—I will drink her blood very nice, you understand?"

She flicked her earlobe with her thumb to denote her utter contempt. Min was now praying for a train, any train, to come along. She and Rina would get on it. If they were lucky, this woman would not. She found herself staring at the woman, just to keep her eyes focused. The woman paced the platform with long strides, talking, talking, bashing, circling, as if she was in a play and Min and Rina the audience.

"Australia will not give me papers to work. Germany will not give papers. The Turks, the Moroccans—they are pigs but they can get work anywhere. Ptuh! I spit on them and their families. If I go back to Russia I will die. They will drink my blood very nice, believe me."

A train sounded in the distance. Min looked down the tracks. Salvation. It was on their side. She interrupted the woman with all the force she could muster.

"Is this the train to Rudesheim?"

She had wanted to spend their first night in a little village; the name "Rudesheim" had charmed her when she looked at the map.

"Yes, yes, is right train, no problem. I am taking you there. Rudesheim is a hole, is nothing, tourists everyplace. You go there for nothing, believe me."

Finally they were on the train, it was moving, there was a possibility that they were going in the right direction. Suddenly getting to where they were going was the most important thing in the world to Min. She wasn't enjoying this. She had a tight feeling across her shoulders, an invisible burden of responsibility for their lostness, the fun they weren't having. There were only two empty seats in the car.

"Let's just stand by the door, Rina," Min said loudly. She had no idea how to get her sister's attention, to enlist her in getting rid of the woman. She and Rina didn't seem to be reading one another at all. The Russian scooped up two of

Rina's suitcases and motioned Rina to sit across from her. Rina followed her as if hypnotized, sat down, and offered her some chocolate. Min stood in the aisle with her legs braced against the rest of their bags. An old woman with yellow braids was sitting on one side of her, looking out the window at the empty industrial landscape—factories, bare trees, dark piles of coal heaped in the midst of grey fields. Min thought she might have been crying. A thin young man in the clothes of a student sat across from her, reading *Last Exit to Brooklyn* in German. The Russian woman leaned forward in her seat.

"How much you make, money? For one day, how much?" she asked Rina.

"Depends. I don't know. Forty, fifty dollars maybe."

The woman's smile unfolded slowly, revealing a gold incisor.

"See? You know nothing. I cannot work Australia, I cannot work Germany. I was take to Australia by my mother, she marry a dog, he was shit, my papers are now no good. You know how much costs to live in Germany? No. You know nothing. Cost thousands of mark here. *Thousands.*"

"Well, maybe you should try Canada, then," Rina said reasonably, licking melted chocolate off her fingers. "If you're from Australia you could probably get a job there. It's all like the Commonwealth, you know."

"You think? Maybe they will have me. I need papers. You have passport. What it look like? Let me see."

Min wanted to scream as Rina reached for her bag. There were too many suitcases in the way for her to kick her sister.

"Rina—" she hissed.

"What? She just wants to look at my passport." Rina handed her passport to the woman. "Like my picture? I don't think it looks very much like me, but the guy wouldn't take another one."

It's all over, Min thought dully. This woman knows a gun, she has one stuffed in her jacket, we'll never see Rina's passport again. I wonder where the nearest consulate is, if it will be too late to get there today. Another train.

But after some minutes of studying the passport, the woman seemed satisfied, and handed it back to Rina.

"Nice," she said, leaning back in her seat. "Very nice."

* * *

Min waited five or six hours, until they were finally flopped on their beds in the inn at Rudesheim, to speak to Rina about it. She searched for a pleasing voice, that wouldn't sound like a cranky, bossy big sister.

"Rin."

"Mmmmmm."

"Rina, we're going to have to work out some kind of strategies, some better form of communication, if we're going to travel together. You've got to—you can't just hand your passport to strangers like you did today."

Rina was lying on her back. She closed her eyes when Min started talking.

"You're so *paranoid*. We were on a train. She wasn't going anywhere."

"Neither would you, without a passport. You have no idea. People sell those things—"

"Okay. Okay. I know nothing. I'll keep it buried in my bra. You'll never see it again. If anyone tries to touch it I'll swallow it, I swear."

"It isn't just the passport, Rina. I don't want to look after you while we're here, you know? Do you understand? We're both adults. I mean, I was always supposed to look out for you and I'd really—I'm hoping we can sort of move beyond that. Or I can."

Lame, Min thought. Move beyond it my ass.

Rina's eyes shot open. She raised herself up onto her elbows and turned her head to stare at Min incredulously, her eyebrows disappearing under the red fringe of her bangs.

"Who said you were in charge? You're not in charge. Relax. You know that poster? 'I do my thing, you do your thing, I'm not here to live up to your explanations—' "

"Expectations."

"Seriously. I don't expect you to handle everything. You're totally making that up. I want to spend some time together, but I mean, I can take care of myself. I am *perfectly* self-sufficient."

"Yeah, but you're a Scorpio."

"What's that supposed to mean?"

"It means, you can be unstable at times. Emotionally. Like Ma."

"I'm not *either*. I'm right on the crust anyhow."

"*Cusp.*"

"Whatever. You really blow me away, you know? I'll just pick up the car and we can split up. No problem. I can read a map. I'll have a blast, I'll be—"

"Rina, Rina, listen to me. I was just kidding about the Scorpio thing. All I'm saying is watch it. This isn't Wyandotte, okay? You're dealing with different people here. All kinds of people. I'm not saying don't have a good time. Just don't go throwing yourself into the arms of everyone you meet. People don't know you, they don't know your family. They assume things because of where you're from and how you look. You're from another planet as far as they're concerned. A rich planet. A planet that *owes* them. Believe me. You're not who you think you are, anymore."

Rina was dubious, twirling her split ends between two fingers, then dabbing them at her mouth like a small paintbrush.

"What do you think, she was like a terrorist or something?"

"I don't know what she was. Not someone I'd trust with my passport."

"I'm not a very good judge of people, Dad says. I never know if they're telling the truth or not."

"That's because you want everyone to like you."

"Maybe. I don't know. I always wanted *you* to like me."

"I liked you."

"No you didn't. You despised me. You put up with me because Ma made you. You thought I was a scab on the face of humanity, that's what you said once. Remember?"

"No."

"You did. And slapped my face in front of these boys."

"What boys? I don't remember that."

"You never remember anything about me. I was seven. I remember it perfectly well. We were at the corner, in the bush, with those boys who lived in the beige house right next to the field."

"Who? You mean Randy? Randy and his brother?"

Min had only the vaguest recollection of ever being with

Rina and the Dupuis boys. Nothing about any slap. She'd have remembered that, surely.

"Yeah, Randy. God how humiliating. I thought you were such a goddess."

"Oh *Rina*." Here we go, Min thought. Rina's face had taken on the puffy, injured look that meant she was probably going to cry, which always made Min feel bad. Was she going to be like this the whole trip?

"You had all these nice clothes, you were pretty and boys wanted to talk to you, and you were smart. I thought you were perfect in every way. Remember whenever we walked anywhere they'd always slow down their cars next to you. And you were Miss Cool. 'Keep walking, Rina,' you'd say. 'Don't pay any attention.' You never paid one speck of attention. I always wanted to run right over to the car and see what they said. But you acted like nobody was even there. I was so proud of you. I would have died to do something for you, anything, but you'd never let me touch a thing, of course. Remember the line you drew in bed? 'Don't cross over the line, Rina, or you are *dead*,' you used to say. I actually believed it. I thought you'd try to kill me. I still sleep with my arms mashed underneath me."

Min flushed at the memory of the line. *That* she remembered, how she used to lie there, cold with anger at having to share her bed with her sister, and draw the line between them with the edge of her hand every night before they went to sleep. But Rina would inevitably cross the line in her sleep—reach out a hand, kick up a trusting leg, try to hug Min's back for warmth in the winter—and when she did, Min would jab her swiftly and fiercely with an elbow, so that Rina cried out in her sleep, or sometimes awakened in surprised pain and tears. Rina was always wanting to hug her, touch her, be allowed to hold her things, and Min, under Rose's constant injunction to be nice to her sister, look after her sister, play with her sister, rejected her utterly. She *had* ignored her, she had been mean. Was she supposed to be making up for it all now? Skinny, freckle-faced little Rina.

"That was mean," she said now to Rina, softly. "I don't remember it. The slap. It was a mean thing to do, though."

But Rina was sleeping already, on her back, snoring lightly

through her mouth. Asleep she looked much the way she had when she was small: blameless, fragile, unsuspecting. Min used to hector her for that trustingness. *How could you be so stupid? How?* Trust wasn't something you just threw around. Certainly it wasn't to be wasted on boys. Min had forgotten all about those boys: nameless, dragging deeply on cigarettes, everyone's hair combed the same, slowing their unmufflered cars to a crawl by the sidewalk. "Hey! Hey!!! You're cute. Wanna go for a ride?" *Simpletons*. Rina loved it when they stopped, her face lit up, she thought it was wonderful to be noticed. Rina was a little sponge around people; Min, closed as a fist. Now as she lay awake in her bed, exhausted beyond fatigue, her body buzzing and quivering, she brooded over the way her childhood and Rina's never seemed to coincide. Wasn't it shared history? Shouldn't there be certain objective facts they agreed upon, truths that existed outside of your imagination? But there was no narrative coherence, no basic thread of commonality: they seemed not to be talking about the same people or events. How could their lives have been so different, lying on either side of that imaginary line on the same sheet, in the same bed? Memory must be a completely personal thing: exclusive, plastic, utterly idiosyncratic. Everybody making up history as they went along, to suit themselves. Yet she believed her own memory: she credited her own stories as having built themselves up purposefully, around some essential germ of truth. And she had closed herself as carefully around that truth as the two halves of an oyster around its pearl. It gleamed round and smooth and white within her, always present: she guarded it, fed it. *We stand on guard for thee*. It was her world, a dominion complete and viable in itself, where she had withdrawn herself many years ago, when it became clear that her family, the people she had been born to live with, existed in different worlds too, worlds of their own.

Especially her mother. The thoughts and impulses that drove Min had appeared to Rose to be written in a kind of runic alphabet, foreign and impossible to decipher. She strove to substitute the clear, bold type of her own ideas about Min, to fit her into the world she knew, the well-ordered universe of kitchen, yard, supermarket, church. To even begin to decipher that other alphabet would have led them both into something shadowy, dark, as open-ended as a drain. Better to stay in her world, the safe world, everything as plain as the sheet hanging out on the line.

Like that day the pictureman came.

The pictureman came every year in early summer, when the grass had greened and things were finally, reluctantly, growing again in the young, suburban gardens. He walked a dusty pony around the neighborhood and took pictures of children sitting astride it, usually the littler children who didn't go to school yet. The year she was six, the year after Rina was born, Min really saw what was happening. The greenish look of the man's face where he hadn't shaved closely or recently enough. The sheen on the seat of his pants. The way he laughed, barkingly, and touched her mother's arm while he showed her the book. The way Rose turned red and told Min to answer the door while she put some earrings and powder on, and picked up the baby.

But mostly the pony. His name could have been Sorrow, or Loss, he looked so parched and forlorn standing on his three short legs in the gravel driveway like his other foot hurt, like he had been left out in the sun for weeks with nothing to eat or drink, and had withered to this shell, this crust of a horse. Bits of dung clung to his tail and backside, two or three flies nosied around his sad eyes, and a tattered old blanket was thrown across his back like a sweater someone had forgotten there. Adding her weight to the burden of his lost life, his brokenness, was unthinkable to Min.

"Min, honey, come on, don't be a pill. Your sister's starting to cry. Look here, this nice man is going to lift you up onto the horsey so we can get a picture of you."

"That's right, a real nice picture." The pictureman grinned his green face at her, his camera balanced atop its tripod under a black leather veil, like a severed head.

No. Absolutely not.

"Here you go little girlie, you can hold Prince's reins and tell him to giddyap while I shoot your picture so's you can show your daddy what a good rider you are. Come on, now."

Certainly her daddy would have wanted her to have no part in this, the touching, the smiles and winks, the fatal upturned toes of the pictureman's brown shoes.

Awful.

What a pure feeling to scream when he stepped closer to lift her up, what a wonderful bird sound she made in the bright suburban air.

"Just what kind of an act is this, young lady? You straighten up and get over here. If I wasn't holding this baby I'd have half a mind to wallop you right here—"

She had been spared that particular blow by the man coughing—barking, really—and folding the bills her mother had already given him into his shiny pocket, turning his smile on Mrs. Costello from down the street, who was walking toward them with Gina. Gina, whose damp, fat ringlets bobbed and glistened like so many dark sausages around her blank, swarthy little face.

"Here, just take it like this then, just get her standing in front of the horse or something. Can't you hurry it up? I'm afraid the thing's going to do something right in the driveway."

A picture, then, of Min scowling, truly blackfaced, backed up against the sagging animal with her arms flung out to the sides, along his belly, as if to shield him from predators, from the mothers and Gina and her bawling sister and the green-faced man, now headless himself, lurking under his leather veil. A sunny summer day. You could barely see the little white stone from the driveway she had clutched in her left hand.

About that other picture, the shiny eight-by-ten that emerged from a grey folder her mother used to bring down from the top shelf in her closet, Min could tell you nothing. Her as a child, in a frilly white dress and frilly socks, chubby legs splayed across some sleek horse's back, waving and smiling as if you had been standing there in the driveway calling to her, telling her to look pretty now, and she was. She was looking pretty.

It was always like that. Nothing matched up. Moira from next door would knock on the back screen, then cup her hands around her eyes to look up into the kitchen and drone, "Hey, Mrs. McCune, Min took three of my walking doll's best dresses and never gave them back. Mrs. McCune you know what, Min told me and my sister to pull down our panties and pee on the grass in the backyard in front of her. She did. And what else, she cut a bald spot on the back of my brother's head with our sharp scissors and my mother's coming over to talk to you about it right now she said.''

And Min *just didn't remember* most of those things. Oh, maybe Ricky's hair, okay, she remembered *something* about that. Some little thing. But mostly what she remembered never matched up with what other people remembered. As if she and the other people hadn't even seen or heard the same thing at all. Half the time when Moira was telling on her Min didn't have a clue what she was talking about. What was she supposed to do, remember every single doll dress she ever *touched*?

"You're crazy, Moira Silvers," she'd yell down at her through the upstairs screen, the dirty mesh molding to her lips and nose like a mask where she pressed them firmly, hoping this made her look horrible. "Why don't you go home and tell your mother you're crazy? Tell her you lost your mind on your way to the store. Ha, ha, ha. My mother can't even hear you. You're nuts. Go home. Ha, ha, ha.''

It wasn't only Moira, either. Her own mother would say, "Honey, do you remember that time we went to my dear friend Cora Sawitzky's house and she let you sit at that little wooden table all by yourself and gave you that teeny-tiny lamb chop with green jelly on it for dinner? And peas? Remember what you said to her? Boy oh boy, she thought you were really something.''

"Yeah, Ma, I remember,'' Min would say warily, not knowing if her mother was remembering something cute or something bad. Not knowing, period. Because she didn't remember any lamb chop; she certainly didn't remember anything like green jelly. Cora Sawitzky, a tall gloomy house with a funny smell—yes, that could have been. She had gone on various visits with her mother to see these dear friends of hers, each of whom was a little odd, disabled even, in her own special way. One of them couldn't hear, one was so short she was barely a head higher than Min, one had snow-white hair surrounding a baby face, one lived with a sick, whining mother who dragged along behind her like a bad leg. It was plain as could be that Min was the only child who had ever been in any of these women's houses; none of them were married. They had it all planned out before Min even got there where she would sit, what she would probably want to play with, what they would give her to eat for dinner. They all told her first thing where the bathroom was in case she had to "do anything." Like she was a dog! Cora Sawitzky was certainly one of these women. But green jelly—never.

So when something went wrong, when her mother grabbed her jaw in one of her rough strong hands, squinted down into her eyes and said, "Are you telling the truth?" what should she have said? What was the truth, anyhow? Was it what other people remembered, or what you remembered? And if it was what they remembered, how were you ever supposed to know what that was?

Min balanced the map on her knees, and circled the little blue fountains denoting thermal springs. Hat shapes for grottoes, three dots for ruins, something that looked like a roller-skate for "megalithic monuments"—a dolmen? You had to circle what you were looking for here, what you thought was important; otherwise the map reverted to strangeness, inscrutability, you found yourself hurtling inexorably in an uncertain direction, squinting at signs you couldn't read.

She and Rina were heading south on the A 7. They had picked up Rina's car three days ago at the factory. Rina got up early every morning now and looked outside, to make sure it was still there. The car was red, and went very fast. Too fast, Min kept telling her, *Too fast, Rina*. According to the manual, Rina was supposed to be breaking in the engine at moderate speeds.

"Any slower and they'll have me towed," Rina grumbled, easing it back down to eighty.

Rina was a good driver—a fast driver, but a good one, considering there wasn't a single freeway in Wyandotte. She gave a running commentary, talked constantly to the other drivers, to the road itself.

"*Damn*. D'you see that? . . . Okay, here we go, German metal on the move . . . Easy, easy . . . That's it, buddy, signal left, turn right . . . Why you *slimy* . . . I'm moving, all right, I'm moving, pal, look out—Whoa!"

Min tried to abandon herself to the sensation of hurtling through space at her sister's behest.

"Just pick out Bad," Rina said to her, nodding at the map. "That's where we're headed, everyplace Bad. Bad Weezin-Sneezin, Bad Herken-Jerken—" She turned her head and grinned at Min. Her teeth were outlined in dark grey, from the black licorice cats she'd been eating.

"I seem to recall this is one of your picks, tonight," Min reminded her. They were headed toward Sleeping Beauty's Castle, at Sababurg.

"I want to see someplace we at least *know* about," Rina had said.

"The guy behind us is flashing his lights," Min said.

"Frigging demons from hell, these people! What does he *want*, I'm doing almost eighty-five—"

Rina slid into the adjacent lane and a silver Mercedes roared past them, its driver gesturing in the air.

"BLOW ME, BUDDY," Rina shouted, flipping him off. "Passing on the right, a hundred and twenty—where the hell do you think you're going?"

Finally they turned off the autobahn and onto a smaller country road. As they approached Sababurg the sun hung low, cool and silvery in the sky.

"That it?" Rina said doubtfully.

Built of grey stone, the castle rose up from a high hill directly before them—plain, stern, unmagical-looking. Two red-and-white buses were parked in the gravel lot. No briar roses, no clouds, no prince waiting in the courtyard. Min went inside to enquire and found out there were no rooms available, either.

They zipped up their coats and wandered around the grounds, picking their way over boulders and dead-looking bushes. With the sun gone, the air had become chilled, and smelled of rain. Germany seemed a cold, flinty, unloving place. There was a rigidity here, a sense that you were expected to look after yourself and not complain, not step outside the lines, not ask for anything that wasn't offered. Even the paths in the woods were flat, swept, plainly designated by their official markers, every dead leaf present and accounted for.

"Don't worry, we'll come back later and have a nice dinner here," Min said gallantly to Rina, who was feigning interest in some German signs, trying not to act disappointed.

"Hey, turn around."

A picture of Rina: hands shoved deep in her pockets, nose red and streaming, a scowl on her face, hunched next to a sign depicting a black zigzag like a thunderbolt on a white background: a warning of some danger? Thunderstorms? Underground cables?

Min didn't like to see Rina disappointed; she had almost proprietary feelings about Europe, wanting Rina to be pleased with what she found here. *Keep Rina happy.* That must have taken hold after there were just the three of them, and Rina cried so much. She used to cry every night when they went to bed, for hours it seemed. Min did everything she could think of to stop her—called her names, read her books, threatened her, promised her special foods, pleaded with her. She couldn't remember now when it stopped. There was that long time when Rina cried, and then she didn't.

They found a room down the hill, at a white two-story house with an orange roof and a ZIMMER FREI sign in the front window. A chirpy little woman with white braids wound around her head answered their knock, patiently nodded at each of the questions Min tried from her guidebook, and finally took them both by the arms and shoved them toward a tiny blue room with a doll-sized bed, a small dresser, a sink and a heater. The room was like a walk-in freezer; as soon as the woman left, Min turned the heater on high. While she changed for dinner, Rina got some of her clothes out of the trunk of the car; the room was too small for her to bring in any of her suitcases. Min had to lie on the bed so Rina could wash her face and get dressed.

Sleeping Beauty's dining room was dim, damp, and underheated.

"This used to be the dungeon," Rina whispered. Two forlorn, mangy deer heads stared across the room at each other. A larger room behind theirs was filled with Japanese tourists, laughing and yelling and snapping one another's pictures around several long banquet tables.

Rina mumbled something that sounded like "Good napping" as she took her menu from the waiter.

"How is it?" Min asked.

"Land of a Thousand Cold Cuts," Rina muttered, staring disgustedly at the menu.

The food in Germany had been a problem.

"Most of this stuff won't be in there, Rina," Min had said to her sister, who was flipping through her guidebook as they sat down to their first meal, at the inn back in Rudesheim.

Rina had shot her a look.

"Yeah? Well, this one is. 'Throat in Red Wine Sauce.' "

"What?"

"That's what it says. 'An Austrian specialty.' Throat of what, I wonder."

The other choices had been wild boar, venison, bear meat, hare, something called "Butcher's Soup," and a green salad tossed with brains.

"Brains of what, I wonder," Rina said.

"What difference does it make, you're not going to order it," Min said crossly, hungry and irritated herself.

"I know, I know. I guess I'll ask to see the dessert tray."

Rina was a picky eater. Rose always used to say the house ran on Rina's stomach. Every meal they ate was surrounded by the opaque, elastic tension of that small, sensitive organ. Would she like it? Would she eat it? And if she did, would she keep it down? When Rina was a baby, Rose used to pace the floor for hours with her crying, every once in a while sitting on the edge of the couch to plop an enormous aching breast onto Rina's red, sweating face. Rina would contract every muscle in her tiny body as though trying to squirm away from it, and Rose's face would darken with anger, and a grim resolution. By the time Rina started school, it was clear who had won.

"Rina, honey, how does it feel this morning?"

"The top part feels okay, but down near the bottom it kind of itches, it's itching me inside."

"How about some nice hot cereal? That would feel good on an itchy stomach."

"I hate hot cereal. You *know* I hate it. Don't even *say* hot cereal."

"Well then, how about a nice piece of white toast with the crusts cut off, and a little dot of strawberry jam on it?"

"Toast hurts my mouth."

"Doggone it Rina, why do we have to go through this every morning? You give me a royal pain."

"I can't help it if it itches me, Mumma." Tears starting.

"So what do you want?"

"Some of that doughnut Daddy brought home last night with the red stuff inside."

"Rina McCune, you've been told time and time again you can't eat doughnuts for breakfast."

"Then nothing." Back under the covers, loud sniffling.

"Oh jeepers. Here then. Don't start that at this hour."

And Rina would emerge—injured, trembling, her small body martyrized once again by the act of eating—to accept the doughnut.

"Maybe I'll have soup," Rina said tonight. "What can they do to soup?"

Min ordered trout, and a bottle of wine. One of the Japanese, a man in a silvery suit, was making a speech, punctuated by rapid, chopping gestures. The others cheered him loudly, clinked their glasses with their knives, waved napkins in the air.

"Weird place for a convention," Rina said, sniffing her wine. "That's the thing about Europe, you never know what to expect, do you?"

"But you have expectations, all the same. What did you think this place would be like?"

"Oh, I don't know, more like a castle in a picture—you know, big and white with the towers all standing out against a blue sky, swans, flags flying, gardens—"

"Disneyland."

"Yeah. I guess. Not that I've ever been there either. But you look at all those pictures and you think, wow, I've *got* to see that. And then it's never as good as you thought, is it? I think I must be getting old. No, seriously. Everything used to seem so exciting I couldn't *wait* for my life to happen. And now—I'm always disappointed. Nothing is as good as I thought it would be. Not having my own apartment, or sex, or having a job—even traveling—"

"Jeez. Depressing. You like your car, don't you?"

"Yeah. Sure. But even that, you know—I picked it up that first day and we drove it and I started to wonder like, how long it would stay new and then I thought, hey—it's just a car. It's just another *thing*. I hate that feeling. It's a hundred times worse when I'm by myself, too. I hate being by myself. I know there's got to be something else. I want more of a *life*, I want things to happen to me, I want somebody to, like, care about me. I wasn't going to talk about it to you, because you're so . . . but I think I want to have a baby. That's what I want. Oh my god, will you look at this.''

Their dinners were being set before them. Rina's soup was a swirl of dark red, the red of dried blood, with a huge burst sausage floating on its surface, the stuffing an amorphous, herniated mass of fat and bits of meat. Min was given what she ordered: a trout. Lying on its side on a white plate, ungraced by any sauce or vegetable, not even a frond of parsley, its head and fins and tail intact, a paralyzed eye staring bleakly up at her.

Min laid her napkin across the head and tried to pick the skin off the body with her fork. She didn't know if she could deal with Rina and the fish at the same time.

"Rina, what makes you think a baby will make you feel differently? Couldn't it be just another *thing*? I mean, what if you're disappointed in the baby you get?''

Rina took a philosophical stab at the sausage.

"The way I look at it is, at least I'll have given it a shot. But I really don't think I will be. Because it won't be me, see, it will be another being, another person, completely separate. It'll have its own feelings. Don't you ever want that? Something to love outside yourself?''

"I have. I have Peter. And I have my work.''

"Some guy you date. Like high school. I mean *love* love. And work is what you do, it's not what I'm talking about at all, it's not who you are, it's not any kind of normal life.''

"Come on, Rina. Geez. What's a normal life? The way everybody in Wyandotte lives? Husband, three kids, bowling on Thursdays, macaroni casserole Fridays, buy your Christmas cards a year in advance because they're on sale? A Kenmore washer and dryer? That kind of normal?''

"Never mind. You can make things sound so horrible. Actually, I *would* like to have a washer and dryer. So I wouldn't have to go to that depressing Maple Leaf Laundromat every week, or over to Dad's. A washer and dryer would be great. But see, you make me feel like a moron for even saying that.

People aren't supposed to want dryers and babies, are they? They're supposed to want—what are they supposed to want in your great scheme of things? I guess they want Art, or something. To take the perfect picture. Is that what you want?''

Min put down her fork and tipped her head back for a long sip of wine.

"I don't know, Rina. I'm still trying to figure that out.''

"That's your problem right there, if you ask me. You think everything can be figured out. The way Mr. Lancaster used to make us write up science experiments. Purpose. Apparatus. Method. Observations. Conclusions. I mean, what a joke. Maybe it's because I'm a *moron* or something, but I don't think you can figure everything out. There are some things you just have to try.''

Rina picked at a morsel of Min's bony, abandoned fish with her fork.

"See, you're like—you like to *run* things, you like people to act a certain way, meet up to your standards. And I bet nobody does, except maybe Dad. I don't know about this Peter guy. But you and Dad are two pods of the same pea. I mean. Work. Work is the only thing that matters, right? You're probably thinking about it this minute, about some spring and how to get there and what shots you're going to take or whatever, this is all going right past you. But look where it got Dad. He worked himself into nothingness. Into a basement. He has no friends, no interests—no *life*. He sits down there with that decrepit dog, waiting for I don't know what. Another war, or something. That's where obsession gets you, if you want to know what I think. You lose whatever you're obsessed with and wham, you've got nothing. Less than nothing. A gold-plated top.''

"Great. So let's all roll up our sleeves and start rinsing diapers in the toilet, right? Cut coupons. Shop detergents. You are living in some kind of fifties dream, Rina. You've got no job, no husband, a rapidly dwindling inheritance, you're a nutritional nightmare and you want to have a baby. What are you going to do, run an ad in the *Wyandotte Sun* for a father? You've got a tiny apartment. Where would this baby sleep, in your car? How much of yourself would *you* have left when you're a single mother, working two jobs? You're not realistic.

Work is not a period in school you skip because you don't feel like sitting through it, you know. Work is a big part of life for most people. I'm lucky because it happens to be a good part, a part I love. Dad loved it too, his real work. He had—he has a great mind. If he hadn't had us to worry about he might have been able to really use it for something. That's the pity of his life. Not how much work he did, but how much he didn't do. You don't understand that about him. Ma never did either.''

"How do you know what she understood? As if you even had a clue. You've wrote her off as some kind of bad dream, and that's not right, she was a good mother. Brother. Ma was just—Ma. How could she have been any different?''

"You're right. She couldn't.''

There was a long silence. This was an old theme, dear to Rina: what Rose had really been like, what she had known, what the unlived portion of her life might have looked like. Rina lifted the wine bottle, but it was empty.

"This is going nowhere, Rin. Know that?''

Rina looked across the table at Min, sat back in her chair, wiped her face with both hands as if she was suddenly very tired.

"Yeah. Must have been all that blood in the soup. Listen, can we get out of here?''

Flashbulbs were going off in the other room; the Japanese were dancing between the tables and singing "The Beer Barrel Polka.'' Outside on the broad stone steps, Min exhaled great draughts of white breath while Rina looked for a bathroom. The freezing air burned its way through her nostrils, down deep into her lungs. Broad swathes of stars hung overhead, delicately rearranged from their places in the California night sky. She had not seen the stars in Wyandotte.

Both of them were silent during the short drive back to their room. The air in the room was nearly as cold as outside; the old woman had turned off the heater while they were gone.

Rina looked at the thinly-covered bed, then eyed her sister.

"You guys probably sleep bare makeup down in California, I bet. Well, this here Wyandotte girl's sleeping in her clothes.''

"Me too.''

"You get in first.''

"You.''

Rina took off her shoes and coat, dived into the bed, and pulled the covers up to her chin. Min rinsed her face in the tiny sink and followed her. Rina's eyes were already shut.

"Don't cross over the line," Rina said. "Or you're dead."

Tiziano

The first time she felt an earthquake Min was eating dinner with Peter and some friends of his in a highrise apartment in west Lost Angeles. Jenna, one of the women, pointed up with her fork and giggled as the fixture hanging above the table started swaying like a pendulum from head to head.

Peter was on his feet in a second.

"Let's move, find a doorway everybody come on—move," he urged. He yanked their chairs out of the way and grabbed Min's arm, pulling her against him before she realized what was happening. They stood with their arms wrapped around each other, pressed into the doorframe between the dining room and the kitchen, sinking into their knees like sailors in a storm.

While it was happening—for perhaps ninety seconds, though it seemed much, much longer—all she could think was, This is the most *interesting* sensation. She didn't know enough to be afraid, in spite of the rising panic in the faces she saw from where she stood. The belly of the earth was heaving like a panting dog, trying to shrug them off. The dining-room table floated up as if they'd been having a séance, sent dishes sliding into the air, peas into the butter, red wine onto seat cushions. She saw a knife glide off the tabletop and for the briefest moment, stand on end. Outside the windows, the other highrises were listing, incredibly, left and right, like the masts of ships moored down in the streets. Or was it their own building that was swaying? Alarms started to shrill all over the city. Someone in the hallway was screaming "Jack, where are you? Oh my dear god Jack!"

North of them, two seconds earlier, a small town had split at the seams, tipping its inhabitants sideways, scratching needles across the grooves of LPs, coaxing trees out of the ground by their roots, tossing babies from their cribs like dolls. One man would come to with the front end of his car pointed steep as a spade into a deep gash of dirt, the back wheels spinning in air. In Malibu and Topanga, where it had been raining for several days, great slathers of mud slumped off the hillsides, taking buildings, bushes and power poles along with it. For a moment everyone remembered gravity, their loved ones, why they wanted to live. Then everything settled down again.

These were the only times most people in California talked to one another about the future, speculating on the day and the way the big one would hit, turning them all into so much plankton and Phoenix into beachfront property. Then, and when they told you how much their real estate would be worth one day, when they sold it. The future had become démodé, uncomfortably reminiscent of aging and other unspecified losses. Even Walt Disney had had himself frozen, a thumbs-up not so much for Tomorrowland as for today, suspended animation, the eternal now.

In Europe—where she had expected, if not stasis, at least the modest consolations of the past, the languorous comfort of well-worn paths and stones, the familiar shapes of western civilization and art—she felt herself prodded into movement, caught up in a relentless forward propulsion. All the powdery frescoes, the Attic statuary and ancient groves had become just so much background for the amplified roar and press of cities, cities more packed, sooty and insistent than she had remembered them. More alike. In all the big cities of the world now you got stuck in the same traffic, stayed in identical tall glassy hotels, walked under an orangy, leaden, seasonless sky, which seemed to unroll continuously from some vast, endless bolt of firmament. You were carried along in a press of grim, urgent bodies, trying not to stare at faces you thought you recognized, or step in the messes of a thousand dogs, who apparently vanished from the streets at dawn. Everywhere there was shouting, dire headlines warning about nuclear armaments, acid rain, the U.S. military presence on the Continent. "What's going to happen to—" was the question on everyone's lips; the way the blank was filled in varied only slightly from place to place. People here were passionate, enraged, horrified by the future. They would see the heavy armature of Min's cameras, assume she was a reporter, and buttonhole her for a drink in some smoke-filled bar or coffeehouse, an enervating encounter involving many questions, elaborate jokes about corruption and the decayed social order that she never quite understood, hours of sober lecture by people her own age who identified themselves as the *enfants perdus* of France or Italy or Yugoslavia, marching off to premature nuclear doom, or some equally sad, inevitable apocalypse. The weary old globe would be batted and spun back and forth like a balloon over her head, which would be aching from the wine or caffeine, the effort of trying to enlarge enough to contain the conversation, with only her bumbling, half-recollected grasp of Romance languages as a guide.

Yet these same people, men and women alike, turned to Rina with engaging smiles, marveled at her glossy red hair, bought her Sambucca or pastries or espresso, demanded to know her impressions of Italian men or French cheeses. Hilarity and mutual understanding were expressed at one another's mispronunciations. Rina found a niche; on account of her suggestibility, her candor, her disarming lack of knowledge about art, politics, food, history or culture, she was pronounced charming, naughty, unpretentious, refreshing. *Canadian, no? Très charmante*. They loved her.

For her part, Rina had become quite prepared to entertain the future. In fact, she was good and ready for it. The past hadn't been any bargain, she liked to remind her sister. What did she have to lose? At times she seemed perfectly willing to forget who she was or where she was headed, and go off with one of these café people somewhere, anywhere, start a whole new life.

"Smile, Sis," she would say to Min, licking jam from her fingers, a flake of palmier clinging to her lip. "Really. This is as good as it gets."

* * *

Was Min wrong, then, to perceive something slightly sinister in her surroundings, as the decade came to a close, as fall slid gracelessly toward winter and all around them people were battening down, finishing up, storing away? Or was it that she'd lived too long in benign southern latitudes now, where a sunset hot-air balloon ride, say, or a two-hour body wrap qualified as an enriching experience. Even some of the spas had closed their doors, hostile to her enquiries, indifferent to her letters of reference. Ax-les-Thermes, for example, which she had deliberately chosen for its smallness, its unfashionable location in the sodden shadow of the Pyrenees, an unwritten-up, untouristed corner of France. They had stayed in a peculiar, decrepit, Felliniesque hotel across from the baths, which a young couple seemed to have bought solely for their private amusement. Mournful Middle Eastern music blared from an elaborate, new-looking sound system at odd hours. Several small, heavily madeup women with frizzy hair appeared in the dining room each evening with tiny panting dogs, who were seated on cushions and given their own salad plates. The sullen owners shuffled from dining room to hallway to front desk in heavy silk bathrobes and tatty slippers, smoking thin, brown, foul-smelling Turkish cigarettes, their own toy dachshund trailing behind at a body's length on its little sawed-off legs, yapping and nipping at their legs as if to stir things up a bit, get them to act like proper hoteliers. The couple yawned and professed to know nothing at all about the baths, *Rien du tout, mademoiselle, désolé.*

"Like, they don't even know the place is across the street? Is everybody here on drugs, or what?" Rina muttered irritably when Min translated for her. She was still disgusted at having to sit with all those little dogs in the dining room. It had, she said, taken away her appetite.

When they arrived at the baths they were appraised by a heavyset woman in a white uniform, who shook her head pessimistically when she saw them. Did they have notes from any doctors? *Non.* Well. That was that. The *station thermale* was for *curistes* only. She gestured behind her to the dim smelly pavilion where a surprising number of people—most old, some hairless, or missing limbs—were being floated in the cloudy water by tight-lipped attendants like herself, then dragged back to their wheelchairs or benches, wrapped in droopy green robes and taken off to hidden rooms. Rina hadn't liked the looks of the place one bit, and rushed Min back out the door to a bar where they had their usual beer and croques-Monsieurs for lunch. They managed to get a pleasant buzz from a second beer each, amass a huge pile of change from the waiters, and call their father from the phone booth in the street outside, both of them shouting into the Atlantic static until the coins ran out and they were left with sudden, empty space.

"He sounded good, don't you think?" Rina said doubtfully.

"I could barely hear him. I think he was glad we called, though, don't you?"

They avoided each other's looks when the subject of Alex came up. They mailed exaggeratedly cheery postcards, some packets of herb and vegetable seeds, a scarf, a bottle of rose-scented French pet shampoo for Skipper. And though she didn't believe in affirmations or prayers or any of that, several times a day Min caught herself mouthing the words *Make him feel better. Make him feel better.* It couldn't hurt anything. And who could say, really, what might help?

Min was on her own one afternoon in Florence, seeing museums while Rina slept at their pensione. Min thought Rina slept a lot, as if she were already pregnant instead of just thinking about it. "Man, this is my idea of a vacation, sleeping as much as you want," Rina protested. She wasn't much interested in cathedrals or art anyway, preferring to spend her hours feeding the pigeons gathered under *The Rape of the Sabine Women* in the piazza, or browsing the shoe and goldsmith shops on the P.V., as she called it, stopping every so often for *gelato*.

Min loved the museums, and when her feet started to hurt she would sit and watch the people. The Germans, reading aloud from their guidebooks first, then looking up, informed enough to take in the picture. They never skipped around. Most of the Americans went straight for the familiar—the Rembrandts, the Michelangelos, the Leonardos—agreed they were fabulous, held their cameras up in the air to shoot *David* above the heads of the crowd. The Italians tended to bring their families—children, aunts, cousins. They dawdled in large noisy groups past the lesser Ucellos and del Sartos and Gaddis, laughing and jostling one another, stopping here and there to exclaim lovingly. "*Ah, Tiziano, che bella,* La Maddalena." As though Titian were an old neighbor, a cousin who had finally made something of himself; or as if this very portrait had hung above their own satiny white infant beds and they were only now, standing here, remembering it, their cheeks flushed, cooing the way they would over a new baby, their eyes and voices caressing, claiming it, their hands warm and fluid with love, pushing the smaller children forward for a closer look.

And Min felt a great bittersweet shudder of love and sadness, watching these Florentines lingering in the presence of their own history, the honeyed canvases and gilded mirrors, a sense of time not only passing but finally, irretrievably forfeit, great heavy doors in long corridors being firmly closed to her. A part of her life was over, and while she had been in it, living it, she had not imagined that it was anything that could end. There were loves that were now lost to her, other loves that would never be: moments of bliss, openings of the rarest sort that had remained hidden behind a heavy curtain of vague apprehension, torpor, the scrapings and gleanings of everyday life: a kind of life which must, too, finally be acknowledged, and lived. Her younger self, her most brazen, leaping, itching self, which had been filled with dreams and desires ready to burst like seeds from a ripened pod, had gradually disappeared into the shadows of those vanished hours and minutes. Her whole life was no longer before her; somehow, nearly half of it had already gotten lived, and still she felt that she had not really done *it*, whatever *it* was, she had not pushed through to that bright sunlit place she always imagined lay just ahead, where she would feel perfectly satisfied and complete. She had been reasonably happy. Moderately successful. Her work, that fragile evanescent creature with its own existence, still haunted her, the way the baby birds she used to nurse with eyedroppers and torn bits of bread had hounded her childhood with their cheeping, growing ever feebler until one morning they lay there cold and still in their little white Kleenex nests. Was that what was going to happen? Would she never step off a branch herself, into the open air?

All day she had been reading labels and subtracting dates, hardly able to believe what some of the artists had accomplished by twenty-three, twenty-five. Looking back over her life she saw it as a vast empty plain, swept bare of meaning, accomplishment, love, everything she thought it was made of—simply and cleanly gone. What had she done or been, after all? A sulky wayward daughter, an indifferent sister, a demanding erratic lover, a middling-good photographer. That was it. She never felt she had managed to accomplish everything she wanted to in a day; there was always a piece missing, a nagging feeling of incompleteness. And here in the Uffizi, standing by a window watching the rain streaming in the gutters below, the grey afternoon dark with clouds, shading too soon toward evening, she realized with absolute clarity that *it didn't matter*. It didn't really matter to anyone but her. The background she saw herself against, these hallways filled with paintings and sculpture that limned the ancient, grave threshold of the soul, that approached its innermost places—she was the merest speck against all this. She could take her photographs or not take them, as she chose, and no one would care, or be the worse for it, but her. No one was waiting for her to step off the branch. Soon enough, human history would close itself around her paltry absence, claim her unbreathed oxygen, and it would be as if she never was. She would disappear, vanish into thin air, and Rina would have her baby, or not; her father would get better, or worse; Peter would miss her, mourn for her, but finally carry on with his life. It didn't really matter. The step, take it or not, was for herself alone.

It was also clear that none of this had anything to do with Peter. It was ridiculous for her to keep saying: I might lose it, I might not do my best work, or any work at all, if I decide to live with him, or marry. The claiming of whatever potency she was to have was up to her. That would be true no matter what the rest of her life was about. And the rest of her life— not the exalted, the hoped-for, the dramatic, but the ordinary, everyday business of living—was not something she could escape. It had claims on her, like it did on everybody else. The battle she was fighting over that was with herself, not with him. She didn't have to be miserable, to live without his love, in order to do what she wanted. Love had neither depleted her nor rendered her useless. If anything, she was stronger because of it. Giving it up would be, in Rose's words, cutting off her nose to spite her face.

And what if I don't ever *do* it? she thought. Claim my fate, step off the branch into the open air. What is there? She had a vision of herself sitting on a bed in a hotel room, looking out the window, her life running on like the ticking of the portable alarm clock on the bedside table. More cities, more photographs, mornings, afternoons and evenings stretching away endlessly. She would dry out slowly from the inside, like a gourd, its seeds rattling around hollowly in that contained, dark, useless space. You've seen it happen, she told herself. You and Peter and the others, after that night at Jenna's—*She's lost it, she's completely lost it*, you all said to one another. Poor Jenna had unaccountably faded from a laughing golden self to a dull, lusterless one, somehow misplaced her vitality and power, lost hope. *What a shame*, everybody said. *She was so talented. So fortunate. So beautiful*. Poor Jenna. Lost her place in the long line of those of us who are surely destined to be someone, do something. *What a shame*. That night you all counted yourselves part of the rattling orchestra of gourds who made things happen, ran this town, no moss growing under your feet, no rents in your garments, no ashes in your hair. You knew exactly where you were going. You shook your heads at poor Jenna and felt better than ever, the brisk wind of failure blowing off in another direction entirely. You would never grow old, never die, never be alone. Would you?

The Farthest Reaches

When they first arrived at Dun Laoghaire, Min had worried about how she would arrange to meet her relations—not knowing her way around the countryside—since none of them had a telephone. But that afternoon, Cousin Bertie's note arrived at their hotel.

> Come by way of Pennycomequick Bridge. Will meet you in FRONT of DUNNE'S store ARKLOW 12 noon WED. Keep doors, windoes closed and LOCKED. Doen't park on yellow lines ANYWHERES. My BLUE van 21 K T2 behind toilets in case. Wearing BLACK jacket with golden shines BELTED. Arley's father DEAD alredy waked in his OWN BED. 98 years.
>
> — Yr COUSIN
> Bertie

The note sounded slightly ominous to her. Was she expected to decipher a coded message in the capitalized letters? And who was Arley, or his or her father? Bertie—*Miss Bertha McCune*, as Min had addressed her letter—was her father's cousin, the first to reply to her inquiries about living relatives in the area. Now she and Rina were meeting Bertie for lunch. It hardly seemed possible that they were here in Ireland, being met by people they'd never seen before, who claimed them as kin.

"What should I wear?" Rina called from the bathroom, where she was rubbing herself almost cruelly with a thin towel, trying to warm up after another bracing European shower.

"Let's not dress up too much. I mean, they're all farmers. Just some jeans or something."

"Or would you like to see me in that grey sweater-dress I picked up in Paris?"

"That sounds nice."

"What shoes?"

"I don't know, Rina. Something comfortable."

"You know I don't have anything *comfortable*."

"Then whatever goes with grey."

"Black, I guess. God I *hate* every single thing I brought. I swear I'm leaving all this stuff in the last hotel room we have. Don't you get sick of your clothes when you travel? All this mixing and matching. Neutrals. I can't stand neutrals."

"I don't think about it much."

"You should. Wearing neutrals every day is enough to seriously depress a person. Here, put on some lipstick. You'll feel better."

There was no reason to suppose Bertie would look anything like Mac. Nonetheless, Min was looking for a sort of tall, lanky woman with wavy brown hair on the street in front of Dunne's, when she was knocked halfway off the curb and then lifted nearly a foot in the air by a punishingly strong pair of arms.

"Why here's the girl! Just have a look at her! And don't she take after her father's side of the family I says to myself the minute I laid eyes on her. Look at that nose, and them bones in her cheeks there. I seen yer sister drive past already once, looking for a place to park. You know you've to look out for those yellow lines or the peelers will nab you right off. Did you get my note then? Well you must have or I wouldn't be standing here talking to you, would I? There's herself—hello there, I'm yer cousin Bertie—really I'm Bertha but it's such a great lump of a name, isn't it. Just call me Bertie, everyone does hereabouts. And how would the pair of ye's be enjoying Ireland so far?"

Bertie paused momentarily for a lungful of air. She was a

short, stocky, red-faced woman of sixty or so, with a smudge of what looked like red dye on her chin, and cropped reddish hair. She scooped great armfuls of air toward herself as she spoke, as if to fuel the energetic fires of conversation. Her black jacket was indeed wrapped and BELTED around her ample form, the way you'd bandage and strap a leaky pipe that was in danger of bursting.

"What we've seen so far has been beautiful—" Rina enthused.

"Beautiful! Why the whole country's in ruins! It's a complete shambles, is what it is. But ye'll find out for yerselves soon enough. I thought we'd have a bite here at Dunne's, they make a lovely cottage roll. Have ye's ever had a cottage roll? Ye haven't? Well yer certainly in for a treat then, Dunne's cottage rolls is the finest there is. I could use a bite myself, I've got into a dangerously weakened condition running all over the damn countryside already and the day only half started. Davey'll be worked up into a dither waiting for ye's to come over there. Now that little fellow is something ye'll never see the like of on this earth again, I warrant ye. Hurry up or them rolls will all be sold and not a bite of anything left for us pokers."

Bertie's weakened condition in no way hindered her from clearing them a wide path to the counter, and then to a small table by the window. They had three large cups of tea and the cottage rolls: small white sandwiches filled with some sort of dessicated ham. Bertie started in on the family as they ate.

"Oh I'll tell ye's about them all right," she said, between dainty bites of her sandwich. "I'm right up on the family tree, I am. Yer grandfather, now, was a great lazy bastard, you know. It's why he lived to such a grand old age, you see, he never did a damn thing. Oh, he worked over there, but I mean the real type of work we have here. The devil's own time they had teaching him to ride that horse in the army. He was that lazy, that he couldn't see the sense of all the saddling and bridling, the climbing up and then the climbing down again. He had his younger brother—that was my father, Malachi, and as sweet a man as ever lived and breathed—he had him lacing up his boots right until he got on that boat for overseas, and unlacing them at night into the bargain. Now did ye's ever hear of a thing like that?''

"And did you ever know his wife? Our grandmother?'' Min asked, as Bertie helped herself to another sandwich.

"Ye'd better eat up, yer thin as a straw,'' Bertie said to Rina, pushing her plate closer to her. "I guess that's the style where ye's come from, women so thin they can hardly walk. That's one thing ye'll learn about me, no beatin' around the bush of anything. Of course I knew her, I'm a McCune and a Connellan both—bet ye didn't know that, did ye? Yes. I'm more related to ye's than yer own father! I hear he's a tall man too, like his father. I take more after my mother, bless her soul. Connellan blood. She's in heaven now, looking down on the shambles of this poor country and I expect worried sick about it. Some local ladies will not live alone any more it's got that bad. Oh my yes. Drug-takers and thieves and decent people strangling in their own beds. The pair of ye's driving alone could meet someone in a stolen car and that's that, too late even to have a blood test done. I can say I did warn ye both.''

She stood abruptly, giving the table a dangerous nudge with her large purse.

"Time's a-wasting while we loaf around here,'' she announced. "Eat up there, Rina. Ye'll never have a lovelier cottage roll than that. Now ye's won't never find Davey's place without me. Min, you can ride with us, and Rina there, follow us out so's ye'll know the way on yer own. I'll leave ye's at the end of his lane.''

"Just give me a sec to bring the car around,'' Rina said, swallowing and wiping off her mouth.

Suddenly Bertie leaned over the two of them, her comfortable bosom grazing Min's chin.

"I know the two of ye's've slept with men and not been to the preacher, either,'' she whispered hoarsely. Then she straightened up, pressed her napkin lightly to her lips and brushed a few crumbs from her capacious skirt.

"But I take no mind at all,'' she continued airily. "We've plenty of that type of thing here ourselves.''

*   *   *

Riding in Bertie's van was like being locked up in a sheep pen and dragged over rocks. Min was sure she knew how sheep must feel being driven to market, breathing their own sweet overheated smell while they were jounced senseless, without any idea of direction or where they were going. Bertie's lanky mutt Blackie paced and drooled in the back, and smiled an inane doggy smile at Min every time they hit a bump.

"If you find it close you can open yer window. I keep 'em shut because you never know who you might meet anymore on the roads. Ye've really picked the worst time to come, unknownst to yerselfs of course, the inspector's coming up this afternoon to look at the lot of my sheep and I'm up to my ears in it at the moment. But I said to myself, Bertie I says, ye've a bounden duty to bring them girls down and show them a real Irish farm before it's gone the way of the devil like everything else around here. Wrack and ruin. Blackie get yer great fat head in the back or I'll cuff you one—"

Blackie was rhythmically banging the back of Min's head with his nose, as if to let her know she was in his seat and he was ready to have it back now. She silently elbowed him, then turned and waved out the back window at Rina, who was driving with her head leaning way off to the right. She'd been driving like that even when Min was sitting next to her, with her head right in Min's face; she couldn't see properly, on account of having left-hand steering, and didn't seem to trust Min when she told her it was safe to pass.

The rutted road, the mixed smells of dog and sheep and medicine, the half-eaten ham sandwich churning around in her stomach, were nauseating her. As she listened to Bertie, she wondered at the way the Irish talked about their country. Bertie used the same scolding, disappointed tones as the couple she and Rina had met in a pub last night. They spoke about Ireland as though it was an overgrown, slow-witted child, with an angelic face and the best of intentions, who nevertheless blundered its way from one thing to the next, beloved but exasperating. One who repeated the same questions, never grasped the answers, let the precious churned milk spill over the hearth again and again. Who could be dealt with at home, but caused consternation and misunderstandings abroad. All in all, a child who caused its parents feelings of suffering, shame and hopelessness. A dimwit.

The thing about Uncle Davey was the great grinning charm of him. He could probably have charmed bulls into giving milk and cows into singing, if he'd had a mind to. Min thought she'd never met anyone who was so naturally good-humored, the way some people naturally have red hair or big feet.

When she and Rina first drove down the bumpy lane, past the sheds and cow barn and into his yard, she thought she saw a small shirtsleeved figure standing in the low doorway of the old stone house. But as they drew nearer and she looked again, she saw only the empty black opening.

"That's strange," she said to Rina. "Surely they're expecting us?"

Rina shrugged.

"Maybe they want to surprise us."

They put on their sweaters, got out of the car, and walked toward the house. As they approached, the small man suddenly reappeared, decked out in a worn dark-green jacket, a woolen cap and tie. He ran his eyes over them with kindly, undisguised curiosity, and lifted his hand in greeting.

"Aye, you're McCunes just by the looks of ye's!" he announced, stepping down and walking across the yard with the slightest hop to his gait. He sounded so positive and delighted in his identification that Min felt instantly warmed by the pleasant feeling that she had involuntarily done something right, simply by being who she was, having the face she did.

"Uncle Davey!" she exclaimed, hugging the slight, tobaccoy-smelling figure. "I'm Min. How are you? What a lovely place this is!"

"Indeed it is," he said, looking around as though he had just arrived himself. "You're in Ireland now, you know." Turning to Rina, he said, "You must be the other one, then. Rina, is it? That's a fine-looking car you've drove up in, Rini."

"You like it? Here, come on and try out the seats. We picked it up in Germany. It really goes—except for your crooked roads here, and driving on the left. I'm not used to that yet."

"Aye. Well they build the roads in Ireland at night, you

know. I expect they're nothing to what your roads is in North America. Course, we haven't as many places to go here."

Uncle Davey walked over to the door Rina had opened for him, stroked the dash, and squinted at all the controls.

"Yessir, a lovely bit of a car. I'm sure it's the only red car in Ireland."

Rina and Min looked at one another.

"No. We don't never get this color of a car here. They just send over a lot of them little beige jobs from England, and a terrible price we pay for them, too, what with the punt the way it stands. Terrible. Well, maybe you girls would like me to show you some sights, then?"

"Love it!" Rina exclaimed, and helped him into the seat. Min had wanted to look around the farm, perhaps take a few pictures, but Uncle Davey looked so settled in, and Rina so eager to go, that she turned around again and climbed into the back seat.

"Uncle Davey, would you mind wearing your seat belt?" she asked him.

"Eh?"

"Your seat belt. We like to have them on."

"Oh, aye. They're a fine thing aren't they?"

He fiddled with the belt while Rina wheeled out of the yard and back down the lane. Min tried to assist him from where she sat. He managed to loop the belt across his neck and under his left arm, gave a final, satisfied nod, then peered into his pipe. And that was the way he rode, looking half hanged, one side of him hoisted up in midair.

"No one would pass me if I had a car like this," he said to Rina, looking at her over his hunched shoulder. "Nossir. I'd be gone like a shot." He contemplated this, drawing on his pipe, while Rina gave him a my-kind-of-guy grin and eased the car up to fifty, oblivious of the corrugated road scarcely wide enough for a single vehicle.

"Well, you're two fine-looking girls, the both of ye's, by God. Would you like me to sing you a little song? I could've been a singer, you know, if I'd kept it up. They said I had a good voice." And Davey began to sing in a fine clear tenor, a love song. He sang sweetly and unselfconsciously, as if he were a bird serenading the green, green landscape that was rolling by; and this day was so fine, the words so sad and lovely, and Min's heart suddenly so full that she had to swallow several times to keep tears away.

> *"But I will climb a high, high tree*
> *And rob a wild bird's nest,*
> *And I'll bring back whatever I do find*
> *To the arms that I love best," she said*
> *"To the arms I love the best."*

Uncle Davey seemed absorbed and entertained by everything they saw on the drive, and took great pleasure in pointing out the sights to them.

"There's a black cow," he'd say, nodding toward a field in which indeed stood an ordinary cow, of the commonest shade of black.

Or "Here's Tyler's Bridge!" at the approach to a bridge a few miles from his house, which he had crossed perhaps five thousand times in the span of his life. And then he'd look pleased, having checked these items against some internal inventory of what the world contains, and not found them wanting in any way.

But he wasn't out of touch.

"Well," he said to Min, not ten minutes after they first met, "and what does Mr. Reagan think he's doing in the Middle East then?"

He said it as if Mr. Reagan was a neighbor they all had trouble with, someone with no respect for the property of others. And she was caught speechless. She hadn't known quite what to expect before meeting Uncle Davey; but discussing foreign policy hadn't really crossed her mind. After all, he was ninety-four: she'd been prepared for him to be bedridden, deaf, a dotard. She had thought more along the lines of polite, shouted remarks about the weather, crops, cattle auctions—he was a farmer, after all.

But Davey never brought up his age. Barely a scrap over five feet, he still had a puckish, boyish look about him, and moved so lightly you never heard his footsteps, or felt any disturbance of the air at his approach. His way of appearing and disappearing was uncanny. Min would turn to speak a sentence, following on one of his, and he wouldn't be there. Or thinking herself quite alone in a room, she'd smile and murmur a few words aloud to herself, only to be startled suddenly by his impish face right next to her own, wearing an expression that plainly said, Oh well, if it's talking to yourself you're after, I'll be making myself scarce. After the first day they spent with him, Min looked at Rina and said,

"Did we make him up? Did we really spend the afternoon with that elfy little guy, or was it my imagination?"

"What I'd like to know is who made up those towns. Ballylicky, Ballydillydally, Ballybellybutton—"

For the rest of the visit the two of them puzzled over the way life was one continuous rolling stream for Uncle Davey. What happened on the *Bonanza* reruns, or the doings in the Knockananna pub on a Saturday night, had equal weight and reality.

"Think there's life on other planets, Uncle Davey?" Rina asked him.

"I don't know why there wouldn't be."

Nor did any barrier exist for Davey—nor a few of the other Irish they met—between the world of potato blight and fenceposts, and the spirit world. He spoke as earnestly about the voices coming from the Moyne churchyard at night as about the outlandish price he'd heard bid for an ewe and two lambs at auction—and in the same breath, for he had passed the graveyard on his way home from the auction, and hadn't he heard both with the two big, hairy ears you were looking at at that very moment? Talk of the banshee, the wee folk, the thing that snatched Harry O'Bannon's shoes right from under his bed was commonplace; many people here took a sober, kindly interest in their doings, much as they did in the doings of their neighbors—or strangers, for that matter.

"You girls best keep your eyes peeled for the creatures that sit up all night at the side of the road, waiting to snatch travelers what haven't got their wits about them," he said seriously as they dropped him off one night. "You've only to look by that heap of rounded grey stones past the Derry Hotel, you know, and you'll see them perfectly well. That's where they like to sit. Mind me."

One morning Davey brought Min an old book that looked

like a scrapbook or album, its cover a faded flower-printed cloth, with more of the pages slipped away from its binding than still held. Without any searching he pulled an old sepia print from the middle of the book and handed it to her. This was a moment she had waited and hoped for, since she had first decided to come to Ireland. It was as far back as she could go, as close to the source as she could hope to get. A moment of *bestowing*, was how she'd thought of it, being claimed by her relatives, an elder finally explaining to her the secrets of her tribe, naming its members.

"Uncle Davey, who are these people? Are they relations?"

He frowned at the picture as though he'd never seen it before.

"Well, I don't know. Maybe they are." Then he looked out the smeary window to the yard, rapped the pane thoughtfully with the end of his pipe.

"You know I seen a man out there once."

Was he *trying* to be exasperating? Surely he must know, after all her hints and explanations, how important these old pictures were to her.

"What man?" she asked, dispiritedly.

"That man who comes on a white horse. Aye. Well past two o'clock in the morning, and I come down them stairs there"—he waved behind him, to the stairs leading up to the bedrooms on the second floor—"maybe I heard a noise. Maybe I didn't. The moon was all shining in that window—there was a frost come already, you know—and himself sitting right there, right outside the window. Him on his great white horse, just looking at me."

Min looked down at the photograph she was still holding, of three strangled-looking preachers sitting on kitchen chairs in the middle of someone's lawn. She opened her mouth to ask another question.

But he was gone. She heard him laughing with his son, Tom, in the kitchen, over a commercial on the TV.

During their sightseeing that first afternoon, the sky began to fill with patches of low grey clouds—as it did, on and off, most days they were there—and Uncle Davey asked that they stop back at the house for a bit. Min had to stoop to get through the doorway. The kitchen was dark and low-ceilinged, with rough-looking exposed beams from which hung pots, pans, a long-handled bread toaster, and some metal implements that she didn't recognize. Against one wall sat a cupboard that held some crockery, glasses, a breadbox, a sugarbowl, a big dish of butter, and several boxes of shotgun shells. There was a massive black cookstove in one corner, with several chairs set around it, and a worn braided rug on the linoleum floor. The room smelled baconish, with fainter notes of woodsmoke and wet wool. Scarves and jackets, all in dark colors, hung on some wooden pegs to the left of the door, a scattering of shoes and boots beneath them. Only the large television set and the light bulb hanging from the ceiling made it a twentieth-century room. It had a masculine, rough-and-ready air, even to the print on the wallpaper, which had faded to a blurry, tweedy pattern. Something about Davey's house reminded Min of her grandfather's: its plainness and maleness, perhaps, the vague presence of dead women lurking in the rooms like a cooking smell.

"How old is this house, Uncle Davey?" Rina asked, looking askance at the ceiling, as if it might cave in on them any minute.

"Oh, I'd say near about two hundred year, maybe."

"Is this where you were born?"

"No, no. This was my wife's father's house. I've only been here fifty years or so."

"Could I use the bathroom?"

"Well now, you could, if there was one. I've a chamberpot by the bed upstairs, or—" He gestured broadly, indicating the great outdoors.

Min had not seen Rina blush for many years.

"Oh great, thanks, I'll just—I'll be—" Rina grabbed her purse and fled back outside.

"And when exactly did your wife die?" Min asked. Now she'd get him to talking about the family. She had done some homework in Wyandotte, knew he'd had a wife and five children. "I think—wasn't she named Margaret?"

"Ah, the wife. Yes. She was named Margaret, matter of fact. It was in the winter. Must be twenty years or more now."

"Do you miss her?"

He gave an odd little grin, and walked into the parlor.

"Maybe I don't," he said, over his shoulder.

Min followed him and looked around the room while he searched for his tobacco. There was a small table with curved legs next to the window where she stood, and a soft chair with a collapsed-looking seat; she thought it must be someone's favorite spot for reading, or sitting to look outside. Davey was extracting a pinch of fragrant tobacco from a small leather pouch.

"So long as I've got my pipe, see, I've no need of anyone else. Or anything else, if you want the truth of it," he continued, tenderly filling and tamping the bowl. "There. This here pipe is my best friend. I scarce know what I'd do without it. Many's the evening I just sit by the fire and have myself a great old smoke, and there's no happier man in the country. Nossir. You know my mother was a hard woman. Hard as boot leather, she was."

"My great-grandmother."

"She never let us children smoke, or dare try a drop of drink. But I did. I had my first drop behind Hallahan's barn when I was thirteen year old, and never been the worse for it, have I? No sir. Our Savior drank, you know. Oh yes. It says so right there in The Book."

He pointed his pipe at a dusty black volume resting on the mantle, as if he'd just consulted it on this particular article but a few moments ago.

"Aye, he had a drop every now and again, and none the worse for it either. There's no harm in a wee bit every now and again."

Davey leaned closer to Min and peered up into her face.

"Does your sister drink?"

She wasn't at all sure what he meant. Was he asking if Rina was a *drinker*, an alcoholic? Or did he mean, Is that how Rina spends her time, drinking?

"Well, yes, she drinks. Sometimes." And as soon as she said this she felt guilty, and wanted to qualify it. It didn't sound quite right to her; it was too affirmative, she felt like she was confessing a shameful secret about Rina, exposing her in some way. Because she didn't exactly *drink*, in the way she pictured the act when she heard someone say, *He drinks*: a man with a hardened look on his face in a black-and-white movie, jerking his tie off, grabbing an opened bottle of some dark liquid and pouring a hotel-glassful, sloshing this back into his throat in a single toss, just to get started, to orient himself, then wiping his mouth with the back of the hand that still held the bottletop and pouring another glassful, this time for pleasure. Rina never did that, that she knew of.

But that wasn't what Davey meant, either. Because he seemed favorably impressed by what Min said. He gave a small, thoughtful nod, as though this was good news, it was what he had hoped to hear. And something in that nod made it clearer to her what he'd meant by his question. He was defining for her two categories of persons that exist in Ireland: those who drink, and those who do not. *How much* they drank was not for them to discuss or be in any way concerned with. *That* they drank was what mattered here.

Davey went into the kitchen and brought back a small plain glass and set it down on the table by the window. Then he walked to the overstuffed, dark green chesterfield and reached down at the far end of it, out of Min's seeing. Clinking, shuffling. He surfaced holding a large bottle of Bushmills, walked back to the table, held it up to the light and examined the label closely, as if this was the first time he'd seen it. Min stood by the table. She felt the two of them had stepped back in time when they entered the parlor. The wallpaper here was faded garlands of roses, fawn and ocher and brownish pinks. A patterned maroon rug lay under the dining table and chairs, and all about the room were little clusters of figurines, china flowers, doilies, candle stubs, dishes of dusty, cellophane-wrapped candies. Clearly this had been a woman's room; it did not have Davey's imprint anywhere. No wonder the liquor was hidden.

Davey looked from the bottle to Min and smiled broadly. Opening it ceremoniously, he tipped three or four fingers of whiskey into the glass, stood back, inspected it with his head cocked to one side, then poured the tiniest bit more. Min wanted to stop him, to revise her statement. Rina *drinks*, but she doesn't drink *whiskey*. Probably she had not drunk that amount of whiskey in her life. She sensed, however, that she had committed her sister to drinking it now, irrevocably.

Davey moved the glass a quarter-inch to the left.

"That's for Rini," he said. Davey never got Rina's name quite right. He looked at Min.

"Do you drink?" he asked.

"I don't drink whiskey," she stated firmly, sure of her ground now. Hope for Rina might be lost, but she could try to save herself.

"But you'll have a drop of something?" Davey asked, a look of concern spreading over his features.

"I guess I could have a drop, Davey, but just a very, very small drop."

He was already out of the room, headed toward the kitchen. He turned his head around to look at her, as if the two of them were passing a secret back and forth. He brought a footed jelly glass, which he set next to Rina's drink, and returned the Bushmills to the place on the floor beside the chesterfield. More clinking. This time he fished up a bottle of cream sherry, dusty around its shoulders, carried it to the table and poured Min an amount equal to the whiskey. There didn't seem to be anything on this label he wanted to read. Min thought she'd never seen anyone pour liquor with so much tenderness and devotion. He could be celebrating the Eucharist, or baptizing a baby.

Back went the sherry. Davey stood next to Min, and they both looked at the two glasses. She had caught his attitude of reverence; transubstantiation would not have been entirely surprising, at that moment.

Then, as if the thought had suddenly occurred to him, Davey said, "Why, I think I just might join ye's in a drop myself!"

Immensely pleased by this idea, he went to the kitchen yet a third time for a glass. He rubbed his hands together as he retrieved the Bushmills; they made a pleasant, dry raspy sound. The third glass was poured with appropriate ceremony, and Min exhaled deeply. Now they were really getting somewhere.

"Where is Rinty got to, do you suppose?" Davey asked her.

She had been wondering that herself.

"Maybe she's out in the car fiddling with the tape player. She brought a couple of tapes she wants you to hear."

"Oh, she is. Well." The three glasses were looking back at them now, waiting for a sign.

"Why don't you have a bit of yours, then?" Davey finally

said, in a soft voice. "You know it'll go flat sitting there on the table like that."

Min held her breath and took a good-sized swallow of sherry, which she hated. Davey had leaned imperceptibly closer, and was looking up hopefully into her face.

"How does that taste, then?" he asked, with barely contained eagerness.

"Oh fine, Uncle Davey, fine. Just lovely, really."

His face wore a look of complete satisfaction, pride almost, he could have been bringing her back from the dead with an elixir stirred by his own hand. The sun suddenly came out from behind the clouds, and shone into the little parlor window, lighting up the golden liquid in the two remaining glasses.

Davey took his own glass from the table and held it up toward the window for a moment. The beams of light played over the sleeve of his dusty, threadbare jacket, his white cuff, his soil-rimmed fingernails. An air of extreme well-being had entered the room, a sense that the day was lifting with the clouds, and taking a definite turn for the better. He turned his soft, twinkling blue eyes toward Min and brought his glass to his lips.

"Well then," he said.

And drank his drop.

"What a mess," Rina said disgustedly, trying to squeeze out her beige slacks above the tiny basin in their room at the bed-and-breakfast inn. She had started her period while they were visiting Davey's, without the necessary equipment—including a bathroom—at hand.

"Still get cramps?" Min asked her.

"Big time."

"I learned a massage stroke that really seems to help."

Rina rolled her eyes.

"A beer and a shot usually does it, thanks. What're you looking up?"

Min had the Dublin "Golden Pages" opened across her lap.

"Well I was looking under 'Confectionery' because I wanted to take some candy over to our relations tomorrow night and I ended up at convents. I can't believe this. Three pages of them. Daughters of the Cross. Handmaids of the Sacred Heart of Jesus. Little Sisters of Assumption. Poor Servants of the Mother of God. Sisters of the Visitation. Who *are* these women?''

"Maybe they can't get jobs. You know, I used to think you were going to be a nun.''

"ME? Get serious, Rina. We weren't even Catholic.''

"I know, I know, this was when I didn't even know what Catholic was. When you used to go to the convent for piano, remember? I thought you were taking some kind of nun lessons. You always looked so serious when you left the house.''

"Yeah, because I never practised and I was afraid Sister Gertrude would yell at me with her mustache and her rotten nun breath right in my face.''

"Something kind of romantic about it, though,'' Rina mused.

"About what?''

"Being a nun. I mean, you don't need any money. All your meals are cooked by somebody, you don't really have to go anywhere, or do anything, except pray. And I look good in black. With my color of hair.''

"You wouldn't have any hair if you were a nun. I don't think it's a bit romantic. A life of total renunciation. Penances. No *men*.''

"Hmmm. I don't know. They're highly overrated anyhow.''

"Men? You just haven't met any good ones, that's all.'' Rina snorted.

"If such a thing even exists. Personally I find them exhausting. You go out, spend all this money on an outfit they won't even notice, get all ready to go someplace, wait around until they find the perfect parking place, sit there listening to them all night, then lose half a night's sleep while they pound away at your parts thinking they're God's gift. It's like, *draining*, in my opinion.''

"God, you're extreme. Why would anybody want to do that? Peter was never like that, not for a second.''

"What was he like, then?''

"He was—I don't know exactly, he was fun, and considerate, and a perfectly ordinary person. That's the thing I like most about him, I think, he's simply a *person*, just like I am. Nothing complicated. I love that. You know, someone who eats with his mouth open sometimes, farts under the covers, tells little lies sometimes, is afraid of a couple of ridiculous things, wants you to like him. We don't have to do anything special, buy outfits or go out or anything, we can just be together and be—''

"Ordinary."

"Right. Ordinary."

"Listen to you. Your whole life you have hated *everything* about ordinary. Like, you did everything you humanly could *not* to be ordinary, and now suddenly it's the greatest thing that ever was invented."

And Min realized there was some truth in what Rina was saying, that something *had* changed in her, she had come to accept small, commonplace occurrences—gathering shells on the beach with Rina, watching her father prune his tomato plants, sitting by the fire in Davey's kitchen—as meaningful pieces of her life, plain and necessary as water. Things she used to shun as trivial, as holding her back from something better, more glowing, that she thought was happening somewhere else. She would go off automatically in the opposite direction, mistaking defiance and disillusionment for courage and insight. What she had tried to describe to Rina, the everyday comfort she and Peter took from each other, was not to be weighed lightly; it was far more valuable to her than she had acknowledged. Even this trip with Rina had been a kind of revelation. When she could set aside her ideas about family, obligations, what she and Rina *meant* to each other, and all that had passed between them, she had more fun with her sister than she would have thought possible. Rina never let her take herself too seriously.

"Think Irish," she would say whenever Min began expounding on anything, and Min would start laughing. It was a joke btween them, the inscrutable THINK IRISH signs they had encountered next to bins piled high with vegetables, in the bleakest of pubs, on kiosks in the little villages they had driven through. The phrase summed up the unlikely, off-center feeling of meeting these people they had never seen before and calling them family, of driving on the wrong side of terrible twisting roads in the middle of the night, full of lager and singing loudly, of nodding at stories of fairies and banshees and small people who lived underground.

There was even something she had learned to appreciate about the family part of it: the way she and Rina could talk about their parents—even if they disagreed—and their periods, their skin problems, their dreams; they could squeeze each other's zits and brush each other's hair and even sleep in the same bed if they had to, each sharing the minutiae of her life with a person who actually cared, for some crazy reason, about all of it, because her life was connected to yours, however remotely, because yours might mirror her own in some way that could not be predicted, or taken for granted; because, in fact, you were, and always would be, relations.

Davey lived with his son, Tom, who was a bachelor and as shy as his father was forthcoming. They grew potatoes and raised pretty light-brown cattle, and Tom hunted grouse, pheasant and woodcock in the moist marshy woods that lay not far from the house. In his stature and lonely, self-covering silence Tom reminded Min of her father, twenty years ago. When they met she had reached out to shake hands with Tom; he looked at her hand for a long moment (Her *hand*? Shake a woman's *hand*?) before he fished his own from his sleeve, studying his wrist carefully as they shook. By a curious muscular trick he withdrew his arm at the same time he extended it, so that she never fully grasped his palm. Under his tweed jacket he wore an inky-colored sweater, which matched his eyes, and rough woolen trousers. He spoke little, with a forward dip and shake of his head, as though in hopes that his hair would fall forward and provide a dark curtain for those eyes, which it usually did. Tom appeared embarrassed by his female guests and their questions, their colors and smells and exclamations of pleasure or surprise. He flattened himself against the nearest wall whenever one of them came in sight. His movements were generally spare and functional, as if he didn't want any part of himself to get away, to perform unexpectedly.

Unlikely as it seemed, he and Rina hit it off at once. They somehow discovered a mutual interest in country music, and discussed Kenny Rogers's latest album and Dolly Parton's bus tour in hushed, sober tones by the fire, while he cleaned his rifle and Rina filed her nails. The second night of their visit he mentioned something to Rina about a country band playing at a pub in Shillelagh, and she nailed him right then to a promise of an evening's entertainment, much to the reddening of Tom's large pale ears.

Tom did not address Min directly, except to ask one or two discreet questions about the weather in her part of the world.

"I expect it's dry then, is it?" he said, staring at the oilcloth on the table between them.

She explained that it was dry in summer, yes, after all much of California was really desert, but the ocean breezes kept it cool at the coast, and green in winter.

What would they grow there, then?

Well, nobody grew much of anything in the way of crops, if that's what he meant, they grew condos, shopping malls, restaurants, that type of thing.

Oh aye.

But the ocean is fine, the ocean is much as it's ever been, blue and lovely, the same as it is here. Lovely, isn't it, the ocean.

Ah. He hadn't seen the ocean for three or four years now.

But it's only twenty-five miles away!

Not much use though, is it.

But it's *there*, it's beautiful, you swim in it. Don't you?

Can't say I've ever swum, no. I expect it would be a fine thing to know, though.

On Saturday night he and Rina went off to the pub in Shillelagh, Rina in high spirits and high heels humming "I Know A Heartache When I See One," Tom's face scrubbed as shiny as the skin on a new potato.

"I was asking about our relations, Davey," Min said, trying to keep asking out of her voice. She and Davey had stayed at home. They were sitting on two wooden chairs by a kitchen fire that smoked terribly but kept away the dampness, so palpable as to be a presence, one Min imagined lurking just outside the low doorway, a dead-pale woman with long dripping hair, bony fingers that slipped underneath your clothing and rubbed the warmth from your skin, chilling you like cold water. Something about being here made you see things like that. Rina would freeze in those heels.

Davey's eyes traveled toward the parlor, away from the subject.

"Ah, I don't know as you'd want to be messing around in all that. Stubborn as his own father, is your father then? The McCunes are stubborn as posts, you know. There's a McCune over by Tinahely—now, the Tinahely McCunes aren't but third cousins of you, but still they're McCunes—the one I'm telling you of, Frank was his name, he owned a little corner of bogland with soil so poor sheep would turn their noses up at it. And the council wanted to put a road across his place. So they offered Frank a sum—I don't know how many pound, exact, but if it was ten, it was twice what that miserable little soaker of a piece was worth. But he won't sell, and he won't sell, and he's hardly got an ear of corn to throw to the pigs he's that poor. The soles is flapping off his shoes when I seen him at Knockananna Pub, he's that far down in his fortunes, but a body wouldn't dare try to buy him a jar, for he's prouder than he is stubborn by far. Old Frank McCune."

As usual, Min was waiting for the climax, the punchline, the denouement. Davey just sat there, puffing a thin stream of smoke out of his pipe, squinting through it at the muddy yard outside the window.

"So Davey, what happened?"

"Eh?"

"What happened about Mr. McCune?"

"Who?"

"FRANK MCCUNE, that you were just telling me about."

"Oh, that. That was a long time ago. He died, you know. Yessir. Died and left not a living soul behind that anyone could find out. And the county got his land after all, and built their road right across that corner where Frank's bed used to be. You know the house is gone. But there's a great bump in the road right there where Frank's bed used to stand, and every time I drives over that place I think, old Frank McCune's still having his say, still jiggling things around from beyond the grave is what he is. Aye."

"I was asking about my grandmother."

Between the smoking turf and the smoking pipe Min's eyes

were tearing. She could hardly see Davey, who was sitting not five feet away from her.

"Your grandmother. Aye. A body can scarce think of a lovely slip of a girl like that as anyone's grandmother. A grandmother is an old thing, you know. She was never no grandmother when I knew her. She was tall as a tree in them days. I'm a little man, you know. And I was a wee lad. We was cousins back then, and we played some great old tricks, her and me. We was famous for the tricks we'd play when they was wakin' someone. Not a scared bone in her body. She made me touch my first dead creature, our old aunt who died. Bony old thing she was. Never liked to touch her when she was living neither. Wakes was a great thing in them days. The food and the tricks and all the dancing! We scarce have seen a good wake here for many a year. But in them days oh! it was a great thing. The second day of wakin' her they brings her in her bed into the parlor, and after a great amount of whiskey is drank and a great number of rounds and jigs is danced all the people nods off to sleep, snoring to a one of them. The men is all in them long tailcoats that they was wearin' in them days, sleeping in their chairs with their backs to the body of our old aunt they was guarding. And don't this cousin of mine take a needle and thread from the hem of her skirt and quick as holy lightning sew the men's coats to the shroud, and me following right behind biting off the thread when she was done with every one. What a fine row of yelling went up when one of those gentlemen got up to answer nature's call, and the corpse went following along behind him! I always wished we could have saw his face. Aye, we was great leg-pullers in them days, Our Savior only knows. I expect they'll be wakin' me one of these days. I'll be under a great slab pushing up daisies with my toes before we sit in front of a fire again. Nature's callin' your old Uncle Davey sure as Christmas is coming."

Min was on the verge of offering some consolation, when she realized he was simply going outside to relieve himself.

While he was gone it came to her, like a whiff of the chilled wet air he let in when he opened the door, that there would be no answers here. Neither Davey nor anyone else was going to tell her the real story, the story of her grandmother she longed to hear. Because, in all likelihood, none of them knew what it was. In fact, her longing seemed suddenly absurd, anachronistic, utterly naïve, like a child wanting to be reassured that the dragon had not swallowed the princess, the king and queen had indeed lived happily ever after. There were no facts about anyone's life that told the real story about them. Everyone made up their lives as they went along; other people saw what they wanted.

She had seen the great slabs Davey was talking about only that afternoon, at the Hacketstown graveyard where the McCunes were buried. A churchyard filled with flat, unyielding, moss-covered stones, the lettering eroded, completely unreadable. They could have marked anyone's grave. And she realized she didn't care whose they were; it was enough that she had come here and seen them, and the place, for herself. There was a lonely windswept view, across fields stubbled as Davey's chin, toward a dark, loaf-shaped hill, and the Derry River. Just below, the town itself stood, a bright smudge where a bit of light was shining through the thickly padded clouds. Odd as it seemed, she felt as if she were, not being handed a gift exactly, but standing within the gift itself, a great soft pocket in time that had opened up around her and invited her in. She felt old here—a good old, as if she had been able to go forward, rather than backward, in time, to retrieve something, a knowledge that she might someday have as an old woman, but which she needed now, to sustain herself. She required no introduction, no one to give the place to her: it had ever been hers.

Morning in Ireland was a dream, a soft stirring of half-sleeping senses. By the sea the mist rolled steady and deep, swirling in such coils and gusts it could have been born in a great machine hidden out in the silent green of the Gulf Stream. Min stood at the shore, pocketing her hands, the little white waves slurping and swishing at her feet, the fine wet vapor netting her like a fish out of water, a fish in air. Her hair was heavy and damp, her clothes felt somehow old and foolish here, as if she should slip them like a useless skin and slither into the green air, the foaming water, finny with delight, a flying fish sewing the sea to the sky with her leaping needle of a body.

The energy of these waves was lazy, it lulled and deceived. No rolling sets of breakers like the Pacific, no feverish churnings over rocks. What danger could there be, in such a weary careworn sea? Even the screeching gulls stood faced away from it, no backward glances as they rifled a log, groomed their oil-blackened feathers. When she first walked down to the beach they came looming up out of the mist like pterodactyls, huge and fearsome, clawing the air near her face for their breakfast. Their cries were muffled by the moist air; now they flapped away from their log like spirits abandoning the wreck of a ship. She was left alone once more, wandering the damp sands, moving among the slushings of small speckled rocks rolling against one another. Rich odors of making and decay swamped her nostrils: the air was a banquet.

Out at sea there was no horizon, and ahead, hardly a shoreline to follow. Above her stood some small cliffs where she had taken the path down to the beach, and a weaving stone wall fallen to rubble, wobbly as a child's first sand dams. Everything here curved. She watched the mist creep up and wrap the corners of the houses. Roofs wavered and disappeared, the windows became darker patches of grey in the stone walls, small open mouths which swallowed the fog that wound into them. The houses floated, their inhabitants curled in some shapeless hibernation, before the light came to fetch them.

What would it have been like, she wondered, to have been born into this watery world, shooting forth from the mist like a fresh pink planet, your blood clear and cold as the sea? What might you have brought up from the depths and flung upon the shore, into the wrack and tumble of weeds and deadwood, the transparent, eaten-out shells of lost tiny creatures? Here you would know yourself simply by breathing, the fresh lungfuls of sea mist buoying you, the plankton-laced waves your home.

She had come here looking for a homeland, ancestors, lines of blood, for something to claim her as its own. Yet nowhere had she found the faces she saw in dreams, no lips had moved to form the words *You are ours. You belong to us*. The beach was pathless, the incoming tide wiped away her footprints behind her. The land was abraded, carelessly fertile, full of secrets. Busy. There was no room for it to care about her, no time to answer her questions. And what answer could there be, but what surrounded her: mists, ocean, crumbling walls, the sun trying to reach its pale fingers through a throng of clouds.

You are your own ancestor here, the bones moving under your shirt the only ones you can really trace, a memory of swimming the farthest reaches alive as anything else, as your tongue moving across your lips. A family could be like the flock of shorebirds moving just ahead of you. Some are chasing the wave while others hang back, standing on one leg. A few are huddled together, for warmth perhaps; some peck away at the sand in solitude. Several fly off as you approach, others take no notice. They call, they scold, they seem not to be able to warn one another away from sudden deep water.

Springs of Living Water

The room was on the eighth floor, at the end of a long, sticky linoleum hallway. Min couldn't understand why the floor always felt like this, grabbing at the soles of your shoes as soon as you stepped off the elevator. Was it cheap wax? Spilled drinks? Bodily fluids? You'd think the nuns would have it swabbed off more often. The nuns at the convent used to be on their hands and knees doing floors every time she went for her piano lesson. It seemed an exercising penance, one that combined purity, humility and precision in measures known only to nuns. They devised elaborate systems for trussing up their voluminous habits and rigging their veils, though nothing prevented the heavy gold crucifixes from swinging out and hitting their forearms as they inched forward, their sober shoes sticking out behind as if they belonged to dummies, their patient hands inscribing perfect wet semicircles on the creaking floors. She had wondered in the way Protestants do about the privacies of nuns—where they got those rags, for example. Threadbare altarcloths? Tattered, consecrated underwear? Wasn't everything they had sanctified?

It was fitting, somehow, that Mac should be at St. Joseph's, a hospital run by these women with their plain, starched garments and masculine names, whose lives had been given over wholly to the inexplicable. The sexes were segregated here the same way they were in parochial school. Walking down the eighth floor hallway you saw common rooms, Leatherette

229

couches, adjustable beds filled with men; men shuffling behind metal walkers or dragging IV stands along like reluctant buddies; men talking in hushed voices by the Coke machine or the public telephones. You could be visiting a male planet, or a space station, especially if, as Min did, you never got off on any other floor but this one. She was thankful they had been able to obtain a private room for Mac.

"What do you mean, semi-private?" Rina had demanded over the telephone. "How could it be semi-private? It's either private or it isn't."

When he was brought here, Mac appeared not to remember what happened. Jack Barber, the chainsaw neighbor, had stopped by to ask about a dead-looking blue spruce at the corner of their property, and found him passed out on the basement landing with a string of outdoor Christmas lights in his hands, and Skipper whimpering beside him on the dampened mud rug. When two of Min's calls from Ireland had gone unanswered she phoned the doctor, who told her Mr. McCune may have had a stroke and had been admitted to St. Joseph's Hospital for tests and observation. She returned on the next flight from Dublin, while Rina took the ferry to the Continent and made arrangements to ship her car back to Canada.

It had been shocking to walk into the room and actually see him lying flat on his back, with plastic tubing taped to his arm and sprouting from his nostrils, and wires leading from his chest to a machine beside the bed. He looked as if he'd lost another twenty pounds since she and Rina had left: a long, gaunt El Greco body lay under the sheets, scarcely raising them. Someone had recently given him a horrible haircut; ragged tufts stood up here and there on his pale scalp like stubble left in a winter field. And something in the left side of his face had given up; it hung lower than the right side, downcast and melted-looking. Finding him this way it was difficult not to suspect that all these devices were what was making him prone and weak, so weak that when she first came, and touched him ever so lightly on his bony shoulder, it required a great gathering of effort for him to half open his good eye and flicker the lid at her once, twice, before letting it close again.

She had sat for days now, and watched him breathe, sometimes reaching over to feel the sheet, to reassure herself of a movement she could not see. Such a small movement, for everything to depend upon. She sat on a plastic chair near the window, by his right side. From that vantage point he still looked relatively normal, his face that of a weary man in repose. She would hold his cool, smooth hand and stroke the contracted fingers that wrapped themselves around her own like a baby's. She went back to the times she had been at home with him, the two of them sitting in darkness on the couch in front of the TV watching war movies, the shadows in the jungle flickering, gruff voices murmuring, shells singing in the distance, his feet in her lap, her hands absently kneading his toes—the only prolonged touching he ever really allowed, for them to steep like that in the rich comfortable silence of hands and feet. Now he lay inert most of the time—"Alive, but just barely," as Sister Scholastica bluntly put it while punching up his pillows. It was not a kind of life Min was familiar with. Even in Rose's last weeks, she often lay awake all night, calling on one or another of them for a drink of water or help going to the bathroom, as if sleep would be the thief of whatever life was left to her. As if the slightest loss of attention would lead to her death.

Sometimes Mac opened his eyes and looked around the room in puzzlement, in search of a telling clue that would reveal what he was doing here. Min would explain to him, once again, how he'd fallen and been found, how they were still doing tests, how he just needed to rest, and get better. Then he would shift his eyes—the right one struggling up toward alertness, the left one trailing behind—and stare at her mouth, as though if he looked long enough, in exactly the right place, he would be able to see behind her words to what was coming next. Another day both eyes would turn up toward hers, and face her with their dull, milky glaze, the withdrawn and hopeless stare of a prisoner. She talked and talked to those eyes. Described for them all the relatives she and Rina had visited in Ireland, their houses and yards, the wild-looking distant cousin who raised his fingers in the sign of the cross and ran off yelping when she started to take his picture. Told how when it was too rainy to picnic, they would eat in the car, feasting on olives and strong cheeses and soft white bread, and enormous bars of chocolate Rina discovered in a shop in Albi. Went back to the stately old home in Paris which housed the Monets, the blurred watery blue canvases of the artist's last, half-blind years, the way—but maybe he didn't want to hear this? Travel images might be too dense for him right now. Too rich. Well, then. Her life in California perhaps. She walked the beach nearly every morning as soon as she got up, putting herself at the edge of the world, as she thought of it. She might photograph gulls picking over a mass of bull kelp, or a clutch of little sandpipers jerking along after the waves. Sometimes Peter came with her. He used to make fun of the way she strode ahead, impatient, scavenging for images. I'd like you to meet Peter, Mac, he's—what? What would he like to hear? He's good to me, she finished lamely. He works with families, and kids. Remember that brochure I sent you when he opened his new office? We're in love, Mac. We're thinking about getting married. Guess what, he's even taller than I am.

Didn't his eyes soften at that? A little, there in the corners?

Other days his gaze was bleary, ancient, beseeching. When she saw that she would frantically go through the list. Water. You want some water? You want me to call the nurse. No. Legs. You need help moving your legs. Turn on the radio? Turn off the radio. Rina is fine. Yes, Skipper is fine, Mac. We're all doing fine. Hurting. Something is hurting you. Where? What is it? What do you want me to do?

As much liquid as they dripped into Mac, he grew drier and drier. Whatever was wrong with him was siphoning off his precious fluids. Once or twice Min even checked under the bed, certain that there must be some mistake, someone had carelessly hooked things up and the IV's were draining away somewhere else, nowhere near her father. Nor did she ever wholly convince herself they weren't draining in reverse, and compulsively held numberless sips of water to his lips. That was the hardest thing about having him here, in a place that was a world unto itself, revolving upon its own rules, schedules, smells, moral imperatives. He was simply another part here, a tiny part of the vast engine of the hospital, a point of light on a circuit. Intensive Care, where he lay when she first arrived, was lit up day and night like a Vegas casino: there was that same whirring of machines and scurrying feet and bright metal

objects, sudden exclamations of hope or despair, an unexpected press of urgent sweating bodies by the desk, whiffs of
adrenaline-laden air. Min longed to kidnap her father, remove
his drips and monitors and machines and carry him off to some
cool shaded oasis, a green and natural place where a body
could be refreshed, and heal. *Springs of living water* was a
phrase that came to her often as she sat by his bed. *I would
bathe him in springs of living water.*

What a relief when Rina arrived, to have a familiar, to
share the small scraps of information there were to be had about
Mac's condition. She had missed Rina, especially at night,
staying alone in that house with only Skipper's aged noises for
company. Their trip made Min aware that her sister could be
solidly relied upon for certain things, insights and proficiencies
and her own Wyandotte-nourished brand of pragmatism, which
Min herself mainly lacked.

"God," was all Rina could say when she saw him at the
hospital. She kept wetting her lips, drank innumerable sodas,
wept copiously, as if all this moisture might help rehydrate him
in some way.

She and Min pored over Mac's test scores like two anxious
parents who hoped to get their son into the right school. Min
watched the doctors slide him in and out of several gigantic
machines that looked far more suited to monitoring nuclear
fission, or jet propulsion, than tracking the fragile paths of
nerve fibers reaching out from his spinal cord, the tenuous
webbing between parts of his brain. The doctors showed her
these pictures, and Min pretended to discuss them; but she
could not believe they were illustrations of what made him
brush his teeth and walk the dog. Where are his inventions?
she wanted to ask. Show me that shoe buffer, the sprinkler
system, the instant rice cooker. Is this wavy stuff his love for
my mother? Or us? Or every one of those cars that he was so
crazy about? Surely that should show up somewhere.

But no. They showed a mass in his brain about which the
doctors—or the *team*, as they liked to call themselves—were
trying to determine malignancy. The pressure it exerted within
the cap of his skull was causing transient loss of speech and

sight, and an incomplete paralysis of his left side.

"What do they mean, transient?" Rina was suspicious.

"They mean, it could be temporary. They hope it's temporary."

"It's only temporary," Rina assured the neighbors who stopped her when she was leaving the house, or called, hoping they weren't disturbing her breakfast, her lunch or her dinner. They're doing tests. Waiting for results. Nothing certain at this point.

The hospitals in Wyandotte were well equipped. The same companies whose employees' lungs were poisoned, fingers crushed, lymph nodes withered, regularly sponsored fund-raising drives to buy the hospitals the latest in equipment.

"Those Holy Names are smart operators, don't kid yourself," Rina said. "Just look at this place."

St. Joseph's was run by the Sisters of the Holy Names of Jesus and Mary. Min was again surprised that such numbers of young women were still betrothing themselves to Christ. The Holy Names *shoosh-shooshed* down the corridors in full nun regalia, their stiff white blinders causing that odd upper-body half twist, as though they all, young and old, had fused or arthritic neckbones. Their habits were a relief to her; she knew how to deal with this kind of nun, what to say. California nuns, whom you saw rarely, wore short, sporty outfits and moved briskly, their light perfunctory headgear tossing in the offshore breeze. They looked more like gym teachers, political activists, union negotiators, who would expect a firm handshake and a steady gaze, and be affronted by any suggestion of a dip of the knees.

She called Peter nearly every day and poured out her fears for her father, her uncertainties about his treatment, the limited progress he seemed to be making. Her heart felt ragged and torn; his voice was like a soothing liquid poured over it. It had become painful to her to be apart from him.

One night she found herself reading her childhood book of myths, still shelved in the basement, and in it the story of Atalanta, the maiden who could run faster than anyone on earth and had been warned never to marry, and her suitor Hippomenes, who ran against her and won the race by tossing three golden apples—gifts of Venus—into her path, one by one. As a child she had loved the story, and the picture of Atalanta bending forward poised on one toe like a dancer, her golden hair floating behind her, to pick up the third apple. That night she read it several times, and could not put it out of her mind all evening. She kept having images of herself and Peter in the story, running not against but alongside each other, and a notion that in him she had something akin to Atalanta's golden apples, if she would but claim it. When she spoke to him later, she tried to tell him this, explaining the story, and ended up feeling foolish, with a catch in her throat and her heart pounding so loudly in her ears she could hardly hear him.

He didn't quite get the story, he said, but he knew what she was trying to say. Did she want him to come up and be with her, to help them out? No, she said. I want you, but my sister and I are doing something here. Not just yet. I love you.

Most of the hospital duty fell to Min, since Rina literally started shaking as soon as she came in sight of the wide double doors on Riverside Avenue.

"That smell," she would say weakly. "I feel like I'm going to throw up every time I get that cafeteria-medicine-pee smell in my nose. Or faint."

"It's okay, Rina. He knows that happens to you. I don't think he even notices what's going on."

Of course, Min was not at all sure that was true. She had no idea what he thought of as he lay there hour after hour, working so hard just to breathe, to sustain that flicker of movement in the vein at his wrist. No one could tell her what any of this meant to him. The left side of his face twisted painfully now when he tried to speak, or turn his head. Then he would look confused, disappointed in himself, and sink back into the pillow, as if there were nothing he could do but acquiesce in his own decline. A model patient, the nurses called him. Like he's made of wood, or plaster, Min thought. A dummy. Helpless passivity makes their jobs easier. She found it difficult to like the nurses, with their no-nonsense, primary-school teacher approach to everyone. She wanted to strangle the tiny Filipino nurse who treated Mac like he was a toddler. You don't want bedpan, Mr. McCune. You want catheter back in. Angie know.

You good boy now. Wet sheets not nice. No no.

It didn't do any of them any good to have Rina standing by the bed clutching her stomach. So she stayed at the house, looking after Skipper, browsing the want ads. She cooked dinner for the two of them most nights, and actually seemed to enjoy this. After Europe, she said, it was a relief to be able to make what you wanted, to find ingredients with pronounceable names sensibly organized in a nice clean supermarket. The markets in Europe displayed foods that looked too much like what they were, in Rina's opinion. Cooking should involve disguise, should be more like dressing up, putting on makeup. Who wants to know they're eating a fish?

They decided to put up a Christmas tree, and Rina even got out the ladder and strung lights around the front door and the picture window. They still had the fat old Noma lights in bright crayon colors; though the cords were frayed they worked fine, and Min liked them better than the twinkly ones that showed up now on the patio of every restaurant on the coast. The nuns erected a creche in the hospital lobby—quite a nice one, all in wood with near life-sized figures wearing practical cotton outfits and cotton batting beards. Lights went up downtown; big gold tinsel stars were strung across Assumption Street and Styrofoam candycanes strapped with red plastic ribbon to the lampposts by the river. There was no snow on the ground yet; great draughts of cold blew down from the north, and gathered in the streets, waiting for the storm that would blanket everything. Emptied of summer's handholding couples and rows of bedding plants, the new Kiwanis shade trees leafless and bound sadly to their supports by dirty strips of rag, the riverfront was a bleak expanse of industrial loneliness, the river itself cold and metallic-looking against the barges that swam slowly past the town.

Occasionally Min took a break from the overheated hospital to walk down and stand by the water, and watch the little grey waves slap against the concrete embankment. The riverfront was usually deserted. She was still surprised that after living here for over twenty years, she never saw anyone she knew. There was an occasional unemployed factoryman, hands deep in his car coat pockets, his fake mouton collar turned up against the raw wind, nose reddened and streaming from grief, or alcohol. Or a businessman weaving down the sidewalk in a flapping trenchcoat, reeking that blend of Labatt's and Binaca. Men in Wyandotte still stared openly at women, as if they were novelties. Their looks shocked her; they were so far removed from the etheric processes of illness she was absorbed in that they seemed almost obscene, as difficult to grasp as the conversations she heard in the hospital waiting room, or had with the neighbors—all sincere, kind, humorless people who talked over hockey games, beef prices, whether the stores should be allowed to open on Sunday, and seemed inattentive to any inner processes save digestion. Self-reflection had never caught on in Wyandotte.

She had terrible, unforgettable dreams during this period. Lengthy sequences of events, encounters with malevolent strangers, journeys to cold unfamiliar places. In the mornings she was exhausted, far tireder than when she had gone to bed the night before.

I am in a dark room, with ugly purple-red walls. Bargaining with some men who seem to be mobsters. They say they will give up Mac for something I have but I don't know what it is.

The hospital elevator is on a roller-coaster track—big gaps where I see space whooshing by. Clutching the bar on the back wall so I don't fall out.

In a crowd of people, forced to watch a surgery, a doctor drilling a quarter-sized hole in a man's skull and squirting saline solution all over the brain. I wish everyone would be quiet so he could concentrate.

She had gone over possibilities ceaselessly at first. What if it had been discovered sooner? What if he'd gone to a different doctor? Couldn't he have taken something? But after days of this she realized how useless it was. There was no ultimate physical that would tell you everything about each little sac and duct, every platelet and nerve plexus. Even if there was, how long could it last? You'd have to start over again a week or two later. It was frightening how little direct information you had about what was happening inside your body. There was a gap there, between your flesh and your perception of it, a vague shadowy corridor you simply could not enter, which no one could tell you anything about. The doctors and their machines and pictures showed up after processes had already gone awry, cells turned on one another, aneurysms exploded like water balloons, when it was time to bargain. There never had been and would never be a clean slate, for anyone. Rose used to say *Nobody can see their own back.* It was an aphorism Min had never quite grasped, which now made perfect sense. What was the point of trying to interpret your own life, when you couldn't even see half of it?

Mac suddenly rallied one afternoon. His knee began to twitch up and down under the covers, he acted greatly excited and clutched at Min's arm, dragging it down onto the bed so as to bring her face closer to his. Vowels churned around deep in his throat, consonants flew spitlike from his cracked lips.

"Oooohg—eeehrrr—aaahhr," he said.

How distressed he was at his miserable speech! His right arm let go of hers, and thumped the covers in shame and frustration.

"Mac, here. Try this. Can you do this?"

She had been waiting and hoping he would recover enough to use words. There was a notepad on the nightstand. She propped it up on his chest sideways and helped him coil his fingers around a pen. He was left-handed; the letters came out in a slow, laborious scrawl, but they were letters.

YOU HAVE ENOUGH? RINA?

Whatever he meant, whatever troubled him acutely enough to awaken him out of his listless dream, she ached to think that it was for them, that he was still acting on their behalf, being their father, sending messages not out of his own need but concern for his children. He wanted nothing. Yes Mac, we have enough. More than enough of everything, except hours with you. I fear I have not *been* enough, for having been all that you and Ma cared about. We live as though our lives will go on forever, as if we have time and love to squander, the way we squandered the nickels and dimes you gave us on candy, left bits of it dirty and half-sucked in the gutter, to your disappointment. You wanted us to save and measure out carefully, to spend wisely, to plant love only where it would flourish. I have learned something from you. I owe you something. Not because of family, because you are my father, but something from myself, from this place opening up in me, I want to give you something and all I can think of is *charity*, a word I never understood and I don't even know now if it's right. Not the sickly, biblical, washed-up kind but something that watching you causes, a pure sweet feeling of *seeing* you, because I understand now, Mac, about you, and about Ma, and I feel ashamed for having come to it so late, so awkwardly. I want to try to give it to you, this token, this kind of love I could never give Ma because it was already too late then, but I know now, none of it matters because I understand now. Can you hear me, Mac?

One side of his face seemed to be trying to smile at her, even though his eyes had suddenly gone watery and tired as Skipper's. She longed to reach across that wordless gap and part the troublesome curtain; the words were lit up back in there like lights on a tree, if she could only find the way in. Shakily he took up the pad once more. With their ten fingers wrapped around the pen, he managed to write GOING TO SEE YOUR MOTHER.

Was he nodding his shaggy head or was that a tremor? He held up the pad to her like an offering, then exhaled back into the pillow, an expression of contentment and great fatigue written on his face, as if he participated in some gruelling competition, rowed a boat across a wide river, rappelled up a cliff.

Min held the pad to her chest and got up to look out the window. Clouds were gathering in great grey swathes over the river, prematurely darkening the afternoon. Down below the streetlights had come on, and shop windows glowed with warm yellow light. A small crowd of shoppers huddled at the bus stop, holding their Christmas parcels and folded newspapers in front of them as windbreaks. Rina would be starting dinner, maybe fixing herself a gin and tonic.

How ordinary and simple was this faith of Mac's, that he still had a future, that he was headed somewhere, to meet someone he loved. For surely it was faith—and love, too, both manifest in small, simple acts, that moved one ahead, step by step, into the future. And even if it was true that love was the cause of grief, still it was all any of them had to hold up against it—against grief, against time, against death, blowing steadily now like cold winds off the river.

The night he died it finally snowed, the beginning of a constant light snowfall that would continue for almost two days and nights. Min watched it coming down in the darkness outside the window of his room. She had forgotten the loveliness of snow, the way it could suddenly appear in the night as if out of nowhere, sifting weightlessly through the air to cover the earth with a serene pearly light, and stillness.

Rina had come to the hospital, and sat by Mac's bed until she could no longer keep still. Then she got up to walk the hallways with one of his big white handkerchiefs held to her mouth, undone by her grief. She and Min had no need for words; they communicated now with their eyes, or by squeezing hands next to his bedside, in perfect understanding.

For almost three hours Min had watched her father's face in the lamplight, observing what she thought was a kind of active process taking place within him. There were small, nearly imperceptible twitchings around his mouth, momentary furrows in his brow, new, altogether unfamiliar expressions which came streaming across his features like moving shafts of light, and gave him every appearance of a stranger. A separation was happening, or a struggle between two men; one her much-loved, everyday father, the other a being who had never been visible before—or at least, one she had never seen. Gradually, subtly, the two sides of his face subtly evened themselves out, the nerves and muscles finally coming to an agreement. It was not frightening; rather, it felt like a very great thing that she had been allowed to see. And finally the movements eased, his face looked rested, and refreshed. Minutes passed before she realized that the coverlet was no longer moving, that his death had come and gone secretly, a private message of the night.

*   *   *

Rina stayed at the hospital.

"I'll take care of things here with the Holy Names," she said, wiping at her eyes. "You go home and get some rest or something."

Rina had found Mac's sweater, hanging in his hospital-room closet like an old self he would not put on again. She put it on, and stood in the hallway, a dark smudge of army-drab green against the glaring white walls. Crying had reddened and disheveled her; standing there in the sweater she looked like a cleaning lady who had lost her watch and arrived in confusion, too early for her shift, before everyone had left for the night.

Min put her arms around Rina.

"I love you, Rin," she whispered in her sister's damp ear.

"I know," Rina said miserably. "Go on. I can't take any more."

She drove home through empty familiar streets, the houses dark, the stoplights changing for nobody. The tires of the van made a soft crunching sound as they rolled over the fresh snow. She parked in the driveway and walked up the sidewalk to the back door. Mac had installed a small wooden gate into the yard so Skipper wouldn't be molested by other, younger dogs when he was let out; it opened with a groan against the snow that had already drifted up against it.

The yard was competely white and luminous, so pristine that she hesitated by the gate before stepping inside and leaving her footprints in the snow. All around her the air was made silvery-white by the snow; you could not see the sky, or stars, or distinct clouds, only this lightness everywhere. The trunk of the apple tree stood straight and black beside the house, its limbs twisted and gracefully raised. Odd shapes rose up in the garden: the humps of pruned perennials, roses under their winter jars, clods of spaded-up earth. Along the back fence stood the tall dried branches of the tomato plants, hanging hoary and forgotten over the rest of the garden like ancestral figures. In a moment, she would go inside and call Peter, to tell him that she was coming home.

The
Best Modern Fiction
from
BALLANTINE